Fleas Upon Snow

by
Eric Carlton Neperud

This book is dedicated to the flora and fauna the parasites infected.

By Eric Carlton Neperud

THE LIMBO CHRONICLES
     Trees And Weeds
     Limbo
     The Octagonal Knight
     Dragons And Golems
     The Brotherhood Of Giants
     Wizards And Druids

THE YELLOWSONE TRILOGY
     Wonders Of The Wilderness
     Fleas Upon Snow
     The Periphery Of Sorrow

Fleas Upon Snow
by
Eric Carlton Neperud

An ancient woman, bald-headed, ebony-skinned, sits upon a stone promontory jutting into an alpine lake. Sunlight drenches open arms and upturned palms. A sapling woman waits, tall, straight, muscular, golden. Lodgepole pines blanket the radiance. The Prophet speaks, slowly, deeply, deliberately. The woman-child does not understand.

"Can you speak English?"

The Prophet shakes her head horizontally, then nods.

A towering, lanky man, a third of his life remaining, arrives from behind, startling the visitor. Beneath his flowing, white robe the leathery man says, "Mother understands, but speaks her own."

The Prophet speaks in a language unfamiliar to the visitor.

The robed man responds in the same language, then walks away from the Prophet.

"Will you teach me to speak her language?" asks the visitor.

"They who seek will find, of their own choosing."

"How may I address you?"

"Mardono was selected from the one selected." He retrieves a dozen chits from a pouch, each with its unique symbol. "Randomness, chaos, creativity, nature, beauty." He chooses chits and replaces them. "Twelve notes: music, mathematics, language. JO-LAIR-SHAY has been randomly selected."

3

The Earth circles its sun and returns, as does Jolairshay. She attempts a second audience with the Prophet, but rain binds the matron to her cabin. The following day the clouds dissipate. The Prophet bathes in the sunlight. Shadows bend. "I welcome your return, young one. Do you comprehend the language of peace and beauty?"

"I speak the language, but do not completely comprehend."

"Simplicity, chaos, nature, unity."

"I understand. I learned much from Mardono. He speaks of himself, his spirituality. Not yours."

"Mine is mine. Ours is ours."

"Mother, will you speak of yourself?"

"*Please* is not our word, because it is always implied. I am called many things, but do not respond to Mother. It is inaccurate, I never bearing a child. Bardula was chosen. Once I was called Lapaz, after my child...

1.   CHILDHOOD

I was born in Renton, Washington on November 1, 1970. Grain was pleased with the religious significance of the date. Grain is my grandmother. She raised me after my mother died of a drug overdose. It was inevitable. She is the only woman I have heard of who almost died from taking too much birthing medication. I never knew my father. I was born in a hospital that has been torn down to make room for a Kmart. I was reminded I was special every time I saw a blue light. I was named Jimi Jackson, after the rock legend who was born and buried in the area. I moved to Rainier Valley in

Seattle when Grain became my guardian. Grain was the only person who looked out for me. "Finish your grain," she would always say in the morning. I confused Gram with grain. Understandable. They both provided.

Even with Grain's love, I strayed. I followed in my mother's footsteps, and then some. I joined the Madrona Marauders. Guys joined the gang by being beat-in. Girls, by being sexed-in, but weren't respected for it. I had to be beat-in to be respected. I barely survived, and I still have some of the scars. I was required to also be sexed-in, but before the beating. They didn't want damaged goods. As a full member, I could choose who I had sex with. Lapaz was my gang baby. I was beat, she to death, by a rival gang, before she was born. A year later, I died.

"So, the stories are true. You rose from the dead?"

I was surrounded by haze. A white gate opened before me. An old man with a long, gray beard frowned and waited. "What do you wish to do?" he asked.

My reply, "To find the people who sent me here."

"Those you seek are already here."

"How can that be?"

"There is no pecking order here. Everything you desire is beyond the gate."

I found a bazooka and picked it up. My killers drove by. I fired. They burst into flames, then disintegrated. I destroyed everything I saw. After a few days, I became bored. I began rebuilding the remnants of my tantrum. It was more of a challenge to become a positive force than a negative one.

I awoke lying on a bed in the hospital. Grain was in the chair beside my bed. "I'm going to leave the neighborhood. I've exceeded my life expectancy. It's time to rebuild, but not here. I'm not yet strong enough to circumvent the temptations of the city. I must go away, as far as possible."

I had turned eighteen, so I could leave school and Grain without any repercussions. I rarely went to school anyway, so did it really matter? In the newspaper, I read an ad, about Yellowstone National Park hiring for the winter. Nothing could be farther from my neighborhood than the wilderness. I was hired sight unseen to work at some place called Snow Lodge.

2.   THE BUS RIDE

I had never ridden a bus before, except in the city. Sixteen hours were going to seem like sixteen days. I found an unoccupied seat. Please, stay that way. I placed the backpack I used as a purse beside me. Maybe that would discourage someone from sitting next to me. The last thing I wanted to do was have a forced conversation with someone. As each additional person entered the bus my stomach lurched. Don't sit here, I silently pleaded. When the bus doors closed it felt like the last day of school. Relief flowed through me. The only thing that prevented me from being completely relaxed was having to go to the bathroom. Stress often did that to me. I would wait as long as I could. I didn't want to be that girl on the bus who couldn't control her bladder. Someone might think I was pregnant and running away from home. Or maybe just weak. The one thing I learned in the Marauders was not to appear weak. I hoped that peeing would be enough to release the twisting pressure in my gut. If the bathroom became stinky I would be blamed. I didn't know anyone here, so I shouldn't worry what others thought about me, but somehow it still mattered.

We passed through the tunnel that carried automobiles into

and out of Seattle from Lake Washington. Travelling the opposite
direction---into the city---there was a stone archway above the
tunnel's entrance engraved with *Portal to the Pacific*. It was already
beginning to feel like I was leaving the city, but it wouldn't
completely kick in until we passed Issaquah, Seattle's easternmost
suburb. Another tunnel was entered at Mercer Island, the wealthy
homeowners preferring those passing through to do so quietly,
from a distance. Minutes later the bus shot out into the open
again, briefly climbing to the surface of the island, before it passed
over a bridge that connected it to the mainland. Interstate 90
continued eastward through Bellevue, then just south of Lake
Sammamish, a significant body of water, but much smaller than
Lake Washington.

      The bus began to slow down. It pulled into the right-hand
lane. A few seconds later it exited at Issaquah. Did the bus need to
get gas? It stopped at a bus station I didn't even know existed.
Only wealthy people lived on the east side of town. Why would
they have to take the bus? Another dozen people entered. My guts
retightened. There were only so many empty seats. An old man
placed a worn suitcase in the bin above me. He had to be at least
forty. He wore a plaid shirt, jeans, generic hiking boots, and a
ragged trench coat missing some of its buttons. He looked down at
the seat beside me, saying more with his worn-out eyes than he
could ever say with words. I removed my backpack and placed it by
my feet. He sat down, then promptly shut his eyes. He didn't smell
very good. It was a combination of dirt, body odor, and alcohol.
Now I really had to go to the bathroom.

      I waited until we started moving again. I looked around. No
one was in line to use the restroom. Half appeared to be asleep. It
was time for me to use the bathroom. It was becoming almost
critical. I was going to go one way or another. If I wet my seat, it
would have been embarrassing, but it wouldn't have smelled any
worse than the guy sitting next to me. I looked over at him. His
eyes were still shut, but he didn't sound like he was asleep yet.

"Excuse me," I whispered. There was no response from him. "Excuse me," I whispered a bit louder. Still nothing. I tapped his leg with mine. "I need to get up." He opened his eyes. Without looking at me he moved into the aisle. I scooted over to his seat, then up. I smiled at him as I headed to the back of the bus. Expressionless, he returned to his seat and closed his eyes.

Someone had beat me to the restroom, so I had to wait. A few people in the seats near the restroom looked at me. I smiled back at them. Come on. I'm so close. The anticipation of finally being able to go to the bathroom was making it worse. I heard a flush, then the rattling of the door. A woman not much older than me came out. She brushed past me.

With great skill, I was able to close the door and lock it while simultaneously pulling down my pants and flopping on the toilet. UGH! The seat was wet. The woman was one of those...female dogs...that didn't want to make contact with the toilet, so she straddled it, making a mess everywhere except on herself. She had left enough of a mess that some of the urine dripped down onto my underwear and pants. The only thing worse than wetting yourself is having someone else do it for you. After taking care of my business, I took care of that woman's. I was not that type of person who wanted everyone else to suffer if I had to suffer. We looked after each other in the Marauders.

I glared at the woman as I passed her. She was asleep or pretended to be, so I wasn't able to get the satisfaction. She snuggled against the shoulder of her boyfriend or husband. Would she feel so soft against him if he knew what she had done in the bathroom?

"Excuse me." I had to knock my leg against the smelly man---again---for him to react. He moved into the aisle. I slid over into my seat. He returned to his. I had tried the best I could to clean myself and my clothes after the ordeal in the bathroom. Every bad odor I smelled I assumed had to come from me. It was illogical considering the cesspool beside me, but that's how I felt. I was one of those people who bathed twice a day, to lessen the possibility of me stinking. And I brushed my teeth after every meal, even after snacks. How often will I be able to bath in Yellowstone? Would they even have bathtubs? I could take a shower if I had to, but having water flow down on you wasn't like soaking in it. MY GAWD! What if Yellowstone didn't even have showers? It was supposed to be a wild place. What if we had to wash in a creek or a lake? When Grain's power went out one winter she filled the tub with water she had heated in the fireplace. What am I going to do without her to look after me? Was I making a mistake coming to Yellowstone?

The bus continued to make stops, every half an hour or so. Like waves crashing onto a beach then receding, people entered the bus and left.

I was beginning to get hungry. There was a meal break scheduled, but not until four, in Spokane. I left too early to eat lunch. Grain made me a sandwich. She also put a couple of homemade cookies in my lunch and a juice box. I felt both embarrassed having the kid drink, and loved.

We lost more people than we gained the further east we traveled. During one of the stops, I pounced on one of the recently vacated seats while my stinking seat mate left the bus to stretch his legs. Someone else might sit next to me, but they had to have better hygiene than the man I abandoned. No one else did. Sometimes being black in a white world had its advantages. Most of the seats had filled up again once we got to Spokane, but not the one beside me. There was more than one occasion when someone was in the process of sitting down next to me to only pop back up once they got a good look at me. Someone had actually bypassed my seat for the one beside the stinky man. Those in rural communities were supposed to be more prejudiced against minorities because they didn't see many on a daily basis. You couldn't get much more rural than Yellowstone. Would I be the only black person there?

I had to change buses in Spokane. There was a two-hour layover. The bus station was large enough that I was able to have some personal space. There was a store and a restaurant in the station, and others in the area. Time for dinner. I had one bag with me plus my backpack. I didn't want to leave it unintended in the bus station, so I took it with me. A third option was leaving it in a locker, but I wasn't confident of its security, and I didn't want to waste what little money I had on it.

I saw one of Spokane's few black faces through the window of a diner. I placed my bag down on one of the benches of a booth and sat down on the other. The middle-aged woman, who appeared to be the only waitress on duty, placed a glass of ice water in a plastic red tumbler in front of me, then a paper napkin to the left of it. She plopped silverware on top of it, then looked at me and smiled. "What will it be, child?" She reminded me of Grain, except she was closer to the age my mom would have been if she was still alive.

I looked up at the menu on the chalk board. "What's a Reuben?"

"It's a toasted sandwich on rye bread. It has corned beef, sauerkraut, provolone, and thousand island dressing."

"I'll try it. Does it come with fries and a drink?"

"It can."

"How much? I only have ten dollars to spend on food. Half of that I need to save for tomorrow."

"That should cover it. I'll even throw in a brownie for the road."

"How did you know I wasn't from around here?"

"Not many people looking like you or me live around here. Those that do I know. Also, half of our business comes from the Greyhound Station down the street. You heading to Minneapolis or Chicago?"

"Yellowstone National Park."

"You know there's bears in zoo's too, girl."

"I needed a change of scenery."

"Well, if you think Spokane is a bit pale, wait 'til you get to Montana, or is Yellowstone in Wyoming?"

"I think it's in both states."

The one thing I could say about Reubens, they were definitely different than anything else I have ever eaten. Once I got over the initial revulsion of both the smell and the taste of sauerkraut, I kind of liked it. It gave the sandwich a bit of a kick, but not too much. I didn't have enough 1000 Island dressing on it though, so I had to ask for more. I dipped the sandwich in the dressing like it was ketchup.

With tax, the meal came to $4.87. I paid the bill at the register, then rushed back to the table with a one-dollar bill. "No, you keep that," the waitress insisted. "I said you could get that meal for five dollars, and I meant it. Woman of color need to look after one another."

"You really think I'm a woman?"

"Children don't travel on the bus by themselves now, do they? If you feel you're not entirely an adult now, I'm sure you'll feel differently once you spend a winter in Yellowstone." I couldn't agree with her more.

I still had an hour before the bus left. I brought a few paperback books. I intended to save them for the long, cold, dark winter, but I was becoming both bored, and apprehensive about living in Yellowstone. I had to take my mind off my concerns for a while. Why didn't more girls like science fiction? A story about a futuristic society was much more enticing to me than a romance novel. A lot more realistic too.

I was so into my book that I nearly missed the bus. I had to rush on at the last minute, which meant no hope of getting a seat to myself. I looked for the most pleasant person I could find. A pretty girl in her early twenties waved me down once she realized I was looking for a seat. "There's a seat open here." She was everything I wasn't: bubbly, outgoing, white. She had straight blond hair that looked like nylon, but in a good way. She wore a long dress that looked simultaneously attractive and modest. "I'm Sarah Proctor."

"Jimi Jackson, but I go by Lapaz."

"That's Spanish for peace, isn't it?"

"Are you fluent in Spanish?"

"More than I was before I began my mission."

"Your mission?"

"I was called to service to share the gospel with migrant workers in Yakima."

"You look too young to be a preacher."

"L.D.S. women can serve at 21. Men at 19."

"What's L.D.S.? That's not like L.S.D., is it? I know that back in the Sixties some people encouraged taking acid, that it was like a spiritual awakening, but when I took it, it just made me feel like I was going insane."

Sarah laughed, but not in a mocking manner, taking pleasure in the inadvertent humor, not the mistake that I made. "L.D.S. is the Church of Latter Day Saints."

"Oh, you're a Mormon. I've always wondered what Mormon's believed in. You're Christians, but not really."

"We believe that the Middle East isn't the only place Jesus Christ came to. If you would like to learn more, you may have my copy of The Book of Mormon?" Sarah began thumbing through her backpack.

"No thank you. I don't want to take your bible away from you."

"The Book of Mormon isn't a substitute for the bible. Think of it as an addendum, like the New Testament. Please, take it. I can easily replace it."

"No thank you. I don't wish to be converted---not today. I have too many things on my mind to make a rational decision about my spirituality."

Sarah looked disappointed, then embarrassed, but for just a moment, before she perked up again. "I'm sorry. I thought you were interested."

"I am. There is only so many things I can think about at once. And I'm nearly saturated. Cheer up. You'll be back in Utah before you know it."

"I live in Pocatello---Idaho."

"I thought all Mormons lived in Utah."

"Pocatello isn't that far from Utah. There's actually more L.D.S. that live outside of Utah, than in it, including millions in other countries. But the concentration is much greater in Utah. I think its because we live where we do to be close to people like us."

"I can relate to that. I've only been away from Seattle for a few hours and I'm already becoming homesick. It's not just the familiar places, but the people. Even in a large city like Seattle there are parts of it where you don't meet many people like me."

"There are a few African-Americans in Salt Lake City."

"Not many though, I imagine."

"No. How do you get your hair so curly?"

Sarah was friendly and kind, but one can only take so much enthusiasm. Once it got dark I feigned sleep, to quiet her. It took her a couple minutes after noticing I was no longer responding to her to begin a conversation with the older couple behind us. She must have finally worn herself out, because she settled back in her seat and dozed off. Once she was quiet it was safe to open my eyes again. I risked looking at her. Even in her sleep she was smiling. Sometime during the night she tilted her head onto my shoulder. A short time later it began to get numb. I hadn't the heart to remove it. Who would have thought a day ago I would have had a white girl with long blond hair in such close proximity to me?

I began seeing snow beside the road on Lookout Pass in Idaho. Was I the only one concerned about slipping off the road? The bus didn't even stop to put on chains. Snow continued to be present as we dropped in elevation as we entered Montana. Even if the seats were comfortable I don't think I could have relaxed during that harrowing experience. It wasn't until we reached Butte that I got relief from my anxiety. The city near the continental divide was garnished in Christmas lights. The snow, that had created a mood of trepidation, became the foundation for joyous holiday celebration.

Sarah had to change buses in Butte. She may have been a bit too social, but she had created as much of a positive mood as the Christmas lights reflecting off the snow. Having her leave reminded me of not being with Grain for Christmas. I understood that living in Yellowstone meant not being home for Christmas, but the loss hadn't really hit me until Sarah left. Would Grain be feeling lonely on Christmas too? Maybe I could visit her on Christmas. If I just spent an hour or two with her I should have enough time. But what about the trip back to Yellowstone? I needed more time to do that. At least another day off. It didn't make much sense, did it? All that time on the bus for just a few minutes with Grain. How would everyone else in Yellowstone cope with being away from home? Would they become my surrogate family like the Marauders had been?

3.   MONTANA

I was the only person getting off at Livingston, Montana, where the Yellowstone Park bus would pick me up later in the morning. I still had three hours.

"Is there a place to eat breakfast around here?" I asked a Greyhound worker.

"There's a restaurant beside the old train station. Go up that way about four blocks. You can't miss it."

"Is it open yet?"

"It opens at 6am."

"Thanks." That meant I had to wait for an hour. I could either try to get some sleep, or read a bit more. I was too pumped up with adrenaline to sleep. It felt good to be off that bus. To emphasize the point, every few minutes I stood up and stretched. How long will the bus ride into the park be? I got tired sitting on the plastic chair the bus station provided, choosing to sit on the ground instead. I leaned against the duffle bag I used as a suitcase. I was half asleep when the westbound bus arrived. Reading always made me sleepy. Maybe that's why I always fell asleep in class.

I was shocked to see one of the passengers getting off was dark-skinned like me. African-Americans didn't travel much. The last black person I saw got off at Spokane. Why was that? We definitely weren't satisfied with our condition. Maybe it was the money. But even middle-class and wealthy blacks didn't travel much. Maybe we didn't like leaving our city-islands, where we felt we almost belonged.

Through the window, I saw the black boy not only carry his bags from the bus, but those of a girl in her mid-twenties with cropped blond hair and clothes tighter than I would wear. He was one of those rare males that looked both rugged and compassionate. I sat back up in my chair as the four potential Yellowstone employees walked into the bus station. I didn't want their first impression of me as being someone who sprawled out wherever she liked. That I was one of those pushy people who tried to make wherever they were their own.

The black boy freed himself from the bags by allowing them to flow off him one by one onto a cart. "Thank you, Flint," spoke the blond in a soft Texas drawl. "Let's eat." Did that black boy really help that white girl with her bags? Was that how it was still done in Montana?

Flint's eyes gravitated toward me. I understood that look. He wasn't thinking about just helping me with my bags. Maybe he didn't just like white girls. Why were black boys so fascinated with them? Did they have some body parts black girls didn't have? So many famous black men had white girlfriends and wives. What did that tell black women about their worth? If a black man couldn't get a white woman, they had to settle for one of their own color.

"My name's Flint."

"I heard your girlfriend call you that."

"My name isn't really Flint, it's Darrel Bogart, but me and my boys back in Chicago like to use pseudonyms...ah...nicknames."

"I understand the term."

"And Samantha isn't my girlfriend."

The girl was becoming impatient. A frown formed on her brow, and she began to tap her foot. "And maybe not even a friend anymore if you delay me from breakfast any longer."

"Samantha has blood sugar issues. If she doesn't eat every couple of hours she becomes distraught."

"That's the nicest thing anyone called me all week. Usually I hear *raging bitch*."

"Not by me."

"No, you're a gentleman. Not many of those around anymore. Hon, why don't you sit your bag on top of the others, and join us for breakfast." In the manner she spoke those words it sounded more like a decree than an invitation.

"Will they be safe just sitting there?"

"Do you see a lot of people roaming in and out of here? What's the worst thing that could happen anyway, someone steal your panties?"

"I don't have that many pairs."

"Come on, if we don't leave soon we'll have to gobble down our food, and that usually makes me have an upset stomach. When I become uncomfortable I let everyone around me know it. Every ache and pain in great detail. If someone steals your clothes, you can borrow some of mine." Like I could fit in any of hers.

As we stepped into the cold, the iciness cut through me. I thought I had brought warm clothes, but when the wind blew it felt like I was naked. Every step brought a pinch of ice as my jeans chafed. The road was cleared of snow, except where it had drifted against parked cars. Samantha chose to walk on the icy sidewalk instead. If there were cars buzzing around everywhere I could understand, but I had only seen a couple pass by the bus station since I was dropped off an hour ago. Not wanting to make any waves my first day, I followed patiently behind Samantha. Flint followed me. On the surface it might seem like he was looking after me, but guys sometimes followed girls just to look at their butts. I've heard of some girls doing the same---not me---so I couldn't be that critical. If Flint really thought the back of my heavy winter coat was sexy, more power to him.

The other two Yellowstone employees to get off the westbound bus were already in the restaurant when we arrived. My feet, and the bottoms of my legs where my coat didn't reach, were numb. Was this what frostbite felt like? Would my feet fall off after they thawed? Nope. Something more agonizing. They felt like they were being poked with jagged, hot, carving knives. Did I have to choose Yellowstone to run off to, instead of California or Florida? Someone in those states must have been hiring. I could have worked at Disneyland. Going on those rides for free, and eating all that wonderful food, like corn dogs and elephant ears. Maybe I could still work there after I finished in Yellowstone, in March.

There was nothing special about the restaurant. Someone accustomed to four-star, or even three-star dining, might call it a dive. Every town of decent size had a half-dozen of these mom and pop places. With its vinyl tables, booths, and chairs, it reminded me of the diner I ate in in Spokane. It was surprisingly busy for a Saturday morning. Three waitresses were running around like crazy. All the booths were occupied. There was a table open, but Samantha didn't want to sit in a chair. She scanned the room, then rushed to a booth as the two older couples in it got up.

"This table needs to be washed," Samantha told a waitress

as she walked by. The server looked like she ignored the comment, but she returned a minute later and removed the coffee cups and wiped the table with a rag. The cloth didn't look particularly clean, nor did the table after she washed it, but Samantha seemed to be satisfied. She slid over to the far side of one of the benches. I did likewise on the other. Flint followed behind me. Did he do so because he liked me, or because he didn't want to be that close to Samantha before she ate?

Two large wall heaters blasted air into the dining room. Moments ago, I had been freezing, now I was roasting alive. I took off my coat, reducing, but not eliminating my overheating. It always took my body awhile to adjust to its surroundings. I was still cold when I first sat down.

I stretched my arms out on the table. Ugh. The sleeves of my turtleneck got both wet and sticky. It was like the bus bathroom all over again. Not exactly. I hoped there wasn't urine on the table, but in some ways the syrup was even worse.

Samantha was getting frustrated again, and it had nothing to do with my accident. After our table had been token cleaned a waitress hadn't returned to take our order. "Flint, can you fetch us some menus?"

Obediently, he appropriately three of the laminated eight-and-a-half by eleven pieces of paper. They were in as bad of shape as the table. The prices were fair. From the number of locals present the food must have been good too. There may not be another opportunity to buy a meal, so I decided to spend the remainder of my money on a combination plate.

The waitress who had *washed* our table finally returned. She set three glasses of water on the table. "Would you like some coffee or orange juice?" She wasn't exactly rude, but she wasn't polite either. She had a job to do and many other customers.

"I'll have a large glass of tomato juice," said Flint. I grimaced.

"Orange juice for me," said Samantha. "And can you bring

me some lemons for my water? Thanks."

"Coffee for me, please."

After the waitress left, Flint pulled a napkin from the metal dispenser at the end of the table and soaked it in his water. "Let me help with your sleeves." Stunned by the unsolicited assistance, I didn't decline. In an extremely gentle manner he delicately wiped the ends of my shirt. When he was done, the stickiness was removed, but about a cup of water was added.

"Thank you."

He smiled.

The waitress returned with the three drinks, a bowl of lemon wedges, and three sets of silverware held in place by a napkin wrapped around them.

Flint took a big gulp of tomato juice, leaving a substantial reminder of it on his face. Samantha pointed at her mouth. Flint got the hint, wiping his mouth with a napkin. He wasn't completely successful. Samantha pouted, then dipped a napkin in her water and wiped his face for him. She may not have been thinking this, but I felt like that action was saying, "If I wanted him, I could have him. And if he ever got with you, I could take him away from you with a single seductive glance, or a snap of my fingers."

"That stuff looks disgusting." I had never liked tomato juice, not even tomato derived drinks like V-8. If a person enjoyed the taste of tomatoes so much, why not drink out of a ketchup bottle? At least it was sweet.

"It will put hair on your chest." I began to picture Flint's bare, hairy chest. I began to blush.

"Are you okay?" asked Samantha. "It's not the coffee, is it? Whenever I drink it I have to pee all day. Sometimes it even gives me the Hershey squirts." That definitely took my mind off Flint's chest.

The food was delicious. I didn't like tomato juice, but I loved ketchup. I coated my hash browns and eggs with it.

"Now, whose being disgusting?" asked Flint.

By the time I got done adding syrup to my pancakes, they were soaking in it. As were my bacon, ham, and sausage links. I didn't mind. I often used syrup as a dipping sauce for meats.

Halfway through the meal the waitress returned, a pitcher of water in one hand, a pot of coffee in the other. After refilling our beverages, she did the same to the table beside us.

We sat quietly as we ravished our food. Samantha abruptly pushed her plate away from her, then looked at her watch. "It's time to go."

"But we still have 45 minutes," Flint insisted. He had been done with his meal for quite some time. He began to nibble on Samantha's after she pushed it aside. "It's a lot more comfortable here than in the bus station."

"I need to freshen up before the others arrive." How fresh can one be? Did she plan to shower and put on clean clothes?

I grabbed my check and began walking up to the register. Samantha placed her money on top of her check. "They can take care of that here."

I flopped down the remainder of my money on my check. Flint snatched the last piece of ham off Samantha's plate, then folded a ten-dollar bill around his check, giving the waitress a very generous tip. Had I given too little? A routinely gave fifteen percent, no matter the service. I visually examined Samantha's tip. She had given about fifty cents. I felt much better about myself.

The walk back to the bus station was warmer than the one away from it. The sun had finally risen. That may have made a difference. It also may have been because we were freshly fueled, and had an increased ability to produce heat. Or was I already becoming acclimated to a Rocky Mountain winter?

Somehow Samantha was able to consume half an hour in the bathroom. The only time I did that was when I had a particularly bad stomach ache. When she emerged, she didn't look any different, not significantly. Her hair was a bit more combed out, and her make-up reapplied, but nothing to warrant the time she spent in there.

While Samantha was in the restroom, two more Yellowstone employees entered the bus station. They had spent the night in a nearby motel. The two who had arrived with Flint and Samantha returned shortly before that. So, there were seven of us. How many were there going to be coming from the airport? At most a bus held 60 people. Did that mean the other 50 Snow Lodge employees drove? Who would choose to drive in snow and ice? They couldn't drive their cars down to Old Faithful, so why bring them at all?

Flint and Samantha knew the two who had stayed in the Motel. They got reacquainted. Many of Yellowstone's winter employees return year after year. They were like family. They might not see one another until the following summer or winter, but within minutes of reuniting it was like they hadn't been away from one another, like no time had passed, like they had been hibernating and had just woken up. I felt like an outsider again. I didn't have any long-term friends to return to.

Samantha turned to me. "Ah…."

Lapaz sounded too exotic. Too distant. It was easier creating friendships with the familiar. "Jimi."

"Has a roommate been assigned to you yet?"

"I don't think so."

"Then you and I are going to be roommates this winter." That didn't leave much open to discussion.

"I'm surprised you don't already have a roommate lined up."

"She did," Flint interjected, "but they had a bit of a falling out this fall."

"Christine never wanted to have fun. She had to analyze everything she and everyone around her did. She would rather talk about doing something than actually doing it."

Our transportation into Yellowstone National Park had finally arrived. The yellow bus had a picture of a bear on it. A cart, pregnant with baggage, was rolled to the back of the bus by the driver. Flint helped. As soon as the double-door was opened the excitement of those within erupted. It reminded me of pictures I saw of Mardi Gras or of Spring Break. Grain never took me to California, and the Marauders didn't think it was cool to go. The bags were transferred from the cart to the space behind the back seats.

"Doesn't the bus have a cargo hold beneath it?" I asked Samantha.

"It must be full." How much stuff did these people bring?

The bus wasn't just full of bags. The additional seven of us barely fit. I was a bit overwhelmed. I had never been claustrophobic, but if I was, this was a good opportunity to start. All those people talking loudly and bouncing up and down in their seats reminded me of school. The kids here weren't that much older than the ones I would have been finishing my senior year with.

Samantha was warmly greeted. It would have been sad if all the trouble she went to, to make herself presentable, went to waste. Flint was also well received, but in a more subdued manner.

I silently listened to the many conversations. In was nearly impossible to distinguish one from another. The stories were part summer tales, part traveling between seasons, part past common experiences in winter, part planning for the current winter season. Stories of hiking, and skiing, and camping, became muddled. Geysers. Buffalo. Bears. Mountains. Hot pots? Most enjoyable, to me, was hearing about people going to Washington D.C., New York City, and Canada. I've never had the opportunity to travel myself, but when I was a child---even as an older child---I loved looking at National Geographic.

With so many interesting conversations going on, and looking at the snow-covered mountains beside the road, I was thoroughly entertained, which made the trip to Yellowstone pass very quickly. It seemed like just minutes after leaving Livingston that Gardiner was reached, one of the park's border communities, and the headquarters of the company I was to work for. The bus stopped in front of a building with the same bear logo as the bus.

We weren't given any instructions, but there were so many repeat employees there didn't need to be any. I followed Flint into the building. Samantha was still busy reuniting. We left our bags on the bus. A line had already formed. The fifty employees who hadn't taken a bus or flown wanted to beat the crowd. I didn't blame them. As the two groups met, more conversations began.

Processing became a blur. I just did what Flint did. I began by showing someone my copy of my contract. It was taken and I was given another one to sign. I was in the process of signing it when I noticed it wasn't exactly the same as the one I gave the woman. "My position and hourly wage have been changed."

"Some of the people who were going to work at Snow Lodge changed their minds at the last minute. Instead of putting the new hires in their positions, we chose to promote from within, which meant people like you who have never worked in the Park, but were hired a few weeks earlier, were upgraded. If you don't want to be a busser, we can put you back as Kitchen Help."

I was hired as Kitchen Help, so that was what I was prepared to do. Running around handing herbs and spices to the cooks didn't sound too bad. "Is being a busser better than being Kitchen Help?"

"A busser helps a server, by setting tables, clearing them, and filling water glasses."

"We'll I could definitely do that. If would be fun to help the cooks too, though."

"Kitchen Help usually means washing dishes, but you might be serving food to employees, or making salads and desserts for the restaurant."

"I definitely don't want to wash dishes." How many hours had I spent over the years washing Grain's pots and pans, and dishes and glasses? Why couldn't she buy paper plates and cups? Or a dishwasher?

"But doesn't Kitchen Help pay more?"

"Servers give part of their tips to bussers."

"So overall I would be making more money?" I signed the form and a few other forms. I received a name badge and three sets of uniforms. "I was told we would be working five days a week."

"Then you're going to have to do some laundry mid-week."

"Or you could wear them more than one day," Flint whispered to me. "I spot clean my pants and shirts if they look too bad." Like that was going to happen. Sometimes I switched clothes midday if they were starting to smell. The dorm was supposed to have a laundry room. It would have to be a large one if a hundred people had to wash their clothes twice a week?

An orientation was given in a small auditorium at 10:30. It was mainly for the benefit of the newbies. I was quite bored with it. Ninety-percent of it I already learned from the literature that was sent with my initial contract.

At 11:00 we returned to the bus. Those with cars were already on their way to Mammoth Hot Springs, the northern most location in the park, just six miles from Gardiner. The ride up the Gardner River canyon was more subdued than the ride from Livingston. The initial burst of socialization had expired. Lack of sleep due to traveling, and from the excitement of the season beginning, had finally taken its toll. Somewhere along the route we passed the Forty-Fifth Parallel and entered Wyoming. I always liked Wyoming's license plate, the one with the bucking bronco. It would almost be worth it to live in Wyoming just to get that license plate.

4.   WYOMING

The bus dropped us off at an Employees Dining Room, what most people just called the E.D.R. It was time for the free meals to begin. The food wasn't really free. A certain amount was taken out of every paycheck to compensate for food and lodging, but the amount was reasonable, much more economical than the *real world*.

On the way to the bus, I saw two skiers climbing the hill behind a cluster of cabins. Diagonal tracks followed them. Flint followed my eyes and smiled. "That would be Charlie Peterson and Andy Lincoln. Two of our most colorful Snow Lodge employees."

"Aren't they going to miss lunch?"

"They probably have already eaten. Even if they haven't, a ski run is more than adequate compensation for missing lunch. You'll see in a couple of weeks. You'll get hooked too."

"It doesn't look very safe. That hill's pretty steep."

"Don't worry. Andy is reasonably practical. If he didn't think it was safe, he wouldn't do it. Now, for Charlie, the more dangerous the better. That boy doesn't have much common sense. Never challenge him to do something unless you can live with the consequences."

"How can someone be that careless?"

"We are all unique. What's inside you or me isn't inside Charlie. Something tells him to push himself to the limit. Only he knows what that is."

The same level of active enthusiasm that was in the bus ride down to Gardiner had returned in the EDR. It was amazing what a modicum of subsistence did to a congregation.

"What would you like?" the server behind the plexiglass protected serving counter asked Flint.

"Let's make it simple and easy. Give me a bit of everything. And when I mean a bit, I mean as much as would fit on my tray."

"You can only have one cheeseburger at a time."

"Then let's hurry it up so I can come back in a couple of minutes." By the time the server was done slopping food on Flint's multi-slotted tray it looked more like what was scraped into the garbage than fresh food. As Flint carried the tray to the beverage station, a fry fell off. He set his food down, then snatched up the fry and put it in his mouth. I nearly dropped my tray. "Haven't you heard of the three-second rule?" he said. "If you pick up food that has fallen on the ground within three seconds it's still probably clean enough to eat."

"Probably?"

"There are no guarantees in life."

My tray looked like Flint's tray's anorexic cousin. I had a cheeseburger on it like he did, but just a few fries, and a small salad.

"Aren't you going to put any dressing on your salad?"

"You can't taste the lettuce if its soaking in that stuff."

"Isn't that the point? Personally, I don't eat salads, on moral grounds. If I eat that much roughage I deny that second cheeseburger an opportunity to reunite with the first one."

I filled a plastic tumbler nearly to the top with ice then added coke to it. I liked to water down my soft drinks. They were always too sweet. Why couldn't they make them with half the sugar? Flint also filled his tumbler with coke, but without the ice. "You get more for your money if you don't add ice."

"But isn't food, and drink, in the EDR all you can eat?"

"What I meant was *when* you have to pay for a fountain drink. Watering it down is going against nature. Do you really think you know more about coke than God?" I wasn't sure if Flint was serious, until the ends of his mouth curled up.

"There's Barry." Flint started to walk towards a table with just one open seat. Was he really going to abandon me, now, after all we've been through? The best three hours of my life. I smiled, then began scanning the dining room for another place to sit. Flint, noticing I hadn't followed him, waved me over. I cautiously clutched my tray as I weaved my way towards him. With all the people coming and going, sitting and standing, it reminded me of being in kindergarten.

"But there's only room for one." I grimaced internally. It got close to sounding like a whine. I didn't like people who whined.

"I'll get up then." A large girl stood up. "I've been done eating for ten minutes." She wasn't fat. She just wasn't petite. She was nearly as tall as Flint. She filled out her frame well, with an equal dose of toned muscle and femininity. She had mid-shoulder length dishwater blond hair. It wasn't particularly messy, but it wasn't fixed up either. She was one of those girls who spent two minutes on it every morning instead of half-an-hour. Her eyes were a shade greener than hazel. Every year or so I would notice someone who stood out. They didn't always happen to be the prettiest or the most hansom, but something about their features or the way they carried themselves made them appear interesting. It had to do more with the inner person surfacing, because physically they weren't much different than anyone else.

"No. Sit. I want to introduce you all to Jimi. She is new to the Park. I'll find another chair."

"I'm Christine Faith." The chocolate brunette extended her hand. I shook it. Her straight hair was tied back in a ponytail. It fell to the middle of her back. She looked like one of those girls you would see in the Swiss Alps or on a farm in the Midwest. Average height. Enough meat on her bones to get her through a winter. Busty, but in a very clandestine manner.

"Samantha mentioned a Christine."

"And you probably weren't able to mention much yourself. She likes to saturate a room with her voice. She *doesn't* like you disagreeing with her. And God forbid if someone wants to discuss something."

"She asked me to be her roommate, because the two of you had a falling out?"

"You weren't given a choice to decline, were you? Just be attentive to her and the two of you should get along. Whatever you do, don't interrupt her when she's on a roll. It's like trying to stop a mad rhinoceros in the middle of a charge. I often wondered what happened in her childhood to make her who she is? Did she not get enough attention at home? Were her parents extremely authoritative, and she wasn't allowed to vocalize her own opinions?"

"She is fun to be around."

"She is that. Never a dull moment around her, especially when you want to sleep. There are no uncomfortable pauses and no idle time."

Flint returned with a chair. He sat in one of the corners of the table, leaving the more desirable location, on one of the sides, for me. "It looks like you've already met Christine Faith. And this is Matilda Enrique."

"Howdy." For someone so large, her sweet, quiet voice seemed out of place. She stared at me intensely with those green eyes. I couldn't sustain such scrutiny, so I had to turn away. When I looked back at her a few seconds later she was still examining me. I turned away again, like I had been looking at something I shouldn't have been and got caught.

"And this is Barry Henry." He nodded. "He has been my roommate the past two winters. Make that three now." If Matilda was a female giant, Barry was her male counterpart. He was a good three or four inches taller than Flint, and outweighed him by a hundred pounds. He looked like a mountain man with his untrimmed beard and hair and plaid shirt. He also looked like someone who played football, but had retired from it. There was a thin line between being massively strong and massively fat. Barry may have had the ability to pick up boulders a few years back, but now that boulder was attached to his gut.

"There's going to be a Safety Meeting in our room tonight." When Barry spoke, he sounded like a bear with a mouth full of honey.

"So soon?" Flint sounded disappointed.

"One can't start off the season unsafe."

"I think this year I might not go to any of the meetings. I'm turning 30 and...."

"Enlightenment doesn't have an age limit. Strong winds deliver great transformations."

Flint whispered into my ear, "Barry says things like that sometimes, whatever pops into his head. He believes he's a conduit for God. Coming from God, there has to be some meaning behind it."

"Why are you so against people discussing safety issues?" I whispered back to him.

"*Safety Meeting* is a term Barry and his disciples use when they mean they want to get high."

"Oh. It seems a bit contradictory to me. Whenever I was stoned I did some very stupid things."

"I think the first Safety Meeting was actually to discuss safety. Somewhere in the conversations, members of the committee learned they all were pot smokers, so why not kill two brain cells with one meeting."

"So, are you also part of this Safety Meeting Committee?"

"I *was*, but I only get high socially. Barry and some of his friends do so as a lifestyle."

"I'm not criticizing you. I used to get high myself. I was just curious."

"Should the two of you get a room?" Matilda smiled as she spoke, but I noticed there was a bit of sadness behind her words. Had she and Flint hooked up? Or was she wanting them to do so this winter? Our ears and mouths being so close together did look erotically clandestine. I blushed.

Flint looked at the clock on the wall. "CRAP! I need to go." Without giving further explanation, he got up and rushed out the door, leaving his tray and partially-eaten food.

Five minutes later someone made an announcement that the busses would be leaving at noon. It was about 11:50. "I need to use the little girl's room before we leave." Christine stacked Flint's dishes on hers, placing the two tumblers and the silverware on the top tray. She headed to the dirty dish drop. She threw the silverware in a soapy bin, and the tumblers in a dry one beside it. She knocked both trays on the inside of a garbage can, then placed them on top of a stack of dirty trays that were on the verge of tipping over.

I had to use the restroom too, but being a fairly private person, I preferred to do it alone. I always thought it weird that girls went to the bathroom in groups. Sharing was great, at times, but did everything have to be shared?

As soon as I saw Christine walk out I walked in. There was a line of girls waiting to use the stalls. I should have gone to the bathroom when Christine did. If it took too long would the bus leave without me? But if I didn't go would I be able to make it all the way to Old Faithful---where Snow Lodge was located?

What then? Asking the bus driver to stop, so I could run into the snow and pee behind a tree? What if someone else saw where I peed? The evidence wouldn't be that obvious on the grass, but on snow…. I would have to cover it up. My hands would get cold or my gloves wet. Maybe I could just kick snow onto it, but then my shoes would get wet. And what if I stepped in it by mistake, or slipped on the icy snow and landed in it?

There was only one more girl in front of me. I can't give up now. But a minute or two more might be all it takes for me to miss the bus. The doors of both stalls opened simultaneously. I rushed into one. I latched the door shut then pulled down my pants and underwear with one yank. I dropped onto the toilet seat. I was in mid-fall when I remembered what had happened on the bus. It was too late to prevent the potential accident. I didn't have time to clean myself up this time. Woo. The seat was dry. The urine rushed out of me like I was a horse. The stall door rolled towards me. Either I hadn't latched it properly or the latch was broken. I pushed the door away from me with my left hand. What was I thinking? The door bounced off the bracket and headed back towards me. This time I kept my arm outstretched. The door may not have completely been shut, but it was shut enough to retain my modesty. With my right hand, I pulled off a wad of toilet paper, wiped myself dry, then attempted to pull up my underwear and jeans. I lost the grip on my underwear. I ended up pulling up just my jeans. Ugh. I not only gave myself a wedgie, it was nearly impossible to walk. As I leaned my back against the stall door I pulled my jeans back down, then pulled my underwear up before pulling up my jeans.

I rushed out of the bathroom, through the EDR, and out towards the bus. There were still a few people in the EDR, but I didn't know if they were heading down to Snow Lodge or were staying in Mammoth. It was the only other location in the Park that opened during the winter. I don't know why I was in such a hurry. I wasn't the only one still heading towards the bus. Now busses. Another had joined ours. Of course, we needed two busses. Those who drove had to also get to Old Faithful. If busses were able to drive down, why weren't cars?

The doors were shut on my bus. The driver opened the door for me. "We're full. You'll need to get on the other bus." She re-shut the door. But that's my bus, with my stuff on it.

Christine walked past me towards the other bus. "Come on. You don't want to walk to Old Faithful, do you?"

"But my stuff is on this bus."

"Doesn't matter. We take care of each other. Your gear will arrive at Old Faithful, eventually."

"Eventually?"

Christine laughed. "Come on."

There was an empty seat near the front. Apparently, the people who worked at Snow Lodge were the troublemaker types that liked to sit in the back. Christine plopped onto the open seat and slid over to the window. I dropped down next to her.

The bus pulled away from the Mammoth Hot Springs Hotel a few minutes later. Only two other people entered the bus after I did. I had cut it close.

We passed a restaurant, a general store, a gas station, then chalky-white terraces, shelves created by thermal runoff, still overflowing with steaming, pale blue water. The water flowed from one level to the next, leaving brilliant red, yellow, and orange deposits. I wish I had about an hour more in Mammoth to see them up close. The bus made a switchback a half-a-mile from the terraces, then headed back towards them. Before it reached them, it turned back on itself one more time. The higher we got the deeper the snow got. I was becoming concerned. Was it safe for the bus driver to make those tight turns on that ice? The busses stopped in a parking area at the entrance to Terrace Drive, a short one-way auto loop at the top of the hot springs.

The bus door opened, and people got up and left. Were we actually going to hike to the top levels of the terraces? I was both exited and put out. I wanted to see them, but I didn't want it to delay our arrival to Old Faithful. I heard the cargo hold being opened and became even more confused. As I stepped down onto the packed snow my questions were answered. In front of the busses, on both sides of the road, were what looked to be pairs of yellow tanks mating. People began transferring the luggage from the busses to the snow machines. I tried to find my one bag, but couldn't.

Matilda noticed my helpless, blank look. "I know it's a bit chaotic. Just lend a helping hand where you can. We don't head to Snow Lodge until all the snow coaches are loaded."

Matilda picked up a large suitcase in each hand and headed

towards one of the snow machines in the middle of the pack. I
picked up a bag that looked like an elongated duffle. Something
moved around in it. I think they were skis. There wasn't a handle
on it, so I carried it over my shoulder. I headed for the same snow
machine as Matilda. I handed it to the person who was loading it.

"We're full here. Take it to another coach."

The one in front of it didn't look like the others. It was blue
and had just one compartment. Unlike the yellows that had just
treads, this one also had skis in front, making it look a bit like a
motorized sled. There was nothing inside it yet, but no one was
there to load it either. Christine came by.

"We're going to ride in the blues and use the yellows to haul
our luggage. The blues are faster. It doesn't make much sense for
our luggage to get to the dorm before we do."

Christine disappeared again. I carried the bag to a yellow
snow machine that was still loading. By the time I had finally
figured out what I was doing, the buses had been completely
unloaded. People began to enter the blue snow machines. I
scanned the area to find someone I had met. I didn't see anyone,
so I climbed into the closest vehicle.

The seats were arranged like a sectional. They wrapped
around the sides and back of the snow machine in a horseshoe
shape. There were two bucket seats in front. They were both
occupied, as were most of the others. The driver wore a khaki
uniform, including his oversized baseball cap, the ones truckers
sometimes wore. He looked behind him as his coach filled. It was
Flint. He never mentioned he was a driver/tour guide. How did he
change so quickly? Did he do so in the coach before the busses
arrived? I smiled at the thought. "Everyone scoot over. We can't
leave until there are twelve of us. Scrunch together. You're going
to know each other quite well by the end of the winter, so you
might as well start now. Hey, Jimi." I felt both pleased and
embarrassed I was singled out. I also I felt like I was a sardine. I
was sandwiched between two men in their mid-twenties with

beards. Why did so many of them wear facial hair here? Was it that cold, or did they choose to not shave because they were isolated, and they felt they didn't have to care about their appearance? I was never that fond of boys with beards. The hair tickled me when I kissed them, and it covered up their lips too much. I don't think I ever made this close of contact to people before, even while having sex.

Flint counted the people behind him. "Mike. Can you recruit one more person, so we're not the last one out of here."

A boy in his early twenties scuttled out of the coach like a monkey. What was the turning point where a boy became a man? It surely wasn't when he fathered a child. I knew too many boys in Rainier Valley who did. They became even more immature afterwards, running from the mother and their emotional and financial obligations. But calling someone a boy wasn't always derogatory. If a male was full of life I thought of him as a boy. If he was the more serious type, a stodgy male of any age, I always thought of him as a man. I think that's why I liked Flint. He had some characteristics of both a boy and a man. The best of each. Mike scuttled back in. A boy very similar to Mike, in motion and demeanor, entered after him. Flint stepped back towards the door and pulled it shut. He returned to his seat. A shift of gears and we were off. The engine had been running all this time, with the heater blaring. With so much body heat the temperature in the coach had long passed from being too cold to too hot. After we had safely maneuvered past the coaches that were still loading passengers, Flint turned down the heat.

We passed some interesting rock formations on the right, then we entered a short canyon, with a creek flowing below on our left. We passed over a bridge that had been constructed to create a shelf large enough for the road. Ahead, the creek became almost level with the road as it fell over a waterfall. An icy rind coated its perimeter. Would it be completely frozen by the end of the winter, making the water appear as if it had solidified mid-fall? As we came out the top of the canyon the land opened up. A snowy plain stretched for miles on our right, to abruptly end at the base of similarly hued peaks.

Flint shared some of his tour guide knowledge with those of us who were new to the Park. "We just passed through the Golden Gate. Rustic Falls was on the left. We just entered Swan Lake Flats. The peak to the left is called Bunsen. Those mountains on the right are part of the Gallatin Range."

There was so much to see. It was difficult to take it all in. There was one particularly prominent mountain on the right and back a bit. The top part of it was obscured by clouds. "What's that mountain back there?" I asked. The sun had finally made its appearance, but that didn't mean the sky was completely clear. Every few minutes a cloud would cover it, making it a tad darker, and less cheery. Overall it had turned into quite a nice day. At times, it was almost too bright, when the sun hit the reflective snow.

"The big one? That's Electric. It's on the park boundary. I've climbed it a couple of times in the summer. I wouldn't recommend it in winter. You get access to it from the south. The land to the north belongs to CUT."

"A lumber company, this close to Yellowstone?"

"CUT in an acronym for Church Universal and Triumphant. It's a cult that owns a lot of land north of the Park."

"What do they believe in?"

"Don't really know. And don't really care. I just keep my distance from them. Some of them walk around with guns."

"Is that legal?"

"A lot of people walk around with guns in Montana and Wyoming. We like to hunt and to be able to protect ourselves if the occasion arises, except maybe in Missoula. A bunch of hippies live there."

"I thought you were from Chicago?"

"I was, but I consider Yellowstone my home now, so

Montana and Wyoming have become my home states. And Idaho. There's a sliver of it on the western border. You can't eat a steak without a potato now, can you? I even have registered my car in Wyoming."

"You have one of those cowboy license plates."

"A silhouette of a wrangler. One of my most cherished possessions."

"Not too many dark-skinned cowboys, are there?"

"There used to be. I read somewhere that twenty percent of the original cowboys where of African descent. Can you imagine? It hasn't been wildly publicized, because that might diminish some of its glamour."

"Don't you ever feel isolated out here? Being a squid in an ocean of pearls."

"There are black pearls too, you know. Everyone is unique in Yellowstone, especially in the winter. How many people do you know back home, black or white, who would even consider working out here? Everyone has prejudices, even here, but none are appraised higher than any other. You are allowed to be an individual. Not just allowed, but encouraged. Some people may love you. Others, hate you. We aren't the only minority here." Flint was referring to the large Lesbian community in Yellowstone during the winter. Butch women were drawn to the wilderness, but few frilly men.

"One of the reasons I sought you out was because of my sexuality," spoke Jolairshay.

"We are who we are. Homosexuals have been sought and despised for the same reason: unconventionality. Popularity and hipness aren't reasons for joining."

The snow coach entered a forest. Most of the trees were burnt, so forest may not have been the most accurate descriptor. But the snow muted most of the bleakness the fires created. Flint returned to tour spiel, throwing out names like Sheepeater Cliffs, Frying Pan Spring, Beaver and Lemonade Lakes, and Roaring Mountain. The latter was seen to the left of us spewing steam and hissing.

"Is that a geyser?" I asked.

Flint stopped the snow coach in front of it. He was eager to arrive at Old Faithful, but tour guide duties superseded, or maybe he did it just for me. He opened the hatch on top of the vehicle, allowing those who wanted to poke their head out and look, a few seconds each. "It's just a steam vent. Geysers are more intermittent. We'll pass a geyser basin in a few minutes. We won't have time to stop today, but you'll be able to see it if you take a tour sometime this winter. All coach rides, as tours or transportation, are free to employees if space is available. The only problem is you may have to wait until the last minute so see if you are bumped by a paying customer."

"Can we leave the hatch open?" someone asked.

"Normally I wouldn't, but because you're employees, sure. I can't let anyone up there when we're moving. Don't want anyone getting whiplash or falling out." That deflated the person who asked, but just a bit. He still got his fresh air and a view of the sky. It was like we were in a convertible---in Alaska. "Anyone want to move around a bit before we start moving again. Those in front could let others enjoy the view."

"I get the hint." The boy beside Flint got up and half-walked, half-crawled to the back. "Don't expect any tip from me now."

"Jimi, would you like to sit up here? Those who haven't been in the Park before should have a good view of the scenery at least once."

Being cramped outweighed me not wanting to appear like I was being given special treatment. The one black boy in Yellowstone helping the one black girl. I guess it all averaged out. White people have been helping each other, to the detriment of others, for thousands of years. The view was much better. Not only was I facing outward instead of inward, the window wasn't steamed up at all in front. All those hot bodies in back all scrunched together covered the glass with a substantial opaque water vapor coating---now frozen.

Flint stopped at the geyser basin he had spoken of, but not to view the spewing water. Bison, more commonly known as buffalo, crossed the road in front us. The largest ones were about a third the size of the snow coach. Snow clumped in their brown coats, retaining its solidity, the beasts' internal furnaces being significantly dampened by their thick fur. Their slightly darker heads were enormous, twice the size they should have been relative to the size of their bodies. Black orbs looked dully ahead. Slightly above them, horns jutted out. "Look out the top if you want. I'm leaving as soon as the road is clear."

"Have you ever hit one?" I asked.

"No. And I haven't heard of any other coach driver doing so, but there was a snowmobiler a couple of years back that did. The bison walked away, but he didn't." The last buffalo crossed the road. "Everyone, back in your seats." The snow coach began moving again.

We came to an intersection. "To the left is the Grand Canyon of the Yellowstone River, or as it is more commonly called, just Canyon. To the right is Norris Geyser Basin. Anyone need to use the restroom?" Flint paused---at most---for a second. He really didn't want any more delays. "Good. There will be one more potty break opportunity before we reach Snow Lodge."

The road followed a creek much wider than the one that created Rustic Falls. It also had its waterfall. We would have missed it if Flint hadn't pointed it out. It could only be seen from behind us. "That's Gibbon Falls." It was at least twice as tall as the first falls. Flint also mentioned Artist Paint Pots, Monument Geyser Basin, and Terrace Spring. He didn't stop at any of them, but they were named, and a few of them even described.

Sometimes Flint would glance over at me in a manner that

told me he was interested. I hadn't come to Yellowstone to have a relationship, but I wasn't opposed to one either. Flint probably had a new girlfriend every season, summer and winter. When I was younger I may not have minded a quick fling, but if I was going to invest emotionally in someone I wanted it to last more than a few weeks. I may only be eighteen, but I've had as many experiences as someone twice my age. I was ready to settle down, at least on an emotional level. I wasn't sure Flint had quite reached that point in his life yet. "Don't be afraid to visit me in the dorm. Barry doesn't smoke weed all the time. He has to be coherent to work. He's a cook. Heavy machinery isn't involved, but he can get cut or burned."

"What's the deal with Barry? You mentioned his drug use and him being some kind of prophet. He sounds odd even for Yellowstone standards."

"Barry almost didn't return this winter. He was arrested for drug possession during the summer. Because the fires in the Park had scared away many of those who had committed to work during the winter, hiring became more lenient. That's why newbies like you were hired. Working during the winter had been a privilege, granted to those superior summer employees with seniority. Barry hadn't always been a philosopher. After he got arrested he was determined to change his errant ways. He almost lost his lifestyle, his freedom to periodically work and travel. He couldn't waste his life by partying all the time. He had to take life more seriously. That is when God entered his life, but a god of his own choosing. The strange things he spoke of to his stoner friends seemed very profound to them in their drugged-induced stupors. During the fall, Barry transformed into this pseudo-prophet. Being stoic, large-bodied, and whimsical, it wasn't too surprising that many saw him as a modern Buddha. I continue to be his friend, but never a disciple. One cannot be both."

We passed another junction. Flint was uncharacteristically quiet about it. A few minutes later he pulled off the road into a parking area. "Everyone take a bathroom break who needs one. We'll be leaving in five minutes. If I'm not back by then, make it ten." Flint rushed towards a row of portable outhouses. I debated whether to go or wait until we reached Old Faithful. I've used an outhouse once, at a carnival. I haven't used one since. How could something smell that bad? I nearly vomited. With it being cold, maybe it wouldn't stink. It had been quite warm the day I used the outhouse. I did have to go, and the snow coach wasn't a particularly smooth vehicle. Bouncing accelerated the termination of the digestive cycle.

I rushed out the open door of the coach and headed to the remaining unoccupied potty. Only two others from the vehicle had to go bed enough to tempt fate, so I didn't have to wait for one to become available. I held my breath as I opened the door. I locked the door behind me. I made sure it wasn't going to open up on me this time. This was ridiculous. I couldn't hold my breath the entire time. Maybe if I was a guy I could, but for a girl it was too time consuming, even if she just had to pee, and I didn't. I did mention the snow coach ride not being particularly smooth. My guts had been tossed like a salad in a mixing bowl. There was no odor at all. After I sat on the toilet seat I knew why. "YOW!" What must the others think of my reaction, not just in the other outhouses, but in the snow coach, and possibly in the next county. The bacteria that causes odors must have froze to death. I leaped up, fortunately before I began my business. I wasn't going to give up so easily. I gritted my teeth as I pressed my butt back down on the seat. It felt like I was branding it with a hot iron. Eventually, the two temperatures, the seat's and my butt's, would become the same. What I hadn't predicted was the merging of temperatures would be closer to the seat's than my butt's. I completed the task, and a task it certainly was. The battle may have been won---it felt more like a draw---but the war endured. Men may have declared victory, but women were more concerned with personal hygiene, and the toilet paper was about the same temperature as the seat before I sat on it.

The employees on the snow coach clapped as I climbed in. My face reddened. I wasn't sure if it was from getting angry at my greeting, my embarrassment, or the interior of the coach being significantly warmer than the outhouse. Flint was already back in the coach, as were the other two who had relieved themselves. "I believe you've been christened." Better than being sexed or beat in, but something I didn't want to repeat anytime soon.

"Anyone want to sit up here for a while?" I worked my way to the back of the snow coach. I really wasn't upset with Flint, not that much anyway. It was all too much for me. Being that startled, and that cold, then having that embarrassing reception. There were others that probably wanted to sit up there anyway. If I had to go through what I did some good was going to come from it, for someone.

"No, not you, Carl. Someone who is new to the Park."

The snow coach pulled back onto the road. Feeling more comfortable now, Flint returned to tour guide mode. "That was Madison Junction back there. West Yellowstone is to the west. That's the Firehole River on the right. Many thermal features drain into it which gave it its name." Flint also pointed out Firehole Canyon Drive, Fountain Flats Drive, and Firehole Lake Drive. We passed through four major geyser basins before we reached Old Faithful: Lower, Midway, Biscuit, and Black Sand. The thermal area Old Faithful was in was called the Upper Geyser Basin.

We passed under an interchange bridge. Half a mile later I spotted buildings on the right that looked like dorms. They were easy to see through the blackened, limbless trees. We turned off the main road towards them. We passed the first building, stopping in front of the second. There were already some snow coaches there, unloading passengers.

5.   MOVING IN

Flint waited for a snow coach to pull away, then took its spot directly across from the dorm. "That's Lupine Dorm, your home away from home for the next three months. It's pronounced Lu-pine in the summer, but Lu-pin in the winter. I don't know why? It's a tradition that started way before I started working in the Park. Your luggage should arrive in about an hour, unless a coach breaks down, which sometimes happens. That gives you plenty of time to check-in and get a room assignment."

We didn't have to be told twice to leave the coach. Being cramped in there for nearly two hours was a bit much. How did Flint do it for a full day, five days a week? "You coming back to the dorm soon?" I asked him.

"Just have to drop off the coach and refuel it. I should be back before the luggage arrives." Flint shut the door and drove off.

I followed the line of people into the dorm, about half looking like they had lived here before. The Resident Coordinator---RC---had an office in the middle of the bottom floor of the two-story building. Stacks of sheets, blankets, and pillows filled most of the room, making it appear more like a storage room. The RC looked to be in her late twenties. She wore a tan uniform similar to Flint's. *Gwen Moon* was engraved on her white name tag. I had also been given a name tag, but instead of having my last name, it had my state: Washington. And the words were made with a tape gun instead of being embossed. Were hourly employees that disposable?

Gwen obviously had done this job for a while, because it

took just five minutes for her to assign a room, bedding, and a key to the five people in front of me. "Name."

"Jimi Jackson."

"Samantha Salsa says you agreed to room with her. Is that okay with you?"

"She was going to room with Christine Faith, but they're no longer friends."

"We'll have to put you in a room up top. You'll have to share a bathroom with another room."

"With boys or girls?"

"Two girls. You can have a roommate of the opposite sex in the winter, but we don't want to force that on anyone. Room 202." Gwen handed me my key. "Take a pillow and a pillowcase, two sheets, and a blanket."

"Can I take two? I've heard it gets cold here in the winter."

"Gets cold? I'm from Georgia. When it gets down to 70 I wear a sweater."

"I meant colder."

"It does that. Thirty or forty below occasionally."

"You're from Georgia? You don't sound like you're from the South."

"You're one of those people who think someone well off in Georgia grew up in a *double*-wide trailer instead of a single, aren't you?"

"Sorry."

"Not all of us who grow up in the South, did so in the country. Some of us don't even like country music."

"About that extra blanket?"

The look she gave me would have curled milk. "Next."

I took my linens and returned to the lobby, where the stairs were. Two-oh-two was on the left, all the way at the end. The door was open. A pillow and a blanket were already on the far bed by the window. What happened to Samantha's sheets? She wasn't there. She must have dropped off her stuff and ran. She was

43

probably off socializing again. How long would it take for her to talk to everyone in Snow Lodge?

The bathroom door was closed. I knocked on it. No answer. I didn't see a light under the door. That was a good sign. I slowly opened the door. Nope. No one there. The door to the other room was directly across from the door I opened. It was also shut. I scanned the room. It was small, but it had everything: a shower/tub, a toilet, a sink and counter on top of a cabinet. The cabinet was spacious, but there was just one of them. How were four girls going to share this bathroom? There were two towels racks, each with room for two towels each. Most girls used two towels, one to dry their body and one for their hair. I used the same towel for both. This was going to be fun.

I went to the bathroom, more as a preventative measure then because I had to go. Who knows when I would be able to go again without at least one person in one of the adjacent rooms? We had to bring our own towels, and they were still on their way down from Mammoth, so after washing my hands I dried them on my shirt. Better it wet than my pants.

I had to make my bed before I did any exploring. It wasn't an option. I couldn't relax unless everything was in its proper place. Particularly annoying was returning to my room after a stressful day and have it be just as chaotic. I don't know how messy people were able to keep from going insane. The sheets were rough and stiff. The brown cotton blanket was softer. It didn't quite cover the sheets. I stuffed the pillow into the pillowcase, then neatly placed it at the head of the bed against the wall.

I lay on the bed, but for just for a minute. A five-minute nap was what I needed to feel refreshed before the luggage arrived. Just ten minutes, then I will get up. Fifteen minutes later I woke up. I was shivering. If it was after dinner I might have went under the covers, but anything before then was considered taking a nap. And I couldn't take a nap under the covers, because that might turn into a full-blown sleep, and that would be giving in. I found the thermostat and turned it up. It was turned down to 55. It didn't feel that cold, but it was definitely colder than what I was comfortable with. If felt warmer when I was active, but once I lay down the true temperature of the room registered with me.

It took about five minutes for the baseboard heat to warm me through to my bones. If this heater continued to work this well I probably wouldn't need that extra blanket.

I had enough sleep. My mind told me that, but my body screamed for just fifteen minutes more. I wanted to do some exploring before the luggage got here. Not long after that it would get dark. I closed the door behind me and locked it. There wasn't anything of value in it yet, but habits were hard to break.

There was a door at the end of the hallway beside my room. I opened it, to be greeted by a burst of cold air. I had opened my jacket after I had warmed up. I hastily rezipped it. I walked down the semi-exposed stairs.

The two guys I had seen skiing on that hill behind Mammoth were skiing towards me. Charlie and Andy, I think Flint called them. They looked like they were skating more than skiing the way they kicked their skis out. As they came closer to the dorm, they glided in, looking like oarsmen as they stroked their ski poles to retain their momentum. A few feet in front of me they rotated perpendicularly, abruptly terminating their locomotion. The taller of the two pressed the tip of one of his ski poles onto a red plastic square on top of his skis. First his right ski came loose, then the left. The other boy, the more hansom of the two, leaned down and detached his boots from his skis with his hand. They both picked up their skis then thrust them vertically into the snow. They rid themselves of their ski poles in a similar manner.

"Aren't you afraid someone will take them?" I asked. "They're pretty expensive, aren't they?"

The hansom boy smiled widely with his little boy smile. "That's an awful lot of work for someone. For the amount of money it would take to drive or fly here, then either rent a snowmobile or hire passage on a snow coach, a person could have bought two pairs of these."

"You do have a point."

"Have you ever heard of anyone losing a pair of skis, Andy?"

Andy took off his glasses and wiped them with a handkerchief. Apparently, he used them strictly for this purpose, or he would have made them worse. "There was the man who got buried alive in that avalanche. I believe he was wearing skis."

"I forgot about that. I think his next of kin found the skis after the thaw, though, so I think we could say they were just temporarily missing. You're Sam's new roommate?"

"How did you know that?"

Andy put his handkerchief back in his pocket and his glasses back on his head. "You're the only black girl here."

"How about Flint?"

"He's not a woman," Charlie retorted. "Probably shouldn't jump to conclusions. Can't rule out him having an operation during the fall. I haven't seen him since August."

"He's definitely a man."

"You know from personal experience?" Andy grinned wickedly.

"Black girls can only hook up with the black boys?"

"Forgive Andy. He lives gratuitously through others."

"I'm just being very selective."

"I think the word is celibate. Has your relationship with Christine progressed to the next level?"

"We're waiting until the right time."

"After she goes through menopause and your pecker shrivels up and falls off? There is a rumor going around that the two of you are brother and sister."

We heard the rumbling before we saw a yellow bi-segmented snow machine in the distance. Charlie and Andy walked around to the front of the building through the snow. They had trampled down the two-foot high snow enough that I was able to follow them without getting my feet and pants wet. Most of the employees were in front of the dorm by the time the snow coach arrived.

It took just minutes for the coach to be unloaded. A chain had been formed from it to the dorm, through the lobby, into the lower hallway. There were enough bodies that by the time the first piece of luggage was set down at one of the ends of the hallway the last piece of luggage was being unloaded from the coach. The next coach arrived a few minutes later, then another a few minutes after that. They had been spaced so perfectly there was very little down time. In half an hour, all four coaches were unloaded.

After the last one pulled away it was time to find our bags. It was easy for me. I had just one large duffle bag. Some of the employees had four or five pieces. Some of them weren't even luggage, but boxes. Weren't there supposed to be a limitation on how many pieces were allowed on a bus or a plane? Then I remembered that nearly half of the people drove. I finally found my bag. It was at the end of the hallway. The end that I searched last. I had spotted it while it was being unloaded, but I had lost track of it as it was handed back.

I hauled it up the stairs to my room, weaving around baggage and people. I bumped into someone on their way down. He didn't mind too much. He even smiled. I guess it was par for the course on a day like this. It wasn't even dark yet, yet it felt like it had been three days since I've gotten off the bus, the one in Livingston.

I set the duffle bag on the carpet outside my door as I unlocked and opened it. I plopped it down on my bed. I unzipped it and was about to unpack when I realized Samantha probably had more bags than she could carry in one trip, so I headed back into the hallway. Samantha was coming towards me, without anything in her hands. Not so, the three guys behind her. It was worse than I imagined. Samantha would need an entire suite to herself to find room for all of her stuff. "Just set them down on the floor somewhere. We'll unpack after you're gone." Who was the *we* she was referring to? After the last box was set down, the boys waited politely. Were they each expecting a kiss or something? Samantha's eyes glazed over as she looked lovingly at all her things. She snapped out of it. "Thanks, guys." She smiled broadly at them, her eyes sparkling. The guys smiled back, now content, and rushed off.

I just shook my head as I perused all Samantha brought. "Are we planning to have a siege?"

"We are going to be snowbound without any radio or television or shopping malls for three months. I can rough it as well as the next girl, but we don't have to be barbarians."

I turned towards my one bag. I began to unpack it, fitting all of it in the top two drawers of the small wooden dresser across from my bed. Samantha looked at me. Something was on the tip of her tongue, but it hadn't yet come out. "Yes?"

"Oh, nothing. Never mind." Samantha sighed, then began to unpack one of her three suitcases. Her dresser quickly filled. She lifted a bra up by two fingers like it was toxic. "This definitely isn't mine." It was about three sizes too large for her. It was one of those expensive bras with the under-wire support. "Hun, the next time you see Christine, can you return this to her?" Samantha dropped it on my bed.

Samantha finally emptied her first bag and began working on her second. I looked at the bags and boxes, to her, then back to her luggage. "Would you like some help?"

"Thank you, so much." Samantha's enthusiasm for life returned. "You can start on that big box over there."

I tried to move it closer to me, but it wouldn't budge. What was in it? I removed my room key from my pants pocket and used it to slice open the packing tape that had sealed it securely. Cutting the top wasn't enough, so I had to cut the sides too. Once the pressure was released the top two pieces of cardboard snapped up. I bent them further back, then the two pieces that opened in the other direction. It was a TV. It was padded with a couple of dozen video tapes. I unpacked the video tapes first. I stacked them in two neat piles beside the box. "Where would you like the TV?"

"On my dresser. You need to wait until you find the VCR. It goes underneath."

I opened a second box. In it were some books and a Nintendo, and some video game cartridges. Samantha didn't seem like the type to play video games. "Do you want this next to the television."

"Sure. It actually belongs to Charlie. He used to have an Atari when he was in high school. A couple of years back he saw the Nintendo in Cody and he just had to buy it. He doesn't have a TV, so I've become the custodial parent. Sometimes it's the only way I get him to visit."

"I'm sure there are other things that might bring him up here."

"Sometimes he forgets about things like that when he gets into his he-man mode and wants to have some great adventure."

The VCR was found in the next box, packed with towels and toiletries. And pink satin sheets. "I wish I had thought of bringing my own sheets."

"The first summer I worked I didn't even have a cassette player. The longer you work here the more things you discover you need."

I carried the VCR to the top of Samantha's dresser. I waited until I unpacked her last box before I attempted to lift her TV. I found the cassette player she spoke of, and about 100 cassette tapes. "Do you have a case for these?"

"Just leave them in that box. Put it by my nightstand." I shivered. Was she really going to leave that cardboard box out all winter? "The cassette player you can put on top of the nightstand. It has a clock and an alarm I use to make it to work on time."

"I have a windup clock."

"That won't do. That ticking all night will drive me crazy.

We can share the cassette player. What job are you doing again?"

"Busser."

"That might work out perfectly then. I'm a waitress. Unless we're given different days off we might be working a similar schedule." Great. I could put up with Samantha in small doses, but I'm not sure I could retain my sanity if I had to see her at home and at work.

It was finally time. People always said bend with your legs, not with your back. The only problem was your arms were the part of your body that actually did the lifting. I was barely able to lift the television off the ground. I had great leg strength, but my upper body just wasn't that strong. "You're going to need to pick up the other side."

Samantha looked like a rabbit that had just spotted a fox. "I can get one of those guys to come back to help you."

"Come on. Girls can't always rely on guys." It was surprisingly easy with two of us. It wasn't just the weight of the TV, but the awkwardness of it. With each of us having to contend with just half of the girth we were able to lift it, move it five feet, then set it back down, in one continuous motion. "That wasn't too bad, now, was it?"

"It still would have been more enjoyable to watch a guy move it."

Samantha had filled up her dresser with her second bag. She unzipped her last one, examined what was in it, then slid it under her bed.

"You can use my bottom drawer if you like," I volunteered.

"You sure you wouldn't mind?" Before I could reply Samantha had already transferred a majority of her bag into my bottom drawer. She didn't have room for a couple of sweaters. She left them in the bag, then slid it back under her bed.

When everything was in as much order as Samantha cared to put them in she began to look around frantically. "Anything wrong?"

"I can't find my ski bag. They must have left it downstairs. Do you mind?"

I sighed. If I wasn't in dire need of stretching my legs I may have declined---politely. "What does it look like?"

"It's red. It also has a name tag on, with my name."

I walked into the hallway, then down the interior stairs. It seemed particularly quiet in the dorm. The red bag was nearly as tall as I was. Fortunately, it wasn't as heavy. It wasn't the only piece of unclaimed luggage. How long might some of those bags and boxes stay in the hallway and lobby? I didn't see a single person on my way down or up.

Samantha had the window open when I returned to the room. Cold air blew in, but with the exertion of going up the stairs it didn't feel uncomfortable. I also noticed it had gotten dark. When had that happened? So that's why the dorm was so desolate. I was becoming concerned. "What time does the EDR close?"

"Six-thirty." Samantha looked at her watch. "We still have plenty of time. It's only 5:30. It will take us just ten minutes to ski there, maybe less."

"If a girl had skis."

"You didn't bring skis to Yellowstone, in winter?"

"It shouldn't take that long to walk, should it? Are there signs to direct me?"

"Not to the EDR, but there are signs for Snow Lodge. Put out your foot." Samantha placed her foot beside mine. "We're about the same size. I have an extra pair of skis and boots. You may borrow them if you like."

"I don't...."

"Please. I probably won't even use them this winter. I bought a new pair last spring. Once you've worked at Snow Lodge a winter or two you learn what type of equipment is best for you."

"So, you're letting me use your skanky hand-me-downs?" I smiled in an exaggerated manner to show that I wasn't really that ungrateful. "I'm not sure they would be too useful right now. I've never skied."

"Now is as good a time as any to learn."

"You sure we have time? I would hate for you to miss dinner. Almost as much as I would hate for me to."

"If it looks like you're completely inept you can carry your skis the rest of the way to the EDR."

Samantha took off her jeans. I couldn't help but notice she had the right amount of flesh on her butt to look feminine, but not too much to look fat. She had the derriere that men lusted over, and women envied. The door was still open, but her red underwear underneath was more conservative than most bathing suits, so it wasn't completely indecent. To someone who liked to be discrete, and who had never worn a bikini in her life, it was still a bit disconcerting. Samantha put on blue tights. Over that she put on nylon ski pants. She looked at my jeans. "You're going to get cold in just those. You didn't bring any long johns, did you? Thermal underwear?"

"I wish someone would have told me all this ahead of time."

Samantha searched through the drawer I let her borrow. She pulled out something that looked like her tights, but they were white, and not in as good of shape. She handed them to me.

"You don't have to do that?" I insisted as I took the thermal underwear from her. "You may only use one pair of skis this winter, but you'll certainly going to need more than one of these. I can put on another pair of pants."

"I still have an extra one. This one isn't as cute."

I closed the door, then took off my jeans, as I faced away from Samantha. I didn't like undressing in front of anyone. I don't know why I faced the direction I did. Was Samantha really going to see more from the front than from behind? Maybe it was more me being aware of someone watching me than someone actually seeing me. Out of sight meant out of mind. Without an intellectual or emotional connection, I was as insignificant as a stranger on the street or a model in a magazine. But not one of those glamour magazines. I was more like the women you see in catalogs. I leaned over to place a foot into one of the leg holes. I nearly fell over. Then I placed my other foot in the other leg hole. I pulled the bottom of the thermal underwear up to my ankles. As I leaned up, the top of the thermals went with me. It got caught on my butt. I kept pulling. The elastic I held onto tore. "Sorry."

"No worries. I've had them for a while."

I grabbed lower, wadding up a greater amount of cloth. This time the thermals made it over the hump. It fit much tighter on me than it did on Samantha. Not only on the butt, but the thighs too. I put my jeans back on. I didn't have to worry about *them* fitting. I liked to wear baggy clothes. There was still plenty of room left, for two or three more pairs of thermals.

As I put on the ski boots Samantha let me borrow, she wrapped a piece of vinyl around her ankles. "What's that?"

"It's called a gaiter. It helps keep snow out of my boots. A girl is much more comfortable skiing if she stays dry."

"You wouldn't happen to an extra one of those?"

"Sorry. Just try to not get snow above your boots. If you do, brush it away before it can melt. Those jeans will be particularly uncomfortable if you get them wet. I think we're ready."

Samantha carried her skis and poles out of the room. I followed closely behind her with the extras she let me borrow. She went out the door at the end of the hallway next to our room. I heard her thumping down the stairs. I locked the room after me. I don't know if she assumed I would lock up, or she didn't care. I was too conditioned living in an urban environment to take such risks.

She was already on her skis when I stepped onto the snow. "Drop your skis beside you." I did as I was told. One of the skis flopped over as it hit. The other landed right side up, but it slipped away from me. I corralled the errant ski, then set both of them right side up to the right of me. "These skis have something called a three-pin binding. See those three metal pins sticking up on the ski?" I nodded. "They need to penetrate the three holes at the base of your boot."

I put my right boot onto the right ski. It seemed to catch for a moment, then it slid off.

"It helps to point you toe." I did so. This time my foot didn't slide off. "Now pull that metal bar over the end of your boot." It lowered easily to a point, then there was significant resistance.

"It won't go down all the way."

"Just push it harder. When it gets low enough it will catch on that clasp." I used the heal of my hand. With that and a grunt the bar caught. I stood up to try it out. I put weight on it. The ski slid forward, and I went down, not very gracefully. "Wait until you have both skis on." I fell one more time before I was able to secure the second ski. "Think of the ski poles as training wheels. They will be your third and fourth legs until you get better, then you'll mainly use them for propulsion instead of for stability."

I walked away from Samantha, my goal being to reach the road before I fell again. On my third stride, I slipped. I would just have to come up with a new goal, like taking four strides before I fell the next time. It was very complicated trying to move. The toes of my boots were held in place, but my heels weren't. I was able to lift my skis, but they wobbled in the back, making my footing very unstable.

"You're on skis, not snowshoes. Slide your feet, don't lift them. Watch me." The back of Samantha's skis lifted then fell, in a rocking motion. Her skis made contact with the snow the entire time.

It felt unnatural sliding instead of lifting, but I eventually got the routine down. I had to use my full concentration just to stay up, but I did for the most part. My ability got better with every slide, as I followed Samantha down the lighted trail to Snow Lodge. I learned that good balance dampens the jarring, and consequently the falling. As long as I bent my legs a bit, my lower limbs acted as shock absorbers. I was quite pleased with my progress until I came to my first hill. Anyone who had been skiing for more than a few minutes would have called it a rise, or maybe even a mogul, but to me that three-foot gain in elevation seemed like three-hundred. I tried to slide up it, but the slope was just steep enough to counter any forward motion. I would begin to climb, but a moment later my skis would slide backwards. I fell three times before Samantha offered any advice. "Spread your skis out more when you climb a hill." She had called it a hill. I already felt much better about my situation. I was no longer so embarrassed. "This is called a herring-bone." Samantha demonstrated for me. She looked like Charlie and Andy when they climbed that hill behind Mammoth.

Samantha waited for me at the top. I hated to be put under that type of pressure with an audience, but what was a girl to do? The EDR had to be close to closing. It felt awkward spreading my legs out like that while moving, but the maneuver worked.

We came up to an L-shaped building. In its armpit was the EDR. We removed our skis by putting pressure on the metal bar. The clasp dislodged, causing the bar to pop up. We leaned our skis and poles next to the small sheet-metal building adjacent to the much larger wood-sided one.

There were a few people at two of the dozen tables, but no one I knew. The EDR was less than half the size of the one at Mammoth. I looked at the clock. We made it, with about ten minutes to spare. The pans in the steam tables were close to being empty. There was some type of lasagna left, green beans, and garlic bread.

A middle-aged Latino was serving. He greeted us with a dynamic smile. "Good evening. So nice of you to finally drop by."

Samantha returned the smile. "Hello, Milo. I would like a bit of everything you have left."

He placed the food she requested on a tray, then handed it to her. "And who would you be? I'm Milo Santiago, the location manager of Snow Lodge this winter."

"I'm Jimi Jackson, sir. I've been hired as a busser."

"Ah, the front lines. The way to a guest's heart is through

his or her stomach. There are some things we can't change, like it being cold here in the winter, but we can at least give the guests a quality meal."

"I hope it will better than the food you're serving tonight in the EDR," said Samantha.

"It was much better half-an-hour ago. Being a manager, there are many things I must consider. One of them being food cost. Here, take these cookies to make up for eating the scraps. I had made them for tomorrow, but I think we'll still have enough if we let two of them go early."

"Thank you."

Milo placed most of what was left in the metal containers above the steam baths onto my tray, next to the large chocolate chip cookie. He handed me my tray. He walked over to the dish drop and took the few dirty dishes there to a back room. There was also a bit of lettuce left in the salad bar, so I supplemented my meal with it.

"So, Milo is like the mayor?" I said quietly between bites of salad.

"More or less. More in the winter. We don't start working until tomorrow, but he has been here for a week. He made this dinner himself."

"Doesn't he have any assistants---other managers---to help him?"

"He does, but he likes to give them the afternoon off the day before the chaos of training begins."

Halfway through eating my salad I took a bite of the garlic bread. Some of the water from the steam bath must have gotten onto it because it was soggy. "I'm sorry I made us so late to dinner."

"No worries. I'm so tired I don't think I would have enjoyed a good meal anyway." A long day made longer by a ski back to the dorm.

We both ate about half of what was on our trays before we

gave up. We washed down the chocolate chip cookies with what remained of our beverages. We discarded our trash, then set our trays, silverware, and tumblers into the empty dish bin. Milo was also ready to call it a day.

I didn't fall as many times as I did on the way to the EDR, but I still fell. I had become overconfident with my newly developed skiing ability. That and my eagerness to return home. A dorm in the middle of Yellowstone National Park, in winter, was home. Hard to believe.

We took off our skis and thrust them and our ski poles into the snowdrift beside the dorm like a couple of dozen other people had done. There were also at least that many beside the front entrance to the dorm.

I strongly considered sleeping in my clothes. The two things I *had* to do before going to bed were to use the bathroom and brush my teeth. Samantha apparently didn't have an inclination to do either. She stripped down to her underwear, then put on a nightgown with a picture of Bugs Bunny on it. Her breasts were nearly as flawless as her backside. They had fullness to them, but not so much to become cumbersome.

Samantha was apparently too tired to make up her bed before falling onto it. She just pulled the loose sheets and blanket over her.

The bathroom door was shut, so I knocked before entering. No answer. The door to the next room was ajar, so I peeked in. Two women lay curled-up together on the large bed they created by pushing the two single mattresses together.

The butch brunette opened her eyes and turned towards me. "Sorry," I said, as I shut the door.

"Don't leave. We're just napping. We drove straight from Maine yesterday and are exhausted." The beautiful blond woke up. "This is Amy. I'm Lori."

"I think I better go." I shut both bathroom doors and locked the one on my side. There was a rumor about that type of woman working in Yellowstone in the winter. I just didn't think I would be sharing a suite with two of them. I didn't believe there was anything wrong with two consenting adults of any gender wanting to have a relationship, but it still made me nervous. I'm not sure why.

I kept the thermostat low, but I had to close the window. I was worried I wouldn't be able to sleep with someone in the same room as me. What if Samantha snored? From the manner in which she was breathing I think she was already asleep. Why couldn't I be the type of person who could just fall asleep like that? I wasn't able to turn off my brain when I slept. I not only thought about things that worried me, but stuff going on in my life that was exciting. One thing that helped me fall to sleep was reading. It not only took my mind off my worries, but the repetition of reading words numbed my brain. I fell asleep after five pages. Not completely asleep, but my eyes did shut, and I was in a limited state of consciousness. I shoved a book marker into the book, set the book on my nightstand, then turned off the wall lamp over my bed. Samantha's breathing was loud at times, but it never turned into a snore. It was almost soothing, like the white noise a wave machine makes. I remembered---before I drifted off for good---that I had forgotten to brush my teeth. It had been years since I had gone to bed without brushing my teeth. What other things might happen here that have never happened to me?

6.   TRAINING

I woke to screeching static. The alarm on Samantha's cassette-player/clock/radio had been set to radio wake. She was either in a place that got radio reception on that channel the last time she used the alarm, or the switch had been accidentally turned to that mode during the move. My roommate was apparently oblivious to the blaring, because she continued to sleep. Not being familiar with the model it took me awhile---30 seconds, perhaps---to find a way to turn it off.

There was an orientation meeting at 8am, which meant if we wanted to eat breakfast we better make it to the EDR by 7:30. It was now just 6:31, but I still had to shower and somehow find my way back to Snow Lodge. I wasn't confident Samantha would be up in time for breakfast. I wasn't that confident she would make it to the training on time either. If we were going to get along as roommates we were going to have to look after one another. If Samantha wasn't awake by the time I was ready to go I would make sure she got up. She may not like being rolled out of bed, but sometimes tough love needed to be provided. That big grin on my face was going to make brushing my teeth easier.

The first thing I did after leaving my bed was turn up the heat. Being cool helped a person sleep, but it didn't help her wake up. It just made her want to stay in bed. I looked at Samantha. How much warmer did it have to be for her to get out of bed? If I ever got married, I would make my husband turn up the heat. I was starting a honey-do list and I didn't even have a boyfriend. Did that mean I was the husband of this relationship?

59

The second thing I did after getting up was make my bed. I hated a messy room, and the bed was the focal point of a bedroom.

Now I was free to set out the clothes I would wear after my shower. We were just training today so I didn't have to wear my uniform. I chose a clean pair of jeans and another turtleneck. I was told to bring a pair of closed-toe black shoes for work. I chose to wear them instead of my hiking boots, because I still needed to break them in. I looked at my backpack purse. If I took a few things out they should fit. The older I got the larger my purse got. When I was a little girl it was about the size of a paperback. Now, at 18, it was a backpack. What would I carry when I was 30? A suitcase?

I compared myself to Samantha, who was curled up in a ball, with just enough of the covers off her to reveal what she was wearing. I compared her satin nightgown to my boxer shorts and tee-shirt. One of us was definitely more of a girl than the other. I chose comfort over style. Without someone to share my bed it didn't really matter if I looked sexy, did it? I hated to be constricted when I slept. That's why I wore the boxers. A nightgown was too constricting.

I looked under the bathroom door. No light on. Then I knocked softly, not wanting to wake Samantha. I did it out of kindness---and self-preservation. If Samantha wasn't awake she couldn't talk. And I liked it to be quiet in the morning. Unless.... I shuddered contemplating the possibility of her talking in her sleep. I hadn't heard her yet, but it had only been one night, and I was very tired. You have to be awake to hear someone. I opened the bathroom door. Good. The other door was shut. I quietly locked it. I have to remember to unlock it before I leave---this time. That was embarrassing. Amy came to the door. Or was it Lori? Samantha got up. In the neighborhood I grew up in, people didn't answer the door after dark.

I draped my towel across the shower bar, then set my clothes on the floor beside the tub. After shutting the door that led into my room, I used the toilet. As I sat, I examined the floor. It looked clean, but that would certainly change after a couple of days. After I flushed, I put the lid down. I picked up my clothes and placed them on the lid. I turned on the water in the tub. As it warmed, I stripped off my boxers and tee-shirt. After folding them, I placed them at the bottom of my stack of clothes. I felt the water. It was too hot, so I had to add some cold water to it. Perfect. I switched on the shower release. Water sprayed too high, so I had to bend down the nozzle. Carefully, I slid open the back of the shower curtain. Water on a bathroom floor was almost as disturbing as a messy room. I pulled the curtain tightly behind me after I squeezed through the small gap I created between the back wall and the curtain.

The warm water flowing over me was blissful. It was like a massage, but instead of hands on your body, it was droplets of warmth. If God embraced someone it would be in the form of a shower. Some people liked baths better, because the warm water completely encased them, like a womb. I didn't like to soak in the soup that was seasoned with my gunk.

Grain was a very frugal woman. I wasn't allowed to take showers that lasted more than five minutes. If I wanted to take a bath, the tub could be filled with just a couple of inches of water.

The first five minutes passed with me just enjoying the pulsating warmth. It felt decadent. Then I began to feel guilty. What if there was a limited amount of hot water. If I took too long of a shower would I prevent Samantha from having one, or one of my suitemates? I forgot to bring shampoo and soap? Grain had always supplied those things. There was already a bar of soap in the shower, and a bottle of conditioner, and two bottles of shampoo. They must have belonged to Amy and Lori. I felt both guilty about using someone else's toiletries, and a bit grossed out. What other options did I have? I washed off the bar of soap before using it. A small hair was imbedded in it. Fearing the worse, I rubbed the soap against the metal grate covering the drain, which eventually dislodged it. I was under the opinion a person could never be too clean, so after I washed from head to toe I repeated the process in case I missed anything. I shampooed with similar redundancy, then with great personal sacrifice I turned off the water. Keeping to my mantra of a dry floor, I dried within the tub. Once I was confident I wouldn't make a mess I opened the curtain. And there was Samantha.

She was sitting on the toilet. I didn't even consider locking my side of the bathroom. Samantha had been sound asleep. I guess my shower woke her up. I didn't know what to do. I needed to get to my clothes which were scrunched between the raised lid and the toilet, behind Samantha.

"Good morning," my roommate said warmly.

"Couldn't you have waited until I was finished?"

"Some things can't wait. I was careful not to flush while the water was still running."

"I'll come back after you're done." I wrapped the towel around me like I had seen on TV and the movies. Either they had used bigger towels or smaller women. I could either completely cover my top half or my bottom half. I chose a compromise. Neither part was completely covered, but I wasn't indecent. I walked out of the bathroom and shut the door behind me.

I sat on my bed waiting. I heard a flush. That was a good sign. A moment later Samantha walked out.

"I'll just be a couple of minutes more," I said as I walked back in, shutting---and locking---the bathroom door behind me.

When I returned to the bedroom, Samantha was completely naked. She was bent over searching through her dresser drawers. "There it is." She pulled out a white towel with the Playboy logo on it. She left the four drawers open, with clothes sticking out of them as she walked into the bathroom. She had left the door open, so I had to close it for her.

I didn't have a place to put my dirty laundry, so I used my duffle bag. I pulled out the thermal underwear Samantha had let me borrow. They had been protected by both my underwear and my jeans, so I would be able to use them many days before I had to wash them. I placed the duffle bag under my bed, as close to the center as I could, to make it less noticeable. I removed my jeans, put the thermals on, then put the jeans back on.

I made sure everything was tidy before I left. Then I looked over at Samantha's side of the room. I wish there was some way I could separate the two sides of the room. A curtain? A brick wall would be better. That wasn't going to happen anytime soon, so I made Samantha's bed instead. Then I shoved her clothes back into her drawers before shutting them. I contemplated folding them for her. But out of sight was good enough---for today. I looked at the clock on the stereo. I just had a couple more minutes. What else had to be done? Samantha's dirty clothes were scattered throughout the room. I collected them with my feet, relocating them against the far wall. I looked at the clock again. Time to go.

I walked down to my skis. They were easy to find. There were only four or five other pairs present. Did I get the time wrong? Did the meeting start at seven, instead of eight? If I got fired, I wouldn't go home completely empty handed. I already experienced a few things I wouldn't have if I stayed in Seattle.

I was a concerned about finding my way back to the EDR. I didn't want to get lost in sub-freezing temperatures. When a person follows someone, they are less aware of where they are going than if they were relying on their own navigational skills. It was also dark that first time I went to the EDR. Things look different in sunlight than they do with street lights. I remember the trail beginning in front of that first dorm, that was unoccupied during the winter. I headed that direction. Cross-country skiing must have been like riding a bike. I didn't fall at all on that road connecting the residential area to the highway.

I heard something behind me. I turned slowly, aware if I whipped around too quickly I would lose my balance and probably fall. That big girl from the Mammoth EDR was skating on her skis. It took her just seconds to reach me from where she began in front of Lupine. "Hi, Matilda. I don't think I will ever be able to ski that fast."

She stopped beside me. "I didn't either. You'll be surprised what you can accomplish after a couple of weeks. Few people have skied before coming to work in Yellowstone, including me. I've done Alpine skiing, the kind you take a lift up to the top of a mountain, but that's entirely different than the skiing you do here."

"You don't mind if I follow you? I've only been to the EDR once, and that was in the dark."

"Even better, why don't I follow you? That way you're trying to figure out where you're going. If you make a wrong turn, I'll eventually guide you in the right direction."

"Eventually?"

"You learn more quickly by doing than following."

It was actually very easy. I just followed the ski tracks. During the summer, footprints don't show up that well, especially on pavement, but winter had its own unique tracking system. I had some trouble getting up that hill I fell a few times attempting the night before, but the training I learned from Samantha kicked in and I was able to slowly herring-bone up the hill without falling. The trail forked after that. To the left, tracks went towards that large building that looked like a log cabin. I couldn't tell where the right fork went, but I knew I didn't want to go to the log building, so it had to be the correct trail. Matilda was very patient with me. Most people would have immediately told me which way to go, but she waited a moment to see if I could figure it out. Matilda would make a good teacher if she ever wanted to work a year-round job.

Why couldn't I have had Matilda as my roommate instead of Samantha? I think Sam and I will be able to tolerate one another, but better would be able to room with someone you preferred to be around. When I first saw Matilda, I was intimidated by her size. Fright became awe. She would have made a great Marauder. Most people believe a woman's worth is attached to her feminine qualities. But wasn't physical prowess, endurance, and toned muscles also commendable? Some of that was genetic, but a person also had to be physically active, to a forced degree, to become such an athlete. But there was more there than just her physicality. In the way she moved and how her clothes fit her there was definitely a girl underneath. And she was kind, but not in a flamboyant manner which demanded attention in return, gratitude, or reciprocal assistance.

The tracks crossed a meadow that was probably a parking lot during the summer. On the far side of the meadow was a cluster of buildings. We skied past the closest one. *General Store* was displayed in bold letters above its entrance. The next had a sign on it that said *Snow Lodge*. We passed between the two buildings, stopping in the crook of the L-shaped building. Finally, something that looked familiar.

We stopped in front of the abandoned skis and ski poles. We walked into the entry between the EDR and kitchen. We took our jackets off and hung them up on the pegs on the wall, then sat on a couple of chairs as we removed our ski boots and replaced them with our work shoes. Matilda put on hiking boots. Being a cook, the public would never see her, so it didn't matter too much what she wore on her feet. "You probably haven't been to the dining room yet, have you?"

"Just the EDR."

"That's where we're meeting at 8:30. The dining room, not the EDR. I'll show you where it is after breakfast. Milo wants to speak to everyone before we split up by departments."

Breakfast consisted of cereal, Danishes, bread, fruit, and juice. I grabbed a packet of cream cheese, a bagel, a banana, and a glass of orange juice. I sat down at an unoccupied table, which wasn't difficult to find. Most people had either eaten already or decided to miss the Continental Breakfast for an extra half-hour of sleep. Matilda sat beside me. I must have looked unsatisfied with my meal because Matilda said, "Tomorrow we'll have a hot breakfast. No one's been trained yet in the EDR."

"That's okay. It just would have been nice to have a hot meal on a cold morning."

"You think its cold today. It's practically balmy. They're be days in January and February where the temperature won't get above zero."

"Does Snow Lodge close on days like that? In Seattle whenever we got a couple of inches of snow schools closed."

"The only time Snow Lodge closes is when it's scheduled to---in March. On those sub-zero mornings remember to wear an extra layer of clothes and cover you face."

"Do the snow coaches come by to take us to work?"

"We have to ski to work like any other day. It's just part of working out here. To compensate for the beauty and the isolation you have to put up with an occasional uncomfortable day or two. It's just a ten-minute ski to Snow Lodge, five if an experienced skier is determined. But the faster one skis, the more wind chill is created. Another ten degree drop in temperature is probably not a good tradeoff for arriving a few minutes earlier."

I felt embarrassed after asking those questions. Matilda probably thought I was a wimp, a girly-girl. Someone like her wasn't going to respect someone like that. I'm going to have to make a concerted effort to toughen up.

"It's just about time." Matilda took her tray, tumbler, and utensils to the dirty dish drop off. I followed closely behind her. "I'm going to wash up before the meeting." Matilda went into the woman's restroom across from the entry. I followed her. I normally didn't like going into a restroom with someone else, but we were just going to wash our hands. It was a very small restroom. It had two stalls, like the Mammoth one, but they were smaller, as was the sink area. Matilda was precise in the washing of her hands. With the liquid soap and warm water, she washed every bump and crevice of her hands. It reminded me of how a surgeon washed their hands. When she was done with her hands she rubbed warm soapy water on her face. She tore a paper towel from its receptacle, then dried both her hands and her face. There was just one sink, so I had to wait for her to finish before I could jump in. I performed a less thorough washing of myself that including just my hands. I did brush my teeth afterwards. I had put one of those mini travel brushes and toothpastes in my pants pocket. Weren't we the excessively clean pair.

Matilda led me through the kitchen, past the EDR and cold prep areas, then past the storage area and office, and finally past the cooks line. The top part of it was open, revealing an adjacent prep area and the more distant dining room. We passed through a pair of swinging doors, like those found in a saloon in a Western. We entered where the serving area transitioned into the dining room. To the left was the bar. To the right, the beginning of the dining room. Both areas were nearly full. It was just a couple minutes before 8:30. A few employees were smoking at tables next to the bar. Being a liberal mecca, most of the restaurants in Seattle were becoming smoke free.

It was strange seeing someone smoke in what was considered a family establishment. I used to smoke. I gave it up to improve my health, but also to prove to myself that I could. I tried to not be judgmental, to those who hadn't yet given up smoking. But there was a part of me, that sometimes came oozing to the surface, that believed smokers were weak.

"Welcome to the 88-89 winter season of Snow Lodge." Milo Santiago began speaking at precisely 8:30. He didn't attempt to silence the 100 or so employees in the dining room. Once he began, though, everyone became quiet. "I see a few familiar faces, so not everyone abandoned the Park. For those of you who are new to Yellowstone in winter, I thank you for accepting a position in the most unique environment most of you will ever experience in your life. Before we speak about expectations this season, the National Park Service wants me to inform you of some of the unique dangers this winter. As you know, about a million acres were burned in Yellowstone last summer. Some of the dead trees have fallen. Most haven't. Be extremely cautious in burnt areas. With so much of the vegetation depleted, animals might be more unpredictable than normal. Use extreme caution around them." Milo continued for most of the next half-hour. There was nothing special about his spiel, and what I did allow to be processed was soon forgotten.

No one really knew what country Milo was from, but everyone was confident it was from somewhere in Latin America. One person thought he was from Columbia. Another, from Costa Rica. A third, from Chile. He emigrated to the United States when he was a child. He spoke several languages, but none of them very well.

He was very good at motivating employees and speaking to guests. No one knew what else he did. Fortunately, most of the Snow Lodge employees had as much experience as he did, so the lodge, cabins, restaurant and gift shop ran well on auto pilot. He was very positive. He never criticized anyone openly. In a different environment, one in which the employees weren't so self-motivated, he would have floundered. But for Snow Lodge, he was perfect. He stayed out of everyone's way while acknowledging their superior effort and skills.

The restaurant staff stayed in the dining room when the housekeepers, front desk, tour guides, gift shop and maintenance left at 9am. After a few more minutes of expectations, by the Food & Beverage Manager this time, we were split up into Front of the House, and Back of the House. The servers, bussers, and hosts stayed in the dining room with the F&B Manager, while the cooks and kitchen help went into the kitchen with the Food Production Manager.

I was curious what we were going to serve in the restaurant. After the F&B manager went over the menu I began to get bored. Bussing tables wasn't a complex job. Setting, clearing, and washing tables. Filling and refilling water glasses. During peak hours, there were six servers, but only two bussers, so I was going to be kept busy. But I preferred that to waiting around.

I did a lot of daydreaming the next two days. Samantha had shown up on time, but just barely, that first day, and on every day. She occasionally spoke to me, but there were 18 of us in the Front of the House and she had to ration her time, so everyone would have the opportunity to listen to her. She was the only person I knew so far that worked in the dining room, but instead of trying to get to know more people I kept to myself.

Come on, let's get this training over so we can open and begin having days off. I was beginning to get cabin fever. All these geysers and hot springs and lakes and rivers and waterfalls and animals, and we're stuck indoors learning how to wrap silverware in a cloth napkin. How likely was it that Matilda and I had the same days off? It wouldn't be as much fun if she wasn't my tour guide.

Occasionally, I caught a glimpse of her through the opening between the server's station and the line. I smiled whenever I saw her. She once caught me looking at her. She smiled back.

Barry was also back there. He looked much more coherent at work than he did in the dorm. For him to live here in the environment he loved, he couldn't afford to get fired again. Did he get high as soon as he left Snow Lodge, or wait until he returned to the dorm? I felt bad for Flint. Having someone getting stoned around you every day was worse than someone smoking in a restaurant.

"It's time to go." Samantha tapped me on the shoulder. "They let us off early today because we're going to open for lunch tomorrow."

I snapped out of it and looked at my watch. "But it's only three. We still have two hours before dinner. What are we going to do until then?" This was the first day I wasn't dismissed a couple of minutes before dinner was served. It was dark after that, so I just went back to my room.

"We'll, I'm going back to the dorm and take a nap. It's called beauty sleep, not beauty run-yourself-ragged. You going back, too?"

I didn't want to ski to the dorm to only have to ski back a couple of hours later. Less than that when you factor in the skiing. "I think I will hang out here for a while. Is the EDR opened between meals?"

"There won't be any hot food available, but you can always help yourself to a drink, a piece of fruit, or a peanut butter and jelly sandwich."

"I think I'll check it out."

I walked with Samantha to the entry, then continued walking to the EDR. Lori was one of those kitchen helps assigned to the EDR. She had been offered a bussing position because she had worked in Yellowstone a couple of summers, but she turned it down. She was uncomfortable around strangers, so she didn't want a Front of the House position. Once she got to know someone she was fine. She just had trouble talking to people she didn't know.

"Hey, Jimi. I hope I wasn't in the bathroom too long this morning."

"Compared to the other two in our suite you are like a humming bird. You just dart in then dart out."

"Amy and Samantha do like to primp. That's one of the things I like about Amy, that's she's different than me."

"You are both girls."

"Physically we're the same, or nearly so. She's a bit more curvy and softer than I am. Mentally and emotionally we are direct opposites. She's moodier than I am, but she's also more fun to be around than me at times. I'm more centered in my emotions."

"You both go by the name Apollanaris? Is it a nickname you use to make your relationship sound more formal?"

"We got it legally changed to that."

"Can someone legally marry someone of the same sex?"

"Not yet. We had to go through a lawyer. You can change your name to about anything if you're willing to give enough of your time and money."

"Is it that important to you, to have the same last name?"

"It is for Amy. The name is taken from a spring we drank from between Mammoth and Norris when we started dating." Lori blushed. "We call it our love spring."

I didn't want to eat a big meal, so I just put a piece of bread in the toaster. When it came out I plastered it with raspberry jam. I loved raspberries. If I ever had a home of my own I wanted to fill the backyard with raspberry bushes.

Matilda walked into the EDR. Her white uniform was stained with a multitude of colors. She grabbed an orange then sat down beside me.

"Did the other guy at least look worse?" I popped the last bite of toast into my mouth.

"It had been awhile since I prepared food. I wasn't as careful as I should have been. It beats being covered in grease. After I clean the line at night I smell quite rancid." I couldn't imagine Matilda every smelling that bad. She tore apart that orange like she meant business. The tablecloth beneath it was covered with rind and juice by the time she got done tearing it apart. One time I got hit by a stray stream. "Sorry."

"I read an article about orange becoming the next lemon."

Matilda looked confused.

"For cleaning."

Matilda smiled. Her mouth was full of orange, so she couldn't verbally respond.

When she was finished she walked up to a table that still had a wet rag on it. "May I borrow this, Lori?"

"Help yourself. I wish more of...my patrons...cleaned up after themselves. You wouldn't believe how much of a mess grown men and women make."

"I'm heading to the geyser basin before dinner. Want to come along?" Matilda set the washcloth back on the table she got it from.

"Sure. I wasn't quite sure what I wanted to do, except not

71

ski back to the dorm."

"What's good about the geyser basin is you can turn back whenever you wish. You can either come back the way you came, or there are a few loops you can take if you don't want to backtrack much."

7.   THE UPPER GEYSER BASIN

Having only an hour-and-a-half left before dark, we didn't mess around. We skied directly to the geyser basin. As direct as possible. The Old Faithful Inn was in the way, so we had to detour around it. It was an immense building, with two large wings.

"I always wanted to live in a log cabin." I wasn't the type of person who liked to share things with others, but I felt comfortable around Matilda. It was more than that. I didn't want her to only know things about me, I wanted her to think I was a terrific person for liking those things. "My grandmother didn't like when I spoke of things like that. She told me that a colored girl should be thinking about moving up in the world, not about living in a shanty shack. I don't think she was ever able to distinguish rural from poverty."

"I wouldn't mind living in a log cabin deep in some woods, away from everyone." I smiled from ear to ear. We did have some things in common.

Packed snow covered most of the boardwalk surrounding Old Faithful Geyser. Only the timber near the water was bare, matching the earth the runoff flowed through. What mad, reverse universe created frozen walkways and bare soil? There were many rows of empty benches. This time tomorrow many of them would be filled, but not nearly as many as there would be in the summer.

How many people will make the journey over icy roads, and in cramped snow coaches? Yellowstone---especially in winter---was definitely not a place for jetsetters.

Matilda was ready to move on, but I had to see Old Faithful Geyser erupt at least once. Cognizant of my eagerness, she pulled back on her throttle and settled down on a bench beside me. "Is there more to it than the steam?"

"You'll see."

About ten minutes later water began to bubble up, about 40 feet in the air. A few seconds later the column of water fell back down. That was disappointing. As I was about to get back up Matilda put an arm out in front of me, like a mother trying to prevent a child from injury during a sudden automobile stop. Water erupted again, this time higher and higher until it reached a height of 150 feet. I was mesmerized. It was like one of those fountain shows, but with nature creating it. Designed by God, not an engineer. Galactic pillars of steaming liquid reached towards the heavens until forced back down by gravity. Completely unexpected, was the soothing heat created by the steam. It was like taking a hot shower, but outdoors, on a grander scale. But caresses became slaps whenever a harsh breeze re-directed the mist. Cold became frigid after being tempted by paradise. I smiled as I looked at Matilda. She smiled back. This moment wouldn't have been as great if she wasn't sharing it with me.

The show was over. Matilda got back up and circled around the geyser counter-clockwise. Another large building was in front of us, but it looked more modern than the Old Faithful Inn. "That's Old Faithful Lodge. Try to stay on the snow. If your skis get wet from the thermal runoff they will stick. You'll have to take them off and scrape them. You've heard of people licking a frozen metal pole and their tongue sticking to it? Same principle." The boardwalk became a trail. Our skis fell into the two grooves in front of us. We hadn't been the first to ski this way this winter. We didn't have to steer much, our skis becoming trains on a track. The trail continued to wind around the hill Old Faithful Geyser erupted from. Directly across from where we watched the geyser, the trail veered down to a creek. "That's the Firehole River, named for the many thermal runoffs that feed it. To slow your decent, point the tips of your skis inward. Snow will be forced in front of you, which will reduce your speed. This maneuver is called snowplowing. At the bottom is a sharp turn to the right, which takes you over a bridge. If you go straight, you'll get wet. Not the most pleasant experience in sub-freezing temperatures."

Matilda went first, becoming my template. Something brown was beneath the part of the bridge that wasn't over water. Becoming pre-occupied, I nearly forgot to turn. I slid halfway across the wooden structure, then wiped out. Fortunately, part of the railing was still above snow level. "WHAT WAS THAT?!" I yelled to Matilda, who was already up the incline on the other side of the river.

She skied back down and helped me up. We both looked down at the two legs within view. "The troll's first victim. Winters can be harsh in Yellowstone."

"But it isn't even winter yet, not officially."

"Winter lasts for six months in Yellowstone. You remember what Milo said about the vegetation? Let me give you something to think about that might prevent you from falling so often. Most falls by novices are caused by *bailing out*. An inexperienced skier thinks she is going to fall, so she does, feeling it's safer to force a safe, choreographed fall than allowing chaos to dictate. You must train your mind that you won't fall, even if you wobble a bit. Some experience with successful escapes will help."

"Okay." I didn't mind someone giving me advice, unless they were being critical of something I couldn't change. I was a beginning skier, so any advice on improving my skiing was greatly appreciated.

We had to regain almost as much elevation on the other side of the river as we lost going down to it. My herring-bone skills got a work out. I noticed that Matilda barely made a **V** with her skis. Did it take more skill to be able to do that or more muscle? By the end of the winter I hoped to have both. Two-thirds of the way up the rise we passed a fork. "What's up that way?"

"Observation Point. It's steep with many switchbacks. You're not ready for it yet, but maybe later this winter."

"I'm getting better."

"I know you are, but one mistake up there means…. One of my best friends died three years ago from a skiing accident. I don't want the same thing to happen to you. Let's go."

Matilda became quiet. We reached the geyser loop and followed it clockwise. I hit a slippery spot and fell as gracefully as I could on my butt. Matilda was jarred from her revelry and was beside me before I had fully recovered my senses. "You okay?" I nodded. "I'm sorry. I should have been looking after you instead of feeling sorry for myself. A beginner should be walking on the boardwalk, not skiing." She helped my get out of my skis. "I promise to be a better protector."

The Upper Geyser Basin consisted of a variety of geysers and thermal pools. Colors embellished many of the run-off channels, including those that flowed into the Firehole River. Old Faithful Inn in the distance, frocked with snow, was magnificent. "Why can't we stay there instead of Lupine?" I asked.

"It's not very well insulated, but maybe if there's ever enough visitors here in the winter, they'll do something about it."

"I don't think I would like that. Everyone needs a break now and again, even a building. Let's allow it to hibernate. Anyway, I like having just a few people here. Would it make it any better right now if there were hundreds on this boardwalk? I like it being just the two of us."

Being surrounded by bubbling water and steam, I thought this must have been what the world looked like when it began. Matilda must have had similar thoughts. "Have you ever wondered how we got here?"

"Weren't we created in God's image?"

"Do you think a supreme being could be that vain? That's a relic from the Greeks and the Romans. Don't you think someone---thing---that powerful would have proportionately powerful morals?"

"But aren't morals subjective?"

"For lesser morals, perhaps, but what of grand morals? There are absolutes in the universe, like temperature. Responsibility may be one of the grand morals. For a being, or a group of beings, to advance to that degree, they must have developed beyond their self-destructive stage. Would these beings be that irresponsible to reveal themselves and their technology before we are ready?"

"So, you think there might be intelligent life in the universe, other than us? And it may have even visited us?"

"Perfectly logical."

"And your argument is: Because we aren't aware of any extraterrestrials visiting us, they must have visited us."

"It's just an explanation of why we haven't seen any aliens. There are billions of stars. The odds are in our favor of there being other intelligent life out there."

"Unless there is just one intelligence and it created us and everything else. Just because self-made spokesmen have created hokey religions doesn't deny the existence of the one true God."

"I think the problem with the concept of God is its classification. What is the ultimate power in the universe? What do we know?"

"Given the disclaimer that knowledge is concealed behind a series of filters, we think there may have been a big bang. That was infinite power."

"But what came before? Could time just suddenly begin? Could matter?"

"But if there was nothing, the perfection of the first something would be the most beautiful thing that has ever existed:

infinite mass with infinitesimal dimension."

"The perfection would become less so over time, as the universe expanded."

"But doesn't something's imperfection create its personality, its uniqueness?"

"Can the universe expand indefinitely? Will it eventually be slung back into its core of infinitesimal dimension?"

"Is it possible for the universe to lose some of its matter? Perhaps from a black hole?"

"A black hole is a gravity sink that is so strong, light can't even escape."

"But where does the matter go?"

"To begin a new universe. Each universe is in flux, but reality is steady-state."

"So, ultimately each universe is completely consumed by black holes?"

"It's just hypothesis unless one is there, and even then, there are filters."

"So, God is all, and is becoming increasingly imperfect?"

"Or just the opposite. God's omnipotence may be in our collective uniqueness. God grows with each incite, with each creative thought."

"Isn't creativity just an excuse to be odd? Once we deviate enough from the norm aren't we classified as being insane?"

"Chaos is just another name for randomness. If a tree grows a branch on the left side instead of the right is it insane?"

"God is creativity and chaos."

It had become dark before we could tour the entire geyser basin. We were able see all the geysers along the boardwalk on geyser hill, and even some of those to the north of it, but we had to turn around at Grotto Geyser. Water steamed and bubbled from a dozen openings in the rock. After we left the boardwalk we were able to safely put our skis back on. Carefully, I zipped up my jacket. Counter force was particularly treacherous on a slick surface. With the sun going down there was a new nip in the air. When we were active I had become almost too warm, but it only took a couple of minutes of inactivity for me to get cold again. "I think I like this one the best. Old Faithful has its short high burst, but Grotto's eruption is more complex. It doesn't happen as often, but it lasts longer."

"It's my favorite too."

8. SNOW LODGE OPENS

Today was the big day. The restaurant would be serving its first meal of the season in a couple of hours. Sounds of tourists on their winter steeds could already be heard. Have you ever had a car with a bad muffler? That's what they sounded like, like motorcycles being constantly revved up. What a contrast they were compared to the quiet, peaceful solitude of cross-country skiing. It seemed insane to take the largest wild area in the lower forty-eight and infest it with those machines.

As I set tables with paper napkins, silverware, and glass goblets I thought of my first days off and what I would do. I know it was a bit premature. We hadn't even opened yet and I was already thinking of taking a vacation. When I was hired, a map of Yellowstone was part of my welcome package. It covered all the Park, so it wasn't very detailed. In the Lodge's lobby, there was a map of just the Old Faithful area. The winter trails were marked, with levels of difficulty suggested. The easier routes were relatively flat, and anyone could do them, even those who hadn't skied before. The intermediate routes had some elevation gains and drops, but with modest skill and endurance they could be conquered. The difficult routes were only for the most fit and advanced skiers. They had many changes in elevations and some extremely sharp turns. There was just one trail marked in red: Mallard Creek. There were many trails on the map that weren't marked at all. Did that mean they were *too* difficult, or just not monitored and patrolled? The one I was drawn to led to Summit Lake. It was near the continental divide, less than ten miles from Old Faithful.

Samantha messed up my hair as she walked by. It was tied back so she couldn't do any real damage, but I wanted to be presentable as possible for my first customers. It felt like a job interview. Would the guests like me? Would they think I was doing a good job? Servers had more contact with them, but bussers were first to greet them. We had to fill their water glasses immediately, giving them something to drink until the server assigned to them could take their drink order. "You excited?"

"I guess. More nervous. I just want it to be over with. I know once there's actually customers and we start working it will be fine. The worst part is the waiting, the unpleasant anticipation of awkward associations, and failure."

"Relax. It's just a job. You aren't trying to save the world. I love meeting new people. Talking to someone I have never met is like reading a new book." Samantha skipped off to the other busser.

I looked at my watch. Still an hour and a half before we open. Our work schedule for the next week was posted. Matilda and I didn't have quite the same days off. She had Thursday & Friday, while I had Wednesday & Thursday. Amy and Lori, being a couple, were able to have the same days off: Friday & Saturday. It meant I had more time in the bathroom on those days. Since I had caught them napping together I had become exceedingly cautious whenever I entered the bathroom. I didn't want to catch them doing anything more intimate, but I had become a bit curious about the mechanics involved. Samantha and I had one day off in common: Wednesday. That would figure. I know I was making a bigger deal about it than I should. With Samantha being such a social butterfly, I probably wouldn't even see her that day. If I wanted to spend some of that day relaxing in my room alone, I could. With Matilda and I both working in the restaurant, we worked similar hours, but hers were longer. Her shifts started slightly earlier than mine, and ended slightly later.

We were about as prepared as we could be. Time to eat our lunch before we served the guests theirs. The EDR didn't officially open until 11:00 am, but that's when the restaurant opened, so food was always ready for us by 10:45. That didn't leave much time to eat, especially if one wasn't in the front of the line, or needed to use the bathroom. Through trial and error, I learned I didn't have time to both wait and pee. If I wasn't one of the first ones in line it was better use of my time to use the restroom before I ate. I learned my lesson the hard way the day we opened. I cut my eating time too close, but I had to pee. I couldn't be late my first day of work, so I just held it until I had a break. That didn't come until two hours later. Putting on a pleasant face for your customers wasn't easy when your bladder was on the precipice of exploding.

When I returned to the dining room after eating a hamburger and fries, there was already a line in front of the hostess stand at the entrance to the restaurant. There were enough people in it that they blocked the entrance to the gift shop, which was adjacent to the restaurant. When the hostess saw the crowd, she began to panic. Fortunately, Mark---the Food & Beverage Manager---was there. With much grace, he warmly greeted the first guests. He filled out their guest check. He marked the assigned table with a grease pencil on the plexiglas blueprint of the dining room. He then gave the check and four menus to the hostess, who was already beginning to calm down. She led the guests to a table beside a window, handed a menu to each of them after they sat, then returned to the hostess stand. The procedure was repeated many times. In less than ten minutes the line was gone, even with a few more groups arriving before the original groups were sat. "Just remember to mark the table before you seat a group," Mark reminded the hostess. "If you forget, seat them at an empty table before making the correction at the host stand. If a line builds again don't hesitate to send someone for me."

Bussing was a breeze after the initial butterflies. The key was staying on top of things. A busser needs to be constantly moving. On those rare occasions when every glass was full, and every table cleared and washed, it felt like something was wrong. As I became more proficient, more of those occasions occurred. That was the one fault with expertise. Eventually you bore yourself with your efficiency. One of things bussers did to improve such efficiency was pile dirty dishes on a serving tray. A large metal oval platter placed on a wooden stand. If a busser filled the tray a certain way she could clear three full tables before she had to take it to the dirty dish drop. The more dishes on it, though, the heavier it got. I wasn't able to carry a full tray at the start of the season. It was quite a milestone when I was able to accomplish the feat in less than a month. My arms didn't look like Popeye's, but they were significantly stronger when I left Yellowstone than when I arrived.

The first people we sat were snowmobilers. The snow coaches began arriving shortly after that initial line was sat. Up to 2000 snowmobilers entered the Park on any given day, with weekends being the busiest. On those busiest of days, as soon as a table was cleared, and sometimes even before, people in black leather, smelling like exhaust, pounced on it. Oily helmets were placed on window sills, under and on top of tables. Snowmobilers are generally kind people, but they become moody when their quest for a quick meal is unsuccessful. A delay in their adrenaline rush instigates curt replies.

I made it through my first real day of work. I had been so busy, that by the time I had caught my breath lunch was over, and we could begin setting tables for dinner. Cloth napkins replaced paper. We had to fold them a certain way, so that took some time.

Normally they were pre-folded during any slow periods during lunch, but with it being opening day we weren't efficient enough to have any down time. As we set the tables, servers vacuumed their sections, and restocked sugars and ketchups. They helped me and the other busser fold napkins when they got done. Restaurant employees normally worked either breakfast and lunch or dinner. We didn't serve breakfast that first day, but with it being opening day there was extra prep work that needed to be done. Tomorrow would be the fun day. Breakfast would begin serving at 6:30, which meant I had to clock in at 6:00, which meant getting up at.... I didn't even want to think about it.

I still had an hour before dinner, but I was too tired to ski anywhere. It really wasn't that long of a day, but I think the dread of the first day with customers wore me down as much as any actual activity. I sipped hot chocolate as I munched on potato chips. Some people liked those flavored potato chips or corn chips. I was more of a traditionalist. I believed a fried slice of potato lightly salted was as close to a perfect food as God could create. Why did someone need to muck it up by coating it with artificially flavored powder? Drinking the hot chocolate reminded me of dipping Oreos in milk. I dipped a potato chip in the liquid. The sweet/salty combination was quite good. It reminded me of chocolate-covered pretzels.

"There will be no playing with your food." I had been so fixated on my new culinary creation I didn't notice Matilda walking into the EDR. I thought it was Lori at first, forgetting she had the day off. Schedules were messed up the first week to provide ample time to train. I had only Thursday off. Matilda filled a tumbler with ice and Coke and sat down across from me.

"You finally off?" I asked her.

"Not yet. The dinner crew needs some help with their prep work. We'll get our act together by next week. I'm taking a brief unscheduled break."

"Cooks must get a lot of overtime?"

"Occasionally, but the company execs don't like it. They can't figure out how a hostess can work just 30 hours some weeks and cooks 50. It's not like the two jobs are interchangeable."

"You must really rake in the dough during those 50-hour weeks? Paid time and a half for 10 hours."

"Just a couple of hours. In Wyoming overtime doesn't begin until you reach 48 hours."

"It sounds like Yellowstone needs a union."

Matilda looked around. "Don't even joke about that. In a normal year there are more applicants than there are jobs---a lot more. Most people don't work here for the money. It's a paid vacation for most of us. A way to escape adult responsibilities for a few more years."

"Do you have plans for Thursday yet? Probably a massive 20-mile ski with some of your longtime macho friends."

"I don't have that many friends, not good ones anyway. I'm kind of a loner. One of the reasons I work here, especially in the winter. And no, I don't have plans yet for my days off. Some people like to make complex plans for the future. To them the process of making them, and the anticipation of the events to come, are as important as the events themselves. For me, if too much work goes into planning, the event itself feels anticlimactic. I would rather wait until the day arrives, then decide what I'm in the mood for."

"Uh, okay."

"Did you have something in mind?"

"If you would rather be spontaneously, I can wait until Thursday to ask."

"You're going to make me wonder for two days?"

"Sorry."

"Don't be. When people begin to know one another sorry should always be implied when things don't go well for the other. Spill it. What do you have in mind?"

"I thought about going to Summit Lake. But that's too far,

and too difficult for me, isn't it?"

"And probably me too. I'm not in that great of ski shape yet. I won't be doing 20-mile skis for a few more weeks."

"What do you recommend then, for someone who is a beginner, but who doesn't want to go down the bunny slope?"

"How about something close, so if you do have problems it won't take you too long to return to the dorm. How about Fern Cascades? There is some elevation gain...and...a creek. The fires may have burnt down most of the trees, but they weren't able to damage the water."

"Great. It's a date." I wish I hadn't said that last part. I didn't want Matilda to think I was like Lori and Amy. Matilda returned to work, and I added some more hot chocolate to my tumbler. What else could I dip in it?

The one advantage of skiing in sub-freezing temperatures is it woke you up in the morning. I ended up hating working breakfast shifts. All that syrup. Everything was sticky: the dishes, the table, me. The only thing nice about it was the lack of snowmobilers. Occasionally some of them spent the night at Snow Lodge, but the vast majority of breakfast diners were those who had come in on one of the snow coaches. They spent their days taking tours and skiing. Breakfasts were sometimes too slow. When you were tired the only thing keeping you awake was being busy. Being the beginning of the season, we weren't yet sold out. Consequently, our first breakfast was a slow one. Being a manager that not only looked after his employees, but also the company's interests, Milo gave two of the servers and one of the bussers the morning off. He asked for volunteers, and there were plenty of takers. My opinion was if I was there already I might as well get some work done, and get paid for it. Now, if I was given an option of not getting out of bed at all, I might have taken Milo up on his offer.

Having just finished working breakfast, lunch was more tiring that it had been the day before. Working both breakfast and lunch made it a long day. It evened out. I had as many dinner shifts as I had day shifts. It was just served from five to nine in the winter, so on those days, it felt like I was working just half a day. With tips being better in the evening I earned about the same amount of money working either shift.

When I first received my share of the tips, it felt like an unexpected windfall, like I had found money on the ground. Each server paid out 20% of what they made. That doesn't sound like much, but when you bus for three servers that adds up. I was making almost as much money in tips as they were, and I was getting paid a better hourly wage.

It was strange having all that money lying around everywhere. Once when a table was sat before the server could collect her tips, I collected it for her. I was concerned those new to the table might take it. She had become upset with me because she thought I was pocketing the money for myself. Was it because I was black? Or would she have felt that way if anyone had placed the money in their apron? Yes, bussers had to wear aprons. Sometimes we put extra silverware or napkins in the pockets, but I usually left mine empty. Looking at her point of view, it may have looked like I was stealing from her. I never took money from a table again.

I was exhausted at the end of my first full day, but what bothered me the most was my sore feet and legs. I don't think I had ever been on my feet for such a long period of time before. Was I going to feel like this after every shift or would I get used to it? Luckily, I had the next day off. What was I going to do when I worked five of these shifts back to back to back? With working dinner shifts too, I had just two or three of the longer shifts each week. That seemed manageable.

9.   FERN CASCADES

Matilda and I made plans for Thursday, but we didn't specify a time to meet. The EDR closed at 9am, so if I wanted to have a leisurely breakfast on my first day off I had to arrive by 8:30. Matilda had one of the rooms downstairs with a private bath. I had never been in her room before, but I've seen her walk into it from the hallway. I think this is the right room. I hesitated before I knocked. Not to make a spectacle of myself, I struck the door with my knuckles lightly.

I heard a brief shuffle within the room. After a rattling of the door knob, the door was pulled inward. Christine Faith greeted me. "Is Matilda up yet?" So, if Samantha and Christine hadn't had their tiff I might have roomed with Matilda. Or had I knocked on the wrong door?

"She'll be out of the bathroom in a minute. Have a seat." There wasn't a chair, so I sat on a bed. It wasn't made, but the covers were at least pulled up.

Christine was finishing dressing, which mainly consisted of putting on her shoes and socks. She wore a gray shirt over black pants, the typical housekeeping uniform. "Shouldn't you be at work?"

"We don't have to go in until nine today."

"Not enough rooms?"

"It will be another week before we'll be busy enough to work a normal shift. They're thinking about giving us an extra day off next week."

"Must be very slow."

"Most of the housekeeping crew returned. Very little training. Another couple of days and we'll be in midseason form."

The bathroom door opened and Matilda appeared. Her hair was brushed, but not completely dry. She was still in her underwear. I felt embarrassed seeing her that way. I shouldn't. People wore a lot less at the beach or beside a pool. I didn't feel uncomfortable when Samantha wore even less. Somehow because it was Matilda, it felt different.

I nervously said, "I...ah...didn't know when we would be going skiing, so I...ah...thought you might have wanted to eat breakfast. We could drop by the EDR on the way to Fern Cascades."

Matilda smiled merrily at me. She was amused by my ravings, but not in a disrespectful manner. She enjoyed sharing this awkward moment with me. "We can ski to the EDR together, but Fern Cascades is in the opposite direction." I was doubly embarrassed now. She had mentioned something about it being close to the dorm. And now, after remembering it, the map did show the trailhead in that direction.

"Enjoy your ski." Christine put her jacket on then squeezed past the partially opened door, careful not to expose her roommate to anyone who might walk by.

It was awkward having Matilda dress while I sat on the bed, waiting for her. I looked around the room. She had a stack of books piled on her dresser. Most of them were on the suggested reading list my English teacher gave me. "You like reading the classics?"

Now it was Matilda's turn to become embarrassed. "Some people think it pretentious of me. It's just what I like to read. The plots and characters are great, but what I like best is they took place hundreds of years ago. I find history much more fascinating than the present." We almost had that in common. I liked the future better, and Matilda, the past.

Nothing else on Matilda's side of the room stood out. It was as Spartan looking as my room, but not as neat.

"Let's go." Matilda grabbed her jacket and headed towards the door.

"Aren't you going to dry your hair first? Aren't you more likely to catch a cold if it's wet?"

"You catch a cold from a virus. Wet hair might be uncomfortable until it dries, but I won't catch anything from it. With the sun and wind, it will probably by dry be the time we reach the EDR."

I didn't know the girl behind the serving counter very well. The best I could muster was a *hello*. I loved breakfast, but I didn't always like something that heavy in the morning. Why couldn't people serve that kind of food in the evenings? I couldn't help myself. I had to have a bit of everything. My compromise was taking smaller portions---than I would have if I was eating dinner. My favorite was the blueberry pancakes. Frozen berries had a tendency to bleed when thawed, so to prevent the pancakes from being stained purple the EDR server dropped the berries onto the batter after it had been poured on the grill. I loved bacon too, but not as much when it was overcooked. It was this morning. I was a trooper. I made the sacrifice, consuming it without external complaint. Matilda chose to have an omelet. She asked the server to put cheddar and ham in it, being quite specific that she didn't add any onions.

After eating and dropping off her dishes, Matilda walked back up to the EDR server. "Do you have sack lunches for Matilda Enrique?" The server walked back to the prep area. She returned with two white plastic bags with the Yellowstone bear logo on them.

"I didn't think to order any?" I embarrassingly admitted.

"You can have one of mine."

"Thanks." I took a quick peek inside before I placed it in the backpack purse I took everywhere with me. There were three small packets of cheese, crackers, an apple, a can of grape juice, and a four-pack of Oreo cookies. "I feel guilty about eating your dinner."

"We'll come back here for that."

"But don't the sack lunches take the place of two of your meals?"

"In essence, yes. But I have never been turned away from eating lunch or dinner on the same day I pick them up. Sometimes I order them on my off-days even if I don't go anywhere. It's a good idea to have a stockpile of snacks in your room. That way if you don't want ski to the EDR, you have something to eat. You can't just walk down to the Ham Store, like you can in summer."

"There are stores in Yellowstone, in the summer, that sell ham?"

"Ham Store is short for Hamilton Store, the company that runs the general stores in the Park---in the summer."

How much did I miss out having not worked at least one summer here?

I understood why Matilda ordered sack lunches, even on days she also ate in the EDR. But it still seemed wrong to double dip.

In Yellowstone, employees work to exist, but ski to live. Occasionally someone worked at Snow Lodge who didn't go skiing, but for every person who was like that there were dozens who were more adventurous. As previously mentioned, the trailhead to Fern Cascades was behind Lupine. I hated to backtrack towards the dorm, but if we wished to do that ski today that's what we had to do. Between the dorm and the trail, we passed through a cluster of unoccupied cabins and outbuildings. The only area with any sign of life was were the snow coaches were fueled and had their maintenance done. Being a few minutes past mid-morning, we only spotted one yellow double-compartment snow machine.

A hill initiated the trail. Even with using everything I learned about climbing, I still consistently slipped and fell. "IT'S ALMOST ALL DOWN HILL ONCE WE REACH THE TOP!" shouted Matilda from up ahead, above me, trying to be helpful, but instead irritating the hell out of someone who was trying to retain whatever dignity she left at the bottom of the incline. NO MORE DISTRACTIONS!

At the top of the hill, I rested, but not before my skis were securely planted in the snow. I wasn't going to start over. Looking back at my route up, I viewed an eerie sight. The limbs on most of the trees had been burned away. All were charcoal black. The snow was the complete opposite. It was of the purest white, a soothing blanket wrapped around the feet of the aching woods.

"It reminds me of a dog," Matilda stated.

"What does?"

"The burnt trees. Ever see a closeup of a cartoon dog?"

"The hair kind of looks like trees, doesn't it? Deciduous, after the leaves have fallen. Or after a fire."

"Skiing through them makes me think of fleas, on that dog."

"Are we that insignificant?"

"Yes, and that magnificent too. Watch as I kick the snow." A small avalanche cascaded down the hill. It tumbled into a tree at its base. The trunk rocked, shaking some of the soot from its hide. A hint of amber flesh was exposed where the black had flaked off.

"The insignificant can make a difference?"

"Nothing is insignificant, because it's part of the whole. If we don't choose our course, something else will. Everything is connected."

"But isn't it all hopeless? People still steal, and injure, and kill. Technology may have changed, but humanity hasn't."

"Then maybe we should evolve into something non-human. Homo Erectus begets Homo Sapiens begets Homo Maturus."

"Evolution takes many generations."

"Then let's begin? If we are able to split the difference every generation, halfway between morality stagnation and Homo Maturus, the distance will eventually become insignificant."

Slowly, we worked our way towards a canyon. The trail forked, the right branch terminating atop a knoll. Below, the mellow Fern Cascades flowed through the snow. The canyon flattened to non-existence by the time the trail reached another fork. Someone had made their own trail across the creek, across a log, and up a steep incline. The ski tracks, that terminated two-thirds of the way up, were jumbled. "Where were they planning to go?" I asked.

"Maybe nowhere. Sometimes people like to go partway up a hill just to ski down it. Or maybe they were thinking about finding a cross-country route to Summit Lake, that place you mentioned a couple of days ago. It's been tried a few times, but never accomplished. This is not the time of the year to break trail. The snow sets up best in February. If I were to attempt something like that, that's when I would try it."

"Let's do it then, in February."

"I haven't heard of anyone ever finding the route."

"I have full confidence in you."

"You have just learned to ski."

"I'm sure you'll teach me what I need to know by February."

We were both ecstatic when we passed through a small grove of *green* lodgepole pines. Miracles do happen, even in the middle of a travesty.

There were two ways down the hill, if one didn't want to backtrack. Both were steep. The right descent intersected the road at the Howard Eaton trailhead. The left, headed back to the dorm. We took the left route, called the Water Tower, for the structure at its crest.

I looked at the steep downgrade. "I don't think I'm going to make it."

"Snowplow the entire way if you have to. The snow is still fairly fresh, so you won't have too many icy spots. You go first, so I can stop and help if you get into trouble."

"Like if I break a leg?"

"Good luck to you, too."

After the first couple of seconds I felt comfortable in the steady, but slow descent. The trees opened up briefly. I could now see where I was going. The trees closed in on me again---too soon. But I thought I might make it. I could see the bottom. Oh, no, someone was coming up the hill, and a person behind him. I tried to maneuver around them, but I was not yet skilled enough. I missed the first skier, but took-out the second.

"ICE CREAM AND ONIONS!" my brakes---a.k.a. Charlie Peterson---exclaimed gleefully.

Matilda came down the hill five seconds later, yelling something incoherent. She stopped just above the melee. "And I thought breaking trail this time of year was going to be dangerous."

Andy helped untangle us.

Matilda added, "I probably should have told you. Make some noise when you're coming down to warn people coming up."

10. THE TOUR

Solitude became a memory. Yellowstone reopened for business. The roar of snowmobilers was heard from mid-morning until dusk. Even at Fern Cascades. And in the geyser basin.

There were now guests twenty-four hours a day at Snow Lodge. They became part of our ever-changing community. Some tourists stayed just one night. Others, a week. Names were learned, but most soon forgotten. A ski shop rented skis, providing even the most raw novice with the resources to attempt to ski. Lessons were given for an additional fee. Milo was pleased at the greater than predicted turnout. The fires were expected to reduce revenue, but sales were barely lower than the previous winter. Did curiosity---of what remained of the Park---trump the deforestation of a natural monument?

I finally had two days off in a row. I wish I could have spent both of them with Matilda. Amy and Lori invited me to go with them on a snow coach tour of the Park. I was apprehensive, for two reasons. If Matilda got off early I didn't want to miss out on the opportunity to spend time with her, on geyser hill or somewhere else close by. I also didn't want to become embarrassed by the Apollinaris's display of public affection. It no longer bothered me that much in private, but their inappropriate behavior around guests would likely cause the tourists' stares and wrath to extend my direction---guilt by association. I wanted to see Canyon and Lake Yellowstone bad enough that I put those misgivings aside. I shouldn't have been concerned. Amy and Lori behaved as most couples with long-term relationships did: they were virtually oblivious to one another.

Our snow coach was one of the blue ones with the single compartment. It was nearly full by the time we entered. As employees, we were permitted to go on any of the tours free of charge, if space was available. A couple of more tourists would have bumped one of us. The snow coach sat twelve comfortably, and four couples were already present.

I was pleased to see Flint. He requested I sit next to him in the passenger seat up front. The last time I had spoken to him was in this same seat, when I got upset at him for making fun of me for having to use a deep-freeze outhouse. To show that I was over it, I agreed to sit next to him. From the way he smiled at me, it had never been a problem for him.

Gas fumes could be smelled inside the snow coach. I hadn't noticed them the first time I was in it. Maybe it had been a different coach of the same model. I assumed the odor would go away once we started moving. It didn't. The windows began to fog as we climbed over Craig Pass on our way to West Thumb Geyser Basin, a mid-sized thermal conglomeration beside Lake Yellowstone. Flint handed me a plastic bottle full of a blue liquid. "Spray the anti-freeze on the windows. It will clear them." The windows hadn't fogged up last time either. In front. Should I be handling this stuff? It couldn't be worse than breathing in gas fumes.

When the windows did clear, I saw snowdrifts five-feet high beside the road. Flint, reading my mind, or following the script, said, "Craig Pass receives some of the heaviest snowfall in the Park, but by February even Old Faithful will have a snow pack as high as you see beside the road."

Flint spent as much time talking to me as he did talking to the paying passengers, combined. If he always did that he would probably lose his job, but I sensed I was a special case.

Upon our descent, a lake covered in snow was spotted to our right. "Is that Lake Yellowstone?" asked a middle-aged man.

"That's Shoshone Lake," Flint replied. "It's the second largest lake in Yellowstone. We'll be seeing Lake Yellowstone in about ten minutes."

We weren't disappointed. It was many times larger than Shoshone Lake. It also was covered in snow, but not completely, most dramatically in the large bay nearest to us.

The snow coach stopped beside a boardwalk that led down to the lake, after passing through a geyser basin. "WHAT'S THAT?!" Lori shouted.

"A coyote, I think," Amy responded. It was on the ice, more than a hundred yards into the bay.

"What's that sound?" I asked.

"Someone singing?" a tourist hypothesized.

Flint smiled. "It's the lake. When it freezes it makes that sound."

"It's so beautiful," a different tourist commented.

"Sounds kind of sad to me," said a third.

"How long will the coyote have to wait for the ice to reach the geyser basin?" the original tourist asked

"Forever," Flint replied. "As long as there's a geyser basin here. Hot water doesn't freeze."

Heading north along Lake Yellowstone, we entered a verdant grove. So stark in contrast to the monochromatic ruins I have begun to associate Yellowstone with. Everyone perked up, momentarily, until the charcoal rubble returned.

We drove past the majestic Lake Yellowstone Hotel along the northwest shore of the lake, then continued north along the Yellowstone River. Ice coated its sides, but a wide channel still flowed down its center.

Flint stopped beside the river. Curiosity permeated the snow coach, then elation. An otter rested on the distant icy bank. It had something in its mouth. It dropped it on the ice. It flopped for several minutes. After ceasing movement, the otter bit a plug out of the fish.

Next was Hayden Valley. During the summer, it was full of bison, but this time of year most of the herd was missing. Only a few bulls remained. They ate the exposed grass by the river. Being loners, there was significant space between individuals. Barren and bleak, snow-covered grassland became temporary tundra in winter's embrace.

We ate lunch at a warming hut at Canyon---the village, not the natural wonder. I remembered to order a sack lunch this time. One of the couples also ate from the white bags with the bear logo, but the other three, plus the Apollinaris's opted for the snacks the building provided---for a fee.

Hoping to do more than stretch my legs during the break, I looked for the canyon. I wasn't successful.

Flint caught up with me. His attempts at conversations with me in the snow coach fizzled after I responded curtly with one-word replies. I thought I was over him making fun of me. Apparently, I wasn't. I also didn't want to give him the wrong idea about us. He was attractive, but when I'm interested in a person, be it male or female, a physical relationship or just friends, I could only focus my emotions on that one person. It wasn't something I did intentionally. I just liked to invest my entire being when I did something, and that included relationships. If I gave a bit of myself to others, that meant I was giving less to the person I had a relationship with. But being distant, didn't prevent me from being civil.

"It's still a mile away, as the crow flies. More by road."

"Someone should have placed the warming hut closer to the canyon."

"I believe it was placed here for safety and logistical considerations."

"Don't you think some of those should be overlooked for the appreciation of beauty?"

"If a restaurant was on the rim of the canyon, how many pieces of garbage, accidentally or intentionally discarded, will fall into it?"

"I didn't think about that. Having a good view for lunch doesn't outweigh the damage that could be done to the canyon."

"Have you been to the pub yet?"

"It's in the Four Seasons Snack Shop, isn't it?"

"It opens at eight, except on Sundays when it opens at six, to compensate for state law closing it down by ten. Tomorrow will be the first movie night."

"What time does the movie begin?"

"Nine. Then a second showing at eleven."

"I have to work the next day."

"But don't people in the kitchen work late on their Monday?"

I nodded. "I don't have to be back to work until five---P.M."

"Promise me you will do it. We haven't spent any time together since we arrived at Old Faithful."

It would be nice to see a movie, and to get away from the dorm. Maybe Matilda would want to go. "I'll think about it."

"That's at least better than a no."

After lunch, we drove to the canyon. We stopped at an observation point at the base of metal stairs. No one had to tell us to hold onto the railing. The canyon's slope was gradual enough in some places to collect snow. Where it was steepest, reds and yellows of the canyon were very prominent against the white backdrop.

At the south end of the canyon, water dribbled off a frozen cliff. It meandered northward. From my vantage point, it looked like barely enough water to sustain its movement.

Our second stop was at the *Brink of the Falls*. After walking a quarter-mile down slippery steps and a sloping trail, we terminated at a platform beside the falls. The water from the river flowed through the small channel, narrowing as the ice expanded.

My pallor surroundings reminded me of the discussion I had on the bus. "Flint, why must there be prejudice?"

"I think it's a side-effect of creating our uniqueness. Anytime we criticize others for not being who we are---even internally---we seed prejudice. Everyone has prejudices. The powerful are just the ones that are criticized for it. Prejudice has always existed. People are afraid of what lies beyond their schema. If something un-pleasurable occurs outside *our community* we associate all ills to that outsider, be it Africans or Chevys. What is most important is not that we have prejudices, but how we react to them. We must think before we act."

The trip home was less eventful than our trip out. The one stop we made was at Norris Geyser Basin. "Steamboat is the world's largest geyser," Flint enthusiastically shared. I couldn't be a tour guide. There was only so much perkiness I was capable of secreting. "It erupts sporadically, the interval between recorded major eruptions varying from four days to fifty years. Water has been known to shoot more than 300 feet. You see that boulder over there?" Flint pointed to a rock beside the parking lot we were in. "That was shot out of Steamboat Geyser after one of its longer dormant states."

"How far away is the geyser?" asked a tourist.

"Almost a mile. We don't have time to see Steamboat. It's

quite boring anyway when it isn't active. We do have time to walk to a couple of closer, more active, thermal areas."

Everyone unloaded. Flint walked past outhouses on the way to a steaming area ahead. "Anyone need to use the restroom?" The last thing I wanted to do was use one of those things again. Flint paused in front of the two plastic structures. He waited a few seconds. No one headed towards them. Flint resumed walking.

He guided us through a breezeway of a building boarded up for the winter. On the other side, a trail led down to a fairyland of billowing steam, snow, ice, and blue water.

Flint led us to a railed observation point above a churning cauldron of boiling water. The un-burnt lodgepole pines beside it were layered in snow, to an exaggerated extent. They looked like trees in a Christmas cartoon. "The steam and mist does that to them. Normally, Rocky Mountain snow is too dry to stick to things like that."

"How could snow be dry?" I asked. "Isn't it made from water?"

"Frozen water---ice and snow---doesn't have the same properties as liquid water. You can stab someone with ice. You can't with water."

"But you can drown them."

"Slushy snow has water mixed in with the ice crystals. Powdery snow, just has the ice crystals."

"So, what makes Rocky Mountain snow so *dry*? The snow we sometimes get in Seattle is messy, but we can at least make a snowman out of it."

"Humidity. The Rockies are a lot more arid than Seattle. And the temperature. It's colder here than in Puget Sound. When it's close to freezing, especially a few degrees above, some of that snow is going to melt. And it might not all be ice crystals when it comes down."

Flint continued to flirt with me on the way back to Snow Lodge. And I was flattered. He was hansom, kind, and funny---and almost too perfect for me. He was also the only black male in Yellowstone and it had been awhile since I had been with a guy. There were so many reasons I should be with him, but all I could think about was spending time with Matilda.

Amy and Lori began discussing the absurdity of war. It was the same old story: if women ruled the world everything would be better. "What if sports replaced wars?" suggested Lori.

"Like the Olympics?"

"Or just a single sport, but encompassing many aspects of different competitions?"

"And the victors would receive political, ideological, and financial rewards."

"Sports heroes would become even more famous and powerful."

"Better that than warmongers and baby killers."

"Maybe all forms of entertainment could replace wars."

"Is there enough *quality* entertainment out there for that to happen?"

"Successful or creative?"

"Can't they be both?"

"As more money is pumped into marketing entertainment, less creativity will occur. There is an inverse relationship there. To become more efficient and consistent, plots to movies and books will eventually be created by computers. When a lot of money is at stake uncertainty isn't welcomed."

"Which will lead to actors becoming computerized. Just because an actor gets old, or dies, doesn't mean their track record of making profitable films needs to end."

"And singers."

"The roles of computers will expand."

"They will become as powerful as people."

"And they will demand citizenship."

"I read an article that computers one day will be made from flesh, because mechanical components could never replace the complexity of the human brain."

"There may not be a limit to their power."

"Their morals may supersede our own one day."

"And we may be deemed too dangerous for the well-being of their society, like wolves next to a cattle ranch."

"The future won't be all bad. One day we'll produce children without giving birth."

"Clones?"

"Or a combination of a couple's cells grown into an infant in an artificial womb."

"So, there would no longer be the need for two sexes."

"We can all become breeders. And women wouldn't need to receive their gift every month."

"I don't think I would want a duplicate of myself walking around."

"That's only if you cloned yourself. And even clones would have their own traits. Don't identical twins have their own personalities?"

Most of the Appollinaris's conversation was on the way back to the snow coach from Norris Geyser Basin, but enough of it was heard by the mostly middle-aged tourists to freak some of them out. And I thought their public displays of affection would cause problems.

Their conversation caused me some concern. Would romance diminish if a union of two people was no longer required to propagate the species.

And why were so many people in the art community gay and lesbian? If God was creativity and chaos, then homosexuals must be His most prized children.

11. MYSTIC FALLS

When a person is away from home, even if that person has created a new home, it feels incredible to receive mail. It's even better to receive Christmas cards. To guarantee I receive some, I sent mine out before I left for Yellowstone. By New Years the wall beside my bed was covered with them. Samantha received more. She put hers on the window beside her bed, with the colorful fronts facing out. She said it was to share Christmas spirit with everyone, but I think it was just to show off. We had a bit of a friendly competition to see who would receive the most. Samantha won, but by only three cards. I wouldn't be surprised if she mailed some to herself just to beat me. I really don't think she did that, but it did rationalize why I lost. Matilda only received a couple cards, and didn't put either of them up. "My family is here," was her explanation. "Some choices we make are attached with costs."

It was dinner time when the tour coach got back to Snow Lodge. I helped myself to a salad and some fried chicken as I waited for Matilda. She never showed up. She must have eaten an early dinner.

I knocked on her door when I got back to the dorm. Neither she or Christine answered. I became depressed, so I did my laundry. Some people ate when they were unhappy, I did housework. I had planned to wash my clothes before I started work on Friday, but since there was nothing else to do, I decided to get them out of the way tonight. The laundry room was downstairs, next to the RC's room. Instead of heading back upstairs after loading a couple of washing machines, I waited in the downstairs lobby. Matilda might walk by. I tried to read a book, but all I could think about was what Matilda might be up to. Was she with another friend? Had Flint hooked up with her, because I gave him, if not a cold shoulder, at least a cool one? I was becoming irrational. Flint had been in the snow coach with me all day. Before he could eat dinner, he had to refuel his rig and clean it. I finished my laundry. No sign of Matilda. I took the laundry upstairs to be folded, then went to bed early. As usual, Samantha wasn't in the room, so it made it easy. I heard Amy and Lori giggling. I put earplugs in and wrapped my pillow around my head.

    I woke up at 1:30, when Samantha stumbled in. She didn't turn on any lights to be considerate of me, but it would have been less disruptive if she did. She must have bumped into every wall and piece of furniture, including my bed. A few minutes after she found her bed I heard gagging, then vomiting. GREAT!

    The next morning, I was woken by a knock on my door. Samantha raised her head, said something very un-ladylike, then dropped her head back down, missing her pillow, which wasn't difficult considering it had fallen onto the carpet. Her head barely missed the small pool of liquidy vomit that was beginning to crust over. I wore an oversize shirt over boxers---my standard sleeping attire. It wasn't something I would normally wear in public, but it wasn't indecent enough to not go to the door.

    I opened the door, but just a crack. Making it clear the act was an investigation, not an invitation. It was Matilda. "I wanted to see if you wanted to go to breakfast." Noticing my attire, she became embarrassed. "I didn't mean to wake you."

    "I was already up," I lied. "Give me just a few minutes."

    "I don't want you to rush. Take your time. I'll meet you in the EDR." Matilda walked off. I shut the door, then spastically changed into my ski clothes. I looked at my hair in the bathroom mirror as I brushed my teeth. It was a mess. And I should take a shower. I hadn't last night. I had switched to an evening bathing cycle. Apparently, inconsistently. After working with food all day, showering after my shift wasn't optional. I had attempted to also take a shower in the morning, but at 5am I just wasn't in the mood. Also, my skin was becoming dry. The combination of taking too many showers and low humidity---lower than Seattle's.

I stripped off the clothes I had just put one. I hopped into the shower. I washed and shampooed as quickly as I could. I turned off the water, then reached for my towel. It wasn't there. I had forgotten to bring it into the bathroom. There was no way I was going to keep the floor dry this morning. I squeegeed my body and hair with my hands the best I could, then rushed towards my towel in the other room. If Samantha had seen me I would have been devastated. She didn't even move. I took the towel back in with me to the bathroom. I finished drying my body, then the floor. I hated to think what might be on that floor, but I didn't have another option. I would have to make time to wash my towel sometime today. I redressed. My hair still looked frightening, but I brushed it out the best I could, then tied it back. I was tempted to blow dry it, but that would probably frizz it out more. It had been a decade since afros were stylish.

I was almost out the door when I realized I hadn't made my bed. I wouldn't have felt any more naked if I had leapt into the hallway after getting out of the shower. I forgot to put on my thermal underwear. I briefly debated getting through the day without them, then some rare common sense kicked in and I stripped off my ski boots and pants and pulled them on.

Finally, I was out the door. I tried to make up time by running out the door to my skis. I slipped, not only bruising my side, but knocking over half the skis and poles sticking out of the snow. I had to replace them, in their proper orientation, before I could put on my skis. When I finally skied away from the dorm calmness inundated me. I had made peace with the situation. Matilda had probably gotten tired of waiting for me and had skied off by herself. There was nothing I could do about it now.

I was relieved to see her sitting at one of the tables eating some pancakes with…. "What did you put on 'em?"

"Peanut butter. It's a family tradition. You shouldn't criticize before you try it."

Not wanting to appear too afraid to…eat food---and that's all it was, it wasn't like I was eating a rock or an ant---I hesitantly spread some peanut butter on a single pancake. I covered it with syrup, then tore off a piece with my fork. I studied it for a moment before putting it in my mouth. It was quite sticky, and messy. Even being careful with it I somehow got a syrupy peanut butter on the side of my mouth. I chewed, swallowed, then licked my lips. It was actually quite good. How did someone come up with that food combination? Did they not have a piece of bread, but still wanted a peanut butter and jelly sandwich. Syrup had a similar concentration of sugar as jelly.

Matilda was fixated on my face as I ate that first bite. She smiled at the apparent pleasure this new culinary experience provided. I returned to the serving line. The EDR server placed three more pancakes on my tray.

"What took you so long?" Matilda asked, more curious than upset.

"Sorry about that. I had a bathing emergency."

"Like what? Accidentally falling into a dumpster?"

"Better than intentionally doing it. I hate to admit this, but it's been a day-and-a-half since I've taken a shower. I didn't want to be around someone in such a state."

"From the serious of your tone, I thought you may have been confessing to killing someone?"

"After a day-and-a-half a human body can smell like something that has died."

"It doesn't make much sense to me taking a shower before a potentially sweaty ski."

"Where should we go?" I wanted to ask Matilda where she was all last night, but I dreaded what her reply might be, so I didn't.

I allowed my imagination to conceive the worse instead.

"We didn't see all of the Upper Geyser Basin last week. And later I thought we might go to Biscuit Basin and Mystic Falls. They're in the same general direction."

We bypassed most of what we saw the week before, taking the flat trail adjacent to the geyser basin that was used as a bike path during the summer. We stopped at Castle Geyser. The fork beside it was one of the access points into the basin. The geyser was steaming, but no water was spurting out. A sign predicted the next eruption. We still had an hour.

"We better take our skis off," Matilda suggested. The snow on the boardwalk beside the geyser had turned to ice. Past eruptions had sent water in its direction, and had melted the snow that had fallen there. Once the eruption ended, subfreezing temperatures returned, transforming the water into ice. A hundred feet past the ice was a steep descent, followed by a bridge crossing the Firehole River. On the other side was a steep ascent. We kept our skis off until we reached the top of the rise.

As I snapped my boots back into my bindings I noticed the earth around one of the bubbling pools to my left was scuffed up with hoof prints. I peered into the pool that was beside a sign that read *Scalloped Spring*. A bone was in the cavity, on a rise above the water. "Did something fall into that?"

"A few days ago, a bison got too close. It must have boiled too death."

I didn't know how to respond to that. What would it be like to be boiled alive? "Where's the rest of it?"

"Probably down there somewhere. Most of these pools, geysers, and vents are interconnected."

"So, one day the skull of that thing might shoot out of Old Faithful."

"It's possible."

There were a lot of elk and bison in the geyser basin. They were supposed to be more prominent in thermal areas during the winter than in the summer. Quite evident today. They enjoyed a steam bath as much as the next mammal.

The most prominent geysers we passed were Grand and Riverside. The most prominent pools, Beauty and Morning Glory. Neither of the geysers were spouting. The same couldn't be said of Grotto. Whenever Matilda and I passed it together, it was gushing.

Morning Glory was the last thermal feature before the beginning of the Biscuit Basin trail. We had to climb a long, but not particularly steep hill. On the way down its backside we began to see steam from Biscuit Basin. The trail crossed the road to Madison, Norris and Mammoth. We had to wait for a group of snowmobiles to pass. The busiest road in the Park, winter or summer, was the one between the west entrance of the Park and Old Faithful. The buzz and roar of the snow-cycles was constant. As soon as we crossed the road, another group went zooming past us.

There were about a dozen snowmobiles in the parking area. Black leather bodies could be seen through the mist in the distance, beetles scurrying through inclement weather. The wind had picked up. It was particularly cold on the exposed bridge over the Firehole River, that connected the parking lot to the geyser basin. Becoming whipped by the wind, we circled the loop past the pools and vents expeditiously, barely stopping to admire each feature's unique beauty. The wind blew across one of the larger pools, carrying its steam onto the boardwalk beside it. The reprieve from the cold felt incredible. With a courage we weren't aware we possessed, we forced our way out of the decadent cloud. Instantly, we were slammed by the frigid air. In contrast to the warmth, it was nearly unbearable. We briefly returned to the cloud. Then immediately darted off. It was one of those occasions an abrupt separation was more effective than a leisurely emancipation.

At the beginning of the Mystic Falls trail Matilda stopped. "You still want to see the falls?"

It was cold, but I wasn't the type of person who easily gave up. "Onward." I spoke with great enthusiasm, but with little confidence I was making the right decision. If I had been with anyone but Matilda I might have turned around.

The trail to Mystic Falls was a bumpy one. I don't mean that the trail was covered with potholes. The terrain wasn't level. The trail would drop ten feet or so then climb five feet, to only drop five feet before climbing ten more. I snowplowed the first few drops, but after seeing Matilda drop at full speed and make it nearly to the top of the next rise without any self-propulsion, I thought I might attempt to be bolder. I had been skiing for over a week now. I reached the bottom of the first drop okay, but had trouble when I started rising a few yards later. The momentum I created from my drop had been expended about halfway up. I began to slide backwards. I didn't know how to react, so my instincts took over. I landed on my center of gravity: my butt. Matilda had gotten a bit ahead of me. I didn't blame her. Who wanted to travel persistently at a sluggish pace? I tried to pick myself up, but I had settled in a depression, making a difficult maneuver even more daunting. I felt like a turtle on its back.

My flailing attracted a spectator. Was it a wolf? It cautiously moved towards me. I think it sensed my inability to free myself---and my fear. Any moment I thought it might make that final charge. Then Matilda appeared. She was on top of the rise I had attempted to tackle with momentum. Perceiving my predicament, she raced down the hill, yelling as she descended. The canine darted off like it had been stung by a bee.

Matilda helped me get into a sitting position. My heart was racing, my body shaking. "I thought that wolf was going to attack me."

"It was a coyote. There aren't any wolves in Yellowstone anymore. I have never heard of a coyote getting that close to a human before. They usually run away. It must be the scarcity of food this winter."

"And I was its last resort. Should I feel offended?"

"I don't think it intended to eat you. Someone may had fed

it before, or maybe it smelled the food in your pack. Your color doesn't look right."

"Kind or racist thing to say, don't you think?"

"It must be the combination of the workout---you've haven't skied this far before, have you?---and the shock." Matilda opened her pack and pulled out her sack lunch. "You need to eat something." She handed me half her sandwich. It looked---and smelled---funny.

"What is it?"

"Honey, banana, and peanut butter."

After liking the peanut butter pancakes, I was less hasty to judge odd food combinations. MY GAWD! It was even better than the pancakes. It was sweet, flavorful, and hearty. She also handed me a can of apple juice. "It's a specialty of Snow Lodge. It will give you more energy than a meat and cheese sandwich, while still being hardy enough for lasting energy. The color in your face is returning."

"You can't lay off the racial comments, can you?"

"You must be feeling better if you can tease your benefactor. I promised I wouldn't let you get hurt. I guess I didn't do that great of a job at it."

"You prevented the big bad wolf from eating me. That's something. Would you like half of *my* sandwich? To replace the half of yours I ate?" I began to fumble in my pack.

Matilda halted me. "Maybe later, if I'm still hungry after I eat that other half of this sandwich. But I'm going to wait until we reach the falls. These burnt trees are too depressing to eat beside."

Matilda helped me up, then I brushed myself off. One of my skis had come off when I fell, so I had to round it up and put it back on before resuming our journey. No, I wasn't going to head back to Snow Lodge. Not yet. If I came all this way, fell on my butt, nearly gotten eaten, I was determined to not head back until I received my payoff.

A few minutes after we resumed skiing we came to a fork.

Matilda paused at it. "That's the official trail to Summit Lake."

"Can we see how far we can get?"

"That won't be very far. The trail doesn't look like it's been broken yet. Before the snow sets up, one mile will feel like ten."

I was disappointed, but tried to make the most of what was obtainable. "We still have Mystic Falls."

"Yes." Matilda resumed her skiing. The trail to Summit Lake dipped down to a bridge that crossed a creek that was predominantly snow and ice. The canyon it flowed through became more prominent the longer we skied above its bank. "Hold up. We need to take our skies off here."

"It's just a drizzle. We can step across it." I was referring to the steaming runoff from a thermal spring that crossed the trail. The earth was bare of snow for about two feet. I rushed past Matilda, lifting my skis one at a time over the water. My left leg stretched all the way across, but I didn't leave enough room for my right leg. Realizing my mistake at the last moment, I attempted a hop-skip before dropping my right ski. My left ski didn't lift at all. It was stuck. The un-expected jarring caused me to lose my balance. Fortunately, I fell away from the steep drop-off on my left. My right leg, ski still attached, slid into the runoff. I was able to push myself back up onto my skis, but now both skis were wet. As dignified as I could, I shuffled-stepped back onto the snow.

During this series of tribulations, Matilda just watched. It wasn't wise to disturb a wild animal when it was injured. My pride was definitely injured, and no sensible, civilized person would have ended up the way I did. Matilda took off her skis and walked across like she had directed me to. I didn't feel too comfortable in her prescience at the moment---from embarrassment, not fear---so I instinctively backed away from her when she got within a certain distance of me. Both my skis were stuck now. Matilda released my boots from the bindings before I could protest. She lifted one of my skis. The bottom of it was covered with caked-on snow. She slid a ski pole across it, scraping off winter's excrement. She handed it back to me. "See if it slides now." I tested as she cleaned the other ski. It moved much better, but it still felt a bit sticky on the bottom. She traded skis with me. The second slid much more freely. After a few more seconds of scraping she handed the original back to me. I snapped its binding back onto my boot. I tested it. Yes, much improved.

We continued towards Mystic Falls, Matilda leading, I, a few strides behind her. "Sometimes experience does matter."

"I'm sorry. I was trying to impress you with my skiing ability." That didn't turn out too well, did it?

"I hate bossing people around. I think that's why I never interviewed for a management position. When I...suggest something, it's not to retain the upper hand in our relationship. It's to protect you."

"I know. It's just that I would like to occasionally be the one in charge---to be the teacher sometimes, not always the student."

"I would like that too, but it probably won't happen a lot this winter. I know the Park a lot better than you. But when the season is over, perhaps you could...teach me. A place I've never been to. Something I've never done."

"I would like that."

We heard the falls before we saw it. The canyon followed the creek, appearing to constantly curve, to the right sometimes, then to the left. It wasn't the most dramatic falls, being just 40 feet tall, but something about it being encased in snow and ice made it extraordinary. I think it was the contrast of its chaotic movement to the peacefulness of its surroundings. The trail took us to an overlook, about 100 feet from the base of the falls. Orange trail markers continued up the side of the hill, but without ski tracks beneath them. "Where does that go?"

"Near the top of the falls. Then to an observation point, of Biscuit Basin. And after many miles, to Fairy Falls."

"Can we go?"

"We don't have time today, and there is a much easier

approach to Fairy Falls than this one, using a ski drop."

"What's that?"

"A snow coach takes us to a trailhead."

"Does it cost anything?"

"It's free, like a tour, if space is available."

"Let's sign up as soon as we get back to Old Faithful. Does a snow coach come back to pick us up?"

"Nope. Once you get off the coach you are committed to an eight-mile ski back. Most of it's flat. The most difficult part is it gets a bit boring. Part of the trail is beneath power lines."

We ate what remained of our lunches, then headed back to Old Faithful. When we returned to the thermal runoff, I took my skis off without being told, like a big girl.

About the time we began seeing steam from Biscuit Basin, I heard what sounded like two sticks striking one another. The forest terminated a few yards from the basin. We skied through an open area towards the sound. Matilda put a ski pole in front of me, halting me. Two elk with full racks were knocking antlers. Every few seconds they would back away a few feet, then with renewed determination charge their opponent, shoulders forward, head bent. CRACK! The sound reverberated off the sheer rocky cliff beside them. Back and forth they moved after their antlers locked---a primal tug-of-war.

"I've heard of elk not being able to untangle themselves," Matilda shared. "Years later all that remained of them were their eternally intertwined antlers."

"Like Siamese twins."

"But without the intelligence to coexist with another in such close proximity."

"What would it be like to spend your dying days so close to your enemy?"

The longer we stayed watching them the colder we got. Without trees to block the biting wind, a few more minutes is all we could tolerate. We paused for a few more minutes in that steam bath in Biscuit Basin. The abandonment of it was just as devastating as our initial experience. We sprinted home, returning to the warmth of the EDR in record time. The food could be terrible tonight. As long as it was hot, we would consider it four-star dining.

12.   CHRISTMAS

In the real-world people didn't have to work on Christmas. As you might have learned already, Yellowstone wasn't the real world. I was a bit bummed at first, but being busy would take my mind off being away from home---from Grain---during the holidays.

On Christmas Eve some of the employees, including Samantha, went caroling, starting with the guest cabins. They ended up at Snow Lodge, first going upstairs to the few guest rooms up there, then finally ending up in the restaurant. It was corny, but it lifted my spirit.

The restaurant closed early to accommodate the gift exchange. A tree was decorated in one of its corners. Colorfully wrapped presents filled the floor beneath it. Names had been drawn the week before. The only place to buy a gift in Yellowstone was in the gift shop, so most of the gifts were similar, so not very surprising. A few employees brought gifts from home for the occasion, but they were rare. Many of the employees down played Christmas. Homesickness became less of an epidemic if memories remained buried.

After we ate our Christmas meal in the restaurant, presents were distributed by Barry and Samantha, dressed up like Santa and elf. They arrived on a snowmobile. I, in my mildly stained apron, and Matilda, in her substantially stained chef's jacket, sat at one of the back tables with Christine, Charlie, Andy, and Flint. When Samantha delivered a package to Christine, she actually smiled, and Christine smiled back. It was a truce of sorts, for at least one day.

Samantha sat on Charlie's lap.

"I thought you were supposed to sit on Santa's lap." Charlie squeezed Samantha, then gave her a kiss on the back of her neck.

"I like your lap better." She twisted around, then whispered something in his ear. A surprised look on his face turned into a smile. She kissed him, then got up.

Christine examined her present as Samantha got the attention she craved. "Sam?"

"I bought it before...well...you know. I didn't want to just throw it away."

"I didn't get you anything."

"That's okay." Samantha returned to the pile of presents to make her next run.

"I thought you were going for a second piece of cake?" asked Andy.

"I still am," Charlie replied. "I just have to wait a moment to...settle down."

What would it be like to constantly worry about your arousal being noticed? I read somewhere that guys have hundreds of sexual thoughts a day. I sometimes go hours, if not days, without such thoughts. I'm embarrassed whenever my nipples become noticeable. That's one reason I wear baggy clothes. But they are more likely to become that way with temperature changes or exertion than with naughty thoughts. A man's erection can only mean one thing. Why does something so private sometimes become so public? Like bathing suits. No matter what style of bathing suit one wears there is never enough material. Why does it have to cling so? Why couldn't they be made to be worn loosely out of less sheer material?

I was curious what Samantha had given Christine, but was side-tracked when Barry handed me a present. "Abundant rain creates spectacular blooms."

"Ah, thanks."

"A safety meeting tonight?" asked Flint.

"I've given them up. I had an epiphany. Not surprising with it being the anniversary of the child. If Gandhi can go weeks without food, I can go as long without my nourishment." Barry returned to the diminishing pile of presents.

"I don't think I will make it tonight, Charlie," said Flint. "Barry's abstinence has created an opportunity I can't turn down: falling asleep at a decent hour. In fact, I think I'll head back to the dorm now. Good night everyone." He looked at me last. He smiled. His eyes floated to Matilda, then back to me. He sighed, then left. It wasn't completely hopeless between the two of us, but I couldn't invest enough of myself at the moment to make it work.

I finally got around to unwrapping my present. It was a romance novel. Just because I was a girl didn't mean I enjoyed this crap. I wasn't against romance. Just books about it. They never resembled real life. Falling in love with a charming, handsome stranger? When did that ever happen?

Barry returned with another gift for me. For an instant, I thought Grain had sent me another present and it had gotten mixed up with the exchange presents. I had already opened two gifts from her. One was a handmade quilt. The other was a food care package. I loved them both. The latter was already consumed. But Grain would never wrap a present for me in comics. She liked to use that shiny paper that was all one color, usually silver or gold, but sometimes red or green. I read the handmade label. IT WAS FROM MATILDA! "I didn't get you anything. I feel terrible."

"Don't. Gifts don't need to be exchanged. A gift is a...gift. Not a repayment of a debt. Open it."

I was relieved it didn't cost too much. It was one of those reading lamps that many skiers use as head lamps. "Thank you."

"Now we don't have to end the day at five o'clock." I hugged her, and she hugged me back, tightly.

"Shall we go for a ski right now?" I asked.

"Good idea," said Charlie. "It's tradition to ski to Morning Glory Pool on Christmas Night." That must have been what Flint backed out of doing.

Our ski for two became a ski for ten. Charlie believed in *the more the merrier*. Everyone wishing to go on an adventure with Charlie was permitted. No one was excluded. At times, a mixed blessing.

The most direct path to Morning Glory was the route Matilda and I used on the way to Biscuit Basin. At one time, it had been a road, but to reduce the impact to the geyser basin it was converted into a bicycle path. It was wide enough to ski two abreast, and with so many people we ended up skiing in that formation. As we passed Grotto, I noticed it wasn't erupting. Too many people this time.

Most of us took off our skis before climbing the ramp to the platform surrounding the south and east ends of the pool. Charlie thought it more of a challenge to leave them on. If it wasn't for the railing, he would have become stew.

The green and red and blue and yellow pool looked nearly the same at night as it did during the day. The only difference was the extra shadows, created by the direct lighting of head lamps.

"Now turn-off your lights," said Charlie. There was just enough moonlight to illuminate the snow, which illuminated our surroundings. Details merged, but outlines were distinct enough to discriminate between objects, including people. "Everyone hold hands." Charlie began singing that song from *The Grinch Who Stole Christmas*. The one where everyone was holding hands in a circle. We joined in, the value of our contribution varying, depending on our memory of the song and the quality of our voice. After the song ended, Charlie added, "And may this day inaugurate our rebirth. May our transformations benefit self and all."

13. FAIRY FALLS

I spent my next day off catching up on housework. That mainly consisted of doing laundry, mine and Samantha's. No one would disagree that my roommate was a beautiful girl, but if only those guys who lusted after her knew how many times she wore her clothes without washing them. I also took the time to thoroughly clean our bedroom and bathroom. Amy sometimes spot cleaned the sink, and toilet, but no one had yet scrubbed the tub. I resented cleaning the bathroom, but after Matilda presented the problem from a different perspective during lunch my opinion of it was altered.

"Just because the other girls don't mind living in a filthy environment doesn't make them bad people for not caring to clean the bathroom. They may be dirty people, but they're not evil. You are cleaning the bathroom for your benefit, not theirs."

"But they use it too. Eliminating all that grime, and all those germs, also benefits them."

"They don't see it that way. If Samantha put red nail polish on your nails while you were sleeping, would you thank her in the morning?"

"I might apologize to her after I pushed her out the window."

"Even if she was painting your nails for your benefit, to make you appear more attractive?"

"You think I would look better with red nails?"

"Different. The point I'm trying to make is Samantha might think she was doing you a favor."

"But cleaning the bathroom is as much a health issue as a cosmetic one."

"Maybe. Maybe not."

"You sign us up for the ski drop tomorrow?"

"I haven't had time. I'm working today, if you haven't noticed."

"Do you always have to get your uniform so greasy? You could be preparing a salad, and by the time you were done, your shirt would be covered in black grease."

"Maybe I was a mechanic in another life. If you want to reserve a spot on that ski drop coach you're going to have to be the one to do it."

"But I don't know how."

"Just go to the front desk and tell them what drop you want to reserve, and at what time."

"Why do we even need to reserve a spot if we ride on a space available basis?"

"So, some other employees won't take our spots."

"Oh. Okay. I'll sign us up. The earlier the better, right?"

"That way if we get bumped, we still might be able to get on a later coach. Time to add more grease to my uniform." Matilda put our dirty dishes in the dish drop, then placed her floppy chef's hat back on her head. She never ate with it on. Some people loosened their belts when they ate, Matilda made her head more comfortable. There were so many subtle things about a person that made them who they were. It was not how perfect someone was that made them who they were, but their idiosyncrasies, their imperfections. Each additional odd thing she did made Matilda more dear to me.

I never liked entering Snow Lodge's lobby from the housekeeping office, which was the most direct way from the EDR. After going back outside for about fifty feet, Snow Lodge was re-entered through a large room that was frequently inundated with activity. Someone was always folding towels or sheets. Most of the time that person said, "hi," as I walked by, especially if it was Andy or Christine. I felt guilty, like I was taking them away from their work. It wasn't my fault if they chose to greet me. But in some ways, it was. If I hadn't come within view of them they would have continued to work. I rushed past a towel folder as quickly as I could, but still got caught. "Good morning."

I opened the door with the large *Doorway To Reality* sign on it. I paused at the map of the Old Faithful area. Fairy Falls was aways away. And if it was too far, would I have to hitch a ride from a snowmobiler?

There were a couple of guests at the front desk. I waited. I sat on one of the chairs around the fireplace. I never saw it without a blazing fire. That must have been one of the first things the front desk staff did when they came in in the morning. Or was there someone on all night? Keeping a fireplace loaded with wood wasn't a bad way to spend an evening.

I looked back at the front desk. People were still there. I walked over to the gift shop. About half of it was full of nick-knacks. The other half consisted of necessities, like toothpaste and Snickers bars. For a place so small, it was well stocked. A guest was flirting with Amy. If he only knew. He bought a package of tampons and left. If I ever got married I would never subject my husband to buying feminine hygiene products. In return, he would have to wash his dirty underwear.

"Hi, Amy. You and Lori have big plans for your days off?"

"We're going to Gardiner. We have some friends that work in Mammoth."

"I thought we couldn't leave the Park until March."

"It's not easy, but it is possible. All coaches are free to employees on a space available basis, even the ones that leave the Park. If an employee wishes to guarantee a spot they do so by paying half the fare."

"I didn't know that. Does it work for ski drops too?"

"Yep."

"Did you pay for the snow coach to Gardiner?"

"Yep. Our friends are expecting us. Another way to get a free ride outside the Park is sign up to return a snowmobile."

"Some people actually leave one here?"

"I can't figure that out either, but they do. The snowmobile companies are more than happy to allow a Yellowstone employee to ride for free to get their machine back."

"Not sure I want to risk leaving the Park. I might not wish to return."

"It isn't like you're going to L.A. or New York. There is probably as much to do here as there is in one of the border towns. There is an employee Super Bowl trip to West Yellowstone."

"When?"

"During the Super Bowl.... Late January. Because guests won't be paying expenses, it will cost something. I think it was ten dollars last year. Ten dollars to get away for a day? Seems like a bargain to me. The Super Bowl marks the halfway point of the season. That's when people start getting cabin fever."

Another customer came up to the counter. It was my cue to leave. I waved at Amy, then headed back to the lobby. The front desk was finally free of guests. It was now or never. Charlie was the only person I knew at the front desk, and he was off. I recognized both of the people manning it. I had seen them in the EDR and in the dorm. I just didn't know enough about them to say I *knew* them. They were like wallpaper I saw every day. The kind of wallpaper one didn't have a relationship with.

"Can I sign up for a ski drop here?"

"What day?"

"Tomorrow."

The girl flopped a binder onto the counter. "Which time and drop?"

"The earliest you have for Fairy Falls."

She flipped to the appropriate page. "No one has signed up for the nine o'clock yet. We can sign you up, but there is no guarantee a snow coach will run."

"What do you think? Should I sign up for that one, or put my name on the first one someone has signed up for?"

"Why don't you put your name on both?"

"Am I allowed to?"

"We don't want you signing up for everything, but a couple is allowed, especially when it's a coin flip whether one of them runs."

"So, you think someone still might sign up for the earlier ski drop?"

"A lot of people like to wait until the last minute."

"Let's sign up for both the nine o'clock and the ten, then. My name is Jimi Jackson." The front desk girl wrote the name down under each time. "Also put down Matilda Enrique. She's working, so she needed me to sign her up."

"We'll just put *Jackson, Party of Two* down. You may want to check back after dinner tonight. If a ski drop doesn't have two paying customers signed up by ten it won't run the next day."

"So, even if no one signs up by 6:30 or so, that doesn't mean it won't run?"

"If you are seriously about going on the 9 o'clock you'll need to check in again tomorrow morning."

"Thanks." I had dreaded going up to the front desk to sign up for the ski drop. I had made myself sick from the worry of having to talk to someone about something I didn't know anything about. But what really could have gone wrong with talking to another employee? If they wanted to be rude to me they've already had two weeks to do it. I felt great now, like the moment I step out of a dentist's chair. I had all this renewed enthusiasm and energy. Maybe I'll go to Biscuit Basin by myself today. Or...maybe not. I could go to Morning Glory though. Or even better, Fern Cascades. No. I didn't want to go down that hill alone. Morning Glory it was. Maybe the Grand or Riverside would erupt as I passed them. It wouldn't be the same without Matilda beside me, but it would be nearly as fun telling her about them.

Matilda and I checked on the availability of the 9am coach, together, after dinner. No one had signed up for it---yet. "Should we just show up at 10 o'clock?" I asked.

"Nine is better, because that's when the EDR closes. Let's assume someone is going to sign up for it tonight. If they don't we can always go to the geyser basin for an hour."

After breakfast the next day we made the trek back to the front desk. I had mentally prepared myself that we would have to wait at least an hour for a snow coach. "A couple booked a pair of seats minutes before we closed last night. The snow coach should be leaving in five minutes." We had to rush back to the EDR to pick up our skis, then rush to the front of Snow Lodge. We barely made it.

Flint waited beside the snow coach. "Spent too much time putting on our make-up this morning, ladies?"

"We assumed our limousine would pick us up in front of our house." Matilda handed Flint her skis and poles. He placed them securely in the rack on the back of the snow coach.

"Just remember to tip your driver. Hello, Jimi." I handed my skis and poles to Flint. He placed them beside the three pairs that were already attached to the back of the coach. "Sorry about you losing at Twister." He was still speaking to Matilda---I assumed---because I didn't know what he was talking about.

"We'll have to have a re-match one day."

"You can't keep your body off me, can you?"

"Been awhile since you've been on a date?"

"Do you consider last summer awhile?"

"This past summer or the summer before?"

"It feels like the summer before."

"Maybe you'll meet a nice girl at the New Year's Eve Dance. Or even better, an indecent one."

"Who am I going to meet that I don't already know?"

"Sometimes people come down from Mammoth for one of these dances."

Flint smiled, but it quickly faded. "But most of the time they don't."

"So, we're having a dance?" I asked. "When is it?" It came out of my mouth before I could reign it back in.

Matilda smirked. "New Year's Eve."

I blushed. After I recovered, I asked, "Where is it going to be held? The lobby isn't large enough. We're not going to heat up the rec hall just for the dance?"

"Dances are held in the pub."

"Which is the snack shop during the day? It's full of tables. Do people dance around them?"

"Sort of. Not the tables, but the posts after the tables are taken off. Gallon jugs are put on top to cushion any contact."

"Sounds weird."

"It is weird. But fun."

"When does it start? And I don't mean what day. What time?"

"The time the pub normally opens. It ends when the last two people choose to leave."

"And when is that?"

"Five am or so," Flint answered.

"You're kidding?"

"They don't always last that long," Flint clarified, "but occasionally a group tries to outlast the darkness. Most of the time they have to work the next day---later that morning. Sometimes they don't even return to the dorm before starting their shift."

"Don't they...."

"Reek of sweat and stale beer? Yes. That's why the last group that did that was strongly reprimanded and sent home to shower and change into clean uniforms."

"It sounds like you know from personal experience."

122

"I've never been reprimanded, but I have closed a dance or two."

I looked at Matilda who had become strangely silent. "Have you ever closed a dance?"

Flint answered for her. "Your friend here may look demure, but she has been known to become a wild woman on the dance floor." Now it was Matilda's turn to blush.

"I definitely need to go now," I declared with enthusiasm.

"I look forward to seeing you two Saturday. Maybe the three of us can share a dance." I had the impression that Flint wouldn't mind if the three of us shared more than that.

The couple that had paid for the ride was already in the coach. The best way to describe them, was elderly, but that seemed almost like an accusation. They looked more fit and vigorous than half the people half their age. They smiled at Matilda and me, not as grandparents, but as peers. We were to share this adventure. The two of them sat beside each other on one side of the coach, Matilda and I on the other.

Flint stepped into the coach and shut the door. "No one wants to sit up front? You're going to give me a complex. I just hope I can keep this rig on the road while I'm constantly wiping off the windshield." It had gotten cold again last night---below zero. Why did it always have to be so cold on my days off? If I worked here during the summer, it would probably rain every weekend. Flint had kept the snow coach running while he was loading people and equipment, but the heater could only put out so much heat. It would have helped if we had a few more bodies to put out a smidgen more body heat.

Flint sprayed the antifreeze solution on the windshield, then wiped it with a rag. "Can you get that back window for me?" he said as he handed Matilda the antifreeze bottle and rag. I was a bit jealous he hadn't delegated the task to me. I didn't really want to do it---I had to wash my hands a half-a-dozen times after the tour to get the smell off them---but it would have been nice to be asked.

123

He probably thought Matilda could do a better job because she was had more experience. Hey, I'm getting more experience every day. Maybe if I return to Yellowstone next year I'll be driving a snow coach like this.

Matilda handed back the anti-freeze bottle and rag. The snow coach immediately lurched forward. We passed the dorm, then Black Sand and Biscuit Basins. I hadn't warmed up yet. If I was cold in the snow coach, what would it be like outside? Maybe I had made a mistake skiing in these conditions. It had been in the teens when we went to Mystic Falls. The high today was supposed to be ten degrees lower. The elderly woman looked as cold as I. Her husband embraced her, attempting to transmit some of his warmth. Then he rubbed her arms and shoulders. She smiled at him, put her head briefly on his shoulder, then patted his leg. If only someone would look after me like that one day. I glanced at both Flint and Matilda.

While still steering, Flint passed the anti-freeze and the rag back to Matilda. I almost cried.

Shortly after passing the Midway and Lower Geyser Basins, the coach turned left onto a less well-defined road. A couple of miles later it stopped beside ski tracks heading west near the base of a hill. Were all the trails in Yellowstone at the base of hills? "That's the trail to Fairy Falls. The falls are a mile away. There are some colorful hot springs further up the trail."

The elderly couple's skis and poles were first unloaded. A minute later they were heading down the trail, slowly, but consistently. Flint then detached Matilda and my skis and poles from the rack and handed them to us. "Don't forget about the dance Tuesday."

"You making more ski drops today?" I asked him.

"Until noon. Tomorrow I head to Mammoth. Then Saturday I have a tour."

"You must like the variety."

"Sure, but sometimes it would be nice to settle down with

the same route for a while. Good luck on your ski. Try to stay warm."

"It's easy for you to say sitting next to that heater." Flint smiled, climbed into his coach, then drove away.

As we put our skis on, four snowmobiles passed us, the gentle purring of their motors heard many minutes before and after.

The elderly couple was nearly out of sight. If the forest wasn't so burnt they would have been completely concealed by now. "Let's see if we can catch up to them." Matilda began heading down the trail.

I followed her, keeping just a few feet back. "Moving will probably help my blood to start flowing again. I think it has congealed."

"Just keep your extremities covered. I've heard that a person loses half their heat through their head. I think that's an exaggeration, but I know I feel warmer when I keep my cap on." Matilda wore an orange stocking cap with a black ball on top. It could almost be called cute. Almost. My blue felt hat looked medieval. It covered most of my head, including my ears. The part it didn't cover was my face. If I wasn't so dark-skinned my face would be dark pink now, or even red---somewhere between medium to rare. The combination of wind and cold was scorching my face. Matilda had given me the hat. That was the one thing I wasn't able to borrow from Samantha. She wore scarves instead. She didn't want to cover her beautiful blonde hair more than she had to.

We eventually caught up with the elderly couple, but it took some work. They were nearly at the falls by the time we did. The woman had to be at least in her sixties. The man appeared to be about ten years older than that. If only I could be that healthy at that age.

The trail had embraced a jagged hillside for most of the mile. Our perseverance in the bitter cold was rewarded. A tinkle of water fell from a cliff. An icy helix enveloped it. Did the structure begin from the bottom or the top? Would it fill-in one day, concealing the falls completely?

It was only ten o'clock. That didn't dissuade the couple from sitting on a snow-covered log and eating their sack lunch. Why did old people eat so early? Were their digestive tracks so worn out they had to start eating early enough in the day to have their food digested by the time they went to bed? I've heard of people eating their dinner as early as three or four.

We preserved their privacy, continuing to the springs Flint suggested. It took us just five minutes to reach it. Unlike most of the hot springs in Yellowstone, this one also had some green in it where algae began to grow. The water was warm enough to melt the snow in the area and cause steam, but not too hot to prevent things from growing. I was careful to not get too close. I didn't want to risk my skis sticking like they did on the way to Mystic Falls.

"We better start heading back," Matilda recommended. "Once we hit the road we still have almost ten miles to go."

On the way back to Fairy Falls, I bounced over a mogul. Something snapped. I looked down at my skis. I broke a binding. It was more than a mile to the road. Walking through waste-high snow when it was five degrees wasn't how I would have chosen to spend one of my days off.

I hesitated a moment before I said anything to Matilda. Breaking my ski didn't just affect me. It was going to ruin Matilda's day too. I wish we had never come to Fairy Falls. Why did I have to insist on going? Was Matilda going to hate me for having to put her through this? It would take me hours to reach the road, then we'll have to get a ride from someone. Could we even fit on the back of a snowmobile? Ski drop snow coaches weren't supposed to return with anyone. Maybe they would make an exception if there was an emergency. I looked at my watch. It was 10:30. The ten o'clock drop was probably just arriving at the trailhead. How many more ski drops would there be for Fairy Falls today? I think the last was at noon. That would give me an hour-and-a-half to reach the road. What if I didn't make it by then? What if no one signed up for the twelve o'clock?

Matilda stopped when she noticed I was no longer following her. She waited for me to catch up. When I didn't, she turned around and skied back to me.

"I...ah...broke my binding, I think."

Matilda looked down at my ski. "That you did." Calmly Matilda took off her backpack. Why wasn't she freaking out more? Her demeanor diminished my anxiety. If Matilda wasn't concerned, and she has spent more winters in Yellowstone than I had, why should I be? She was looking for something. Was that a spark of inspiration in her expression? She opened her white lunch bag and pulled out a plastic knife. She broke a piece off and stuck it in the loose binding. I tried moving with it. It stayed in place.

I gave Matilda a hug. "You saved my life. How can I repay you?"

"We'll figure something out one day."

Eventually the plastic piece worked its way out, but every half-mile or so it was replaced with either the same piece or another segment of knife.

The elderly couple was finishing their lunch when we returned to the falls. "It's good to be alive, isn't it?" said the woman.

"It's much better than being dead," Matilda responded.

"Not necessarily," said the man. "True, life is the greatest gift, but death doesn't have to be feared. Death is the eternal sleep, and who doesn't enjoy sleeping? We dream during sleep. Some of the adventures are wonderful, and others, dreadful, all created from a subconscious twisting of memories."

"Our souls persist," the woman clarified. "It may be no more than a clustering of memories, but isn't that enough?"

"No heaven?" I questioned.

"Heaven and hell is our own creation. If we lead a life

acceptable to our own moral code, our dreams will likely be heavenly. In contrast, if we lead an immoral life, our dreams will be more like nightmares."

"What if a murderer thinks there is nothing wrong with killing?" asks Matilda. "Heaven to him may be being able to murder without consequence."

"THAT'S NOT FAIR!" I exclaimed.

"Life's not always fair, dear," stated the woman. "One needs to try harder during the difficult times. To appreciate more during the less demanding."

A wave of melancholy washed over me. "Are you all right?" asked the man.

"I was just thinking about you not being here in ten years. Twenty years? I'm sorry. I feel bad for thinking such a thing. And now even worse for mentioning it."

"Don't lessen a person's life by making their memory a burden," spoke the man. "Celebrate their life, not their death. Add them to your memory chain. The Egyptians believed what's buried with them follows them to the afterlife. But the only thing the truly transfers are our memories."

As the four of us headed back towards the road, Matilda and I eventually put some distance between ourselves and the elderly couple. I had no doubts they would make it back to Snow Lodge, but they weren't going to do it at the pace of those 40 years younger than them.

We welcomed the side road once we reached it, but after the fourth or fifth group of snowmobilers passed us we no longer viewed it with so much longing. Most of the snowmobilers waved at us. They probably thought we were as foolish as we thought they were. But after being on that flat, barren road for a few minutes, I was beginning to come around to their way of thinking.

We skied down the road for two miles, until it terminated at the highway. We saw numerous thermal pools to the left of us. There were bare spots on the road, due to their proximity to the thermal features. Wood chips covered most of them, protecting machine from road, and road from machine.

A trail began across the highway. After a hundred yards it curved to the right, paralleling the road to Old Faithful.

We stopped for lunch. I sat down in the middle of the trail, where the snow was packed. "Be careful," cautioned Matilda. "We still have seven miles left. And on a day like today no one wants to endure a wet bum for that long." My intention was to brush off the snow before it made its way into my jeans. I wasn't completely successful.

I piled the contents of my lunch on the white plastic bag it came in. The cheese and apples were rock hard. The only thing I could bite into were the crackers and cookies. Matilda shared her peanut butter and banana sandwich. It was partly frozen, but not to the degree it couldn't be consumed. Our cans of apple juice were half frozen. Our water, being in larger containers, was in a less solid state.

"Don't forget to drink water," Matilda reminded me. "It's easy to become dehydrated in subfreezing temperatures. We drink less because we don't get as hot. That cloud of steam coming out of your mouth and nose is water vapor."

Most of the trip back to Old Faithful was boring. It was straight, relatively flat, and a good portion of it was beneath the power lines the girl at the front desk mentioned. When a person was tired, cold, and sore, the last thing she needed was to ski on a trail rated as easy. But sometimes arriving at a desirable destination required travelling through Kansas.

14. SNOW LODGE DANCES

The big event had finally arrived. The first dance. An excuse to blow off steam. Where the enjoyment is proportional to how much effort the participants put into it.

Dances are held in the employee pub, an A-frame building near Snow Lodge. During the day it's the snack shop, serving hamburgers and chili and fries, soft drinks and beer, hot chocolate and ice cream.

By the time Matilda and I arrived, the place was already packed. Being fashionably late in Yellowstone was impractical. Fun, not fashion, mattered. For many, duration was part of the fun. If someone can put in eight hours at work, they can certainly put in that many dancing.

Flint sashayed across the room as soon as he saw me enter. He grabbed my hand. "LET'S DANCE!"

"Let me take off my coat first. Where should I put it?" Coats, gloves, boots, and backpacks were piled everywhere.

"Anywhere you can find a spot. Just remember where you leave it. And don't put it on the ground."

"Why?"

"You'll see."

I whirled around, searching for Matilda. She was at the bar buying a drink. Being just eighteen, I wasn't allowed to buy alcohol. The pubtender was very strict about selling to minors.

"Now take off your boots," Flint demanded.

"I didn't bring any shoes." Then I looked down at Flint's feet. Apparently, he didn't either.

"You'll slide better in socks, especially after the first beer is spilled."

The dance was actually fun. Usually I felt apprehensive at dances, because I believed everyone was looking at me and judging. At Snow Lodge, no one cared. Even a little bump now and again could be overlooked if it was playful.

It takes about a minute to make a complete circuit of the dance floor. Many of the more active participants repeated the circuit, but most stayed within a radius of a couple of feet. Although I was technically dancing with Flint, it was more of a group activity. The only time people paired up was when there was a slow dance. That was usually when the dance floor cleared, an excuse to use the restroom or buy another drink. I was still dancing with Flint when the first slow song was played. I agreed to dance with him, but felt very uncomfortable when he put his arms around my waste. Matilda was at the bar starting her second beer, or was it her third?

"Thank you, Flint," I said as I walked towards her. "Ready to dance?"

"It looks like someone has done her share already."

"It wouldn't have been polite to turn Flint down. Anyway, you could have joined in."

Matilda took her can of beer with her on the dance floor. Drinks were permitted, as long as they weren't in glass containers. Matilda danced like she skied. With controlled abandon. The way she twisted and bent down would have made any sailor on leave want to spend his paycheck. Flint didn't exaggerate when he mentioned her lack of inhibitions. We didn't have to wait very long for the first beer to be spilled. Matilda had the honor. Our socks got soaked, but it was sure fun to slide halfway across the dance floor.

Shortly before midnight a group of dancers, including Charlie and Andy, put on their boots and left. Charlie had been wild on the dance floor, as expected, but Andy was almost as extreme. The only sign that he wasn't completely comfortable in what he was doing was in his eyes. He looked embarrassed, even as he spun around in feral abandon.

At the stroke of midnight, the old timers returned, with skis on. As the music played, they slapped their skis in rhythm as they danced around the poles. Those of us in socks yielded ample space. They were given a cacophonous applause when the song ended.

The ski dance marked the halfway point of the evening. No one left before that event, even those who had to work early in the morning. Mercifully, I wasn't one of them. I had to work, but it was an evening shift.

Matilda and I returned to the dance floor after she bought another beer. Charlie approached us. It wasn't a big surprise. He had been making his rounds most of the evening, and had finally reached us. "Has the rhythm captured your soul yet?"

"The beer has certainly saturated the soles of my feet," I wryly responded.

"Which the cleaning crew must take care of before the snack shop opens at 10:30. A heavy chlorine solution is used to detoxify this place."

"Have you ever been on the cleaning crew?"

"After every dance for the past three years, including this one. It's one of the fringe benefits of being on the dance floor when the music ends. There are some things that no one wishes to do, but still have to be done."

"So, you must be off tomorrow?"

"I don't have to be at the front desk until 6:30."

"A.M.?"

"Some start work much earlier." Charlie looked at Matilda. She had one of those insane 5am shifts. "Which reminds me. Are either of you off on Wednesday?"

Matilda shook her head.

"How about you?"

"I'm off, but---."

"Then it's settled. You will ski with Andy and me, and anyone else who I can shanghai. We're planning to go to Lone Star Geyser, and maybe make some runs on Howard Eaton or Water Tower on the way back."

"I better order a sack lunch for that day then."

"No worries, if you forget. Andy always brings extra."

After another round of dances, and another couple of beers for Matilda, she began to look flushed. She looked like she wanted to say something, like she had most of the night. "You look like you're hot," I said.

"So are you."

"Let's get some fresh air." Fresh, frigid air. Refreshing before the wind picked up, and our activity waned.

Were the silhouettes in the fogged windows looking out at us, or at the dance floor? Difficult to determine from our perspective.

We leaned against a railing. Matilda held onto my hand. She was about to say something, but instead of words coming out, it was the contents of her stomach. "I need to head home."

"Let's find your boots."

Apparently, no good deed goes unpunished. I became stuck, my beer-soaked socks adhering to the snow. I stepped out of them, then pried them up, one at a time. They were so securely cemented to the ground, I had to use both hands.

I waited a moment for them to thaw inside the building before I put them back on. The melting snow added to the volatility of the dance floor.

Now, where were her things? It was difficult enough finding your own things in a cluster of chaotic piles. It was nearly impossible finding someone else's. But I did after many agonizing attempts.

I took Matilda's boots and coat outside to her. She had vomited again, this time down her shirt. I helped her with her boots and coat, and then her skis. She must have gotten a second wind, because she was able to support herself without assistance. She fell a couple of dozen times skiing home, but she made it. I followed her to her room to confirm she reached it. Somehow, she was able to unlock her door. I left her after she successfully fell onto her bed.

I had trouble sleeping that night. Had Matilda really meant to hold my hand that way? And were those innuendos or just miscommunications? I've never been attracted to a girl before, but I was flattered by the attention. Then again, I don't think I was really attracted to guys either. I enjoyed their attention, and them touching my body, and pleasuring me. And I enjoyed pleasuring them. Would it be that much different with a girl? Was Matilda one of *those* girls? I never saw her with a guy, but I never saw her with a girl either. I couldn't help thinking about what might have happened if I had laid down beside her on her bed. What would it be like to kiss soft lips instead of rough ones? As I hugged my pillow I imagined it was Matilda.

15.   LONE STAR GEYSER

I saw Matilda the next day at lunch. She sat slumped, resting her head on the table in front of her, for the 15 minutes she was there. Not eating at all. Forcing down a glass of milk on the way back to the kitchen. When I asked how she was feeling, she just grunted.

The next few days it seemed like Matilda was hiding from me. The only time I saw her was from a distance, usually when she was working on the Line. A few days after that she seemed normal, too normal, like nothing had happened between us during the New

Year's Eve Dance. It was all very strange, and I became even more confused.

I forgot about the ski I had promised to do with Charlie and Andy. Forgot being a synonym for *hoping it didn't happen*. I knew it would be okay once we actually starting skiing, like after I asked the front desk clerk about the ski drop, but there was still some apprehension. I didn't know Charlie and Andy very well. They were more like people you saw on TV than real people. I saw them every day, but I thought of myself as more of a voyeur than a companion. Maybe if they couldn't find me I wouldn't have to go with them. A minute after that thought flashed through my mind, Andy and Charlie walked in. Great. Just my luck. Who would have thought they would have come to the EDR for breakfast?

After filling both of their trays to the rim, they sat down across from me. I sipped on a glass of orange juice. "Where is the group you hoped to gather?"

"Charlie's reputation proceeds him," Andy replied. "It's too early in the winter to break something."

"Then why am I going?"

"You don't know better yet."

"Hey, I can have a leisurely ski when I want to. Most of the trail is safe."

And it was. After the boys gobbled down their breakfast and picked up their sack lunches, we headed in a direction I hadn't gone before. We passed by some cabins near Old Faithful Lodge then down a short descent to a bridge over a creek. I wasn't sure, but I think it was the Firehole River, upstream from the Upper Geyser Basin. The trail forked shortly after that. A metal sign mentioned Mallard Lake to the left and Kepler Cascades to the right. We went right. After a few minutes, the trail began to parallel a road about fifty feet away. It must have been the highway to West Thumb Geyser Basin and Lake Yellowstone. The boys led. Every minute or so they would look back to confirm I was still with them. My reaction was mixed. I appreciated them making sure I was safe, but it made me self-conscious that I was a beginning skier. Okay, maybe I was an intermediate skier now. I would have skied rings around that person who arrived in Yellowstone three weeks ago.

Half-an-hour later we crossed the highway. Kepler Cascades was below us. It was more violent than Fern Cascades, but still fairly mellow.

We caught the trail again at the end of the parking lot occupied by four snowmobilers. It was perpendicular to the highway until it crossed the Firehole River, which we followed for a couple of miles. The water didn't steam as much as it did closer to Old Faithful, but it was still warm enough to keep it free-flowing. Snow covered rocks and sticks in its interior. The tops of them rose far enough out of the water to prevent them from thawing. It was the prettiest, most peaceful spot I had seen so far this winter. It could have been in New England two-hundred years ago. The mood was so over-powering that even the remote rumble of a snowmobile didn't ruin the ambiance. The only thing that would have made it better was sharing the moment with Matilda.

The trail took a hard turn after we passed a spur trail on our left that went over a bridge. The creek turned with us, but not as extremely.

Steam billowed in the distance. "I hope we're not late," said Charlie. "Lone Star only erupts once every three hours."

We raced the remainder of the way. The cone geyser was climaxing by the time we reached it. It dissipated a couple of minutes later.

"At least we caught the end of it," said Andy.

Charlie sighed. "Half the fun is in the buildup."

"First time I've heard a guy say that," I retorted sardonically.

"I'm hungry," said Andy.

"Masculinity reclaimed."

"Remember to save one of your lunches for Jimi," Charlie reminded him.

Crap. I remembered to order a sack lunch this time, but I

forgot to pick it up. Sometimes when someone else is in charge I let them do all the thinking. It's like not knowing which way to go even if you've ridden to that place a dozen times. A person doesn't put as much effort in knowing where she is going if she isn't doing the driving.

 With mild trepidation, Andy handed me the bag. As we ate, Charlie read the geyser log, then stated, "It's amazing how regular this thing goes off. Every three hours, almost to the minute. There's an entry from Amy: *The husband, kids, and I love the snow. My daughter looks beautiful in her pink dress. My son rugged in his safari outfit. My feet hurt. I should have brought something other than heels to Yellowstone. Going to buy some boots tomorrow. Something cute, made specifically for women. Can't decide between magenta and cotton candy. My husband's upset with me buying another pair. I barely have enough to wear a different pair every day of the month? I'll make it up to him by performing my wifely duties.*"

 "What do you think of Amy and Lori's relationship?" I asked.

 "It means less women for me," says Charlie. "I support all loving, joyful, respectful relationships. There aren't many that have lasted as long as theirs. I certainly haven't had any."

 "Andy?"

 "I wouldn't mine watching---from a strictly scientific perspective."

 After eating every crumb of his lunch, Andy said, "We're halfway through the winter." He still looked hungry. Why did I have to forget to pick up my lunch? I not only felt embarrassed, but now extremely guilty.

 "But we've only been here three weeks," I responded.

 "Andy has a theory that as we age we experience less new stimuli, causing time to pass more rapidly," Charlie explained.

 "We experience half our new stimuli by New Year's," Andy clarified, "so it feels like the season is half over."

 "How about the summer?" I asked

"The 4th of July is not the middle of summer, but it feels like it, because we've probably already done the first iteration of every type of activity by then."

"So, we are middle-age now, although we have only lived a third of our lives? A third of yours. More like a forth of mine."

"You don't have to rub it in."

"Doesn't mean we have to act like it," Charlie insisted.

"What are life's stages?" I asked. I wasn't sure if I agreed with Andy, but I was curious.

"Conception, birth, walking and talking, education, independence, sexual maturity, leaving the nest, becoming prominent, decay, retirement, decrepit and feeble, and finally death and the afterlife."

I spent the next few minutes trying to process it all. A couple of minutes later I changed the subject. "Where does the trail go from here?" The runoff from the geyser had cleared the snow in the area in front of us. There were no tracks to see, and the orange markers were scattered in every direction.

Charlie pointed to the left. "That way leads to Shoshone Lake and Bechler, but we want to go this way." He pointed straight ahead. "That leads to the Howard Eaton trail and Lupine."

I was the first to ski off, and I paid a price for my impatience. I crossed the runoff stream on my skis without difficulty, but had trouble when I stepped back onto the snow. Great. Didn't I promise myself I wouldn't let that happen again? I undid my bindings without hesitation, confident I would remember what Matilda did to remove the ice. I lifted my skis up, one at a time, then scraped them with one of my poles. I didn't reattach them to my skis until we were safely on snow again. I smiled arrogantly when the skis slid freely. Maybe I didn't need Matilda? That soured my mood again, but only momentarily. I needed to stop thinking about her, for at least today.

I got the broken binding repaired at the ski shop the day after I returned from Fairy Falls. I didn't have to work until five, so I had most of the day available. The ski shop was slow enough that they were able to fix it by lunch. I had time to hop over to the geyser basin to see if the Grand or Riverside was erupting.

Part of the scenery along the river, and most of it beside the geyser, was green. It didn't stay that way. There were so many burned trees that even one green one became paradise. The Park must have been breathtaking before the fires.

Climbing was difficult. The entire week had been sunny, which meant watery, melting snow in the afternoon and ice in the morning. Each successive day of sun meant slicker trails the next day. Being my days off, it got cold again, but not nearly as cold as it was when I skied to Fairy Falls, or even to Mystic. It just became colder than it had been, lowering the daytime high to a more typical 25 degrees. To climb even the most modest of slopes I had to dig my skis into the icy snow.

After one major rise, it was mostly downhill to the highway. Speed increases when snow was icy, but maneuverability decreases. Snowplowing wasn't very effective. Skis just scraped over the ice. What would have been a great ski run became a death trap.

Charlie went first, with wild abandon. Many times, his body was in the opposite direction as his skis, but somehow he stayed upright.

Andy allowed the trail to lead him when it was safe, but he gracefully bailed when a turn was going to be too dangerous.

I didn't have any control, so I fell numerous times, none of them of my choosing. I had enough sense to fall on my butt, instead of on my head, so I got bruised, but I didn't knock myself out or break anything.

I caught up with Charlie and Andy at a level straight-away. "There is just one more run," Charlie declared.

"But it's a doozy," added Andy.

At the top of the decline was a sign that said, *Skiers Must Announce Their Descent.*

"We're coming down."

"Not like that. Like this." Charlie yelled like a banshee the entire way down. The trail was so slick, steep, and winding even he couldn't stay on the trail, so he didn't even try. He weaved his way around trees and fallen logs. The icy crust was so hard he barely left tracks behind him.

Andy looked at me. "It's a good day to die." He limped to the edge of the hill, then allowed gravity to take over.

Somehow, we all made it down safely. I even managed to bale before I came to a bridge no one warned me about.

Charlie and Andy spent the remainder of the afternoon skiing down Water Tower. Even Charlie felt one run down Howard Eaton was enough.

16. MALLARD LAKE

Matilda continued to pretend nothing happened at the dance. Maybe I had just imagined it all. But she did hold my hand. That must have meant something more than friendship.

I saw her in the laundry room after dinner. She was taking her last load out of the dryer. I noticed she mixed her whites and darks together. As long as she washed them in cold water the colors shouldn't bleed. Visualizing Matilda's reaction if one of her chef jackets turned pink made me smile.

Why was I so concerned how others looked? I guess it was like picking up litter beside the road. I didn't do it just to protect nature. It was also for aesthetics.

I was careful no one saw my underwear as I put them in an

open washing machine. I know I was making a much bigger deal of it than I should have. It's just how I felt. Having them displayed was no different---to me---than wearing them. I placed the remaining whites safely on top, added detergent, then quickly shut the lid.

"Hey, you want to go to Mallard Lake with me tomorrow?" I asked Matilda as she walked out the door, her laundry basket in front of her.

She stopped and turned back around. That seemed to break the ice. It had been days since we've said more than a greeting to one another. She smiled, as much with her eyes, as with the gentle upturning at the fringes of her mouth. "Sure. We'll meet in the EDR?"

"Leave about 8:30?"

"Sure."

On the hill near the Old Faithful Lodge Cabins we met Barry. I thought he might also be going to Mallard Lake, or maybe to Lone Star Geyser, like I did the day before. But as soon as he reached the bottom of the hill, after cutting many turns on the way down, he immediately began to climb the hill. We waited for him to reach us before heading to the bridge over the Firehole River.

"You look like you're doing laps in a pool," I joked.

Through huffs and puffs he responded, "To some extent I am, but the water is frozen, and the slope much steeper. I'm trying to get in shape for the Resolution Race."

"The what?"

"It's a nine-mile race we have every January. Usually only the most fit compete in it. The winner has bragging rights until the Yellowstone Olympics in February."

"Have you done this race, Matilda?"

"Something has always come up."

"I think you should do it. You're in better shape than most people here."

"I don't know. It's next Friday, isn't it? I have to work that day."

"I do too," said Barry, "but not until four. The race will be over by noon."

"You should do it," I insisted.

"Okay, but if I do it, then you'll have to do it too."

"But I'm not good enough to win."

"And you think I am? To a newbie I may appear to be...a professional athlete?"

"An Olympic athlete."

"But in comparison to most of the people here, I'm middling, at best. It's like comparing a decathlete to a ping pong player."

"I still think you can win the race."

"Let's just hope I don't embarrass myself too much." Matilda turned back to Barry. "You have time to go up to Mallard Lake?"

"I do, but I think I'll continue my laps. Who knows, if I do well enough in the Resolution Race I might even complete the Appalachian Trail this summer. I may not look like it now, but I used to be a prolific hiker. God-willing, I'll be in that good of shape again."

At the river, I turned sharply onto the bridge, then coasted towards the fork in the trail. How easy it seemed now. Three weeks ago, I probably would have fallen into the river, or if I was lucky, just bruised myself as I slammed into the wooden structure. I was first across the bridge, but I let Matilda lead after that. She had done this ski before. If there was anything dangerous ahead I preferred her to be the guinea pig---or hamster or gerbil. The trail immediately entered a forest. It was in one of those rare areas left untouched by the fire. There was also some thermal activity there, near the river. I saw steam. The forest floor was exposed, displaying bright green grass, sustained by the heat and moisture.

The trail climbed moderately, but constantly. It was, at

most, a twenty percent grade, but I was still sweating. My lungs and heart were also working overtime, but it was the overheating that forced me to stop. Matilda must have stopped hearing me drag myself up the hill, or maybe it was the gasps behind her becoming less pronounced. She stopped. She turned her head around, but not her body. The narrowness and steepness of the trail made it difficult to do so without falling. "You need to vent."

"I'm upset I wasn't able to make it to the top of the hill without stopping, but it's not something that's grating me."

"I didn't mean…. I'm talking about your body heat. You lose most of your heat through your head. Take off your cap. If you're still hot, take off more." I blushed, or was that just me being hot? The ambiguity of our pseudo-relationship compelled my mind to go there. My pausing to consider what I said provided her time to also think about it. She also began to blush, or was the hill also taking its toll on her? I took my cap off and put it in my backpack. I felt like a balloon being opened. But instead of air, heat escaped from me. To fill the void, adrenaline rushed in. I resumed my climb, with renewed vigor---which caused Matilda to resume her skiing, with a similar enthusiasm.

I thought we were almost to the top of the hill. I was mistaken. It was stark when the vibrant flora finally yielded to monochromatic death and destruction. Alice leaving Oz to return to Kansas. An English garden being bombed by the Nazis. The trail finally leveled out. We paralleled a creek on our left. Shortly after the trail became less steep---it never truly became level, but less steep seemed like level relative to what we had experienced---it turned sharply towards the creek, crossing it via a bridge. The creek looked dry, which probably meant it was frozen, indicating there weren't any thermal features upstream. We continued to follow the creek for a bit, then the trail made another sharp left turn, this time onto a steep hill. I was confident I was going to wipe out on the way down, on the way back. It was difficult enough making a 90-degree turn, and this was more like 120 degrees. If I didn't fall I

143

was even more certain to drop into the creek---at the bottom of a gully. If I was able walk away from it, it would probably be with some broken bones.

At the top of the hill, I had to stop again. This time I took off my gloves. Another release was felt, but not as strongly as when I took off my cap.

A short drop brought us to another bridge. We paralleled a second frozen creek. The trail continued to rise, but not as steeply as either the first hill or the one between the two creeks. I was ready to take off my jacket when we arrived at a boulder filled bowl. It was more exposed up there. Without trees to block it, the wind became more prominent. I cooled down enough that I no longer needed an additional heat sink. The trail wrapped around the bowl, remaining on its rim. The top of the crater was much higher up on the side opposite us. Much of the stone there was exposed, creating both a beautiful and rugged setting. A few un-burnt lodgepole pines stood atop the cliff. Sentinels? Or cheerleaders? Matilda and I paused at the top of the bowl. The longer we stayed the more we belonged, becoming peers with nature.

The wind continued to whip at us at the top of the bowl. I was actually starting to get cold. Had it been that long ago, that the sensation felt like an anomaly instead of the norm? I put my gloves back on. Matilda zipped up her jacket. She said, "That's a good idea. If we fall it's better the snow doesn't get inside our clothes. After we pass through a few more trees, then skirt a meadow, we have a steep decent to the lake."

"So, we're almost there?"

"About a quarter-of-a-mile more. Near the beginning of the descent is a fork. We need to go right. If you go left nothing dangerous will happen, but you'll have to backtrack, because your momentum will make it difficult to stop for a couple of hundred feet."

I followed Matilda through the forest and meadow she

spoke of. When the trail began to drop, Matilda permitted the change in elevation to propel her, like Andy did on Howard Eaton. The waxless skis Samantha let me borrow weren't as fast as Matilda's, causing her to get farther ahead of me. Which was fine with me. It made it less likely I was going to crash into her. The trail was too narrow to accommodate snowplowing, so I gave myself permission to go along for the ride. My skis slid down the pair of grooves Matilda reinforced. Except for particularly sharp curves I was on auto pilot. Ten seconds into the decent the tracks split. With the skill of a person who had been skiing all of her life, I cut my skis successfully to the right.

Confidence in my ability was at an all-time high. The descent couldn't be more perfect, until…. "TREE!" I heard Matilda's exclamation too late. Even if I heard it earlier I don't think I would have been able to do anything differently, except maybe slamming into the alleged tree. Falling on top of Matilda was better. She was softer. She was on the ground in front of a fallen log, and now I was. After we confirmed neither of us was hurt we laughed---contagiously. Once one of us stopped, we would see the other still chuckling, initiating a new round of hysterics. "I thought I warned you."

"Do you think I can ski and think at the same time? My true protector would have cut a path through that tree before I reached it."

We took off our skis and climbed over the log. After replacing them, we traveled another hundred yards before reaching the lake shore. I stopped at the shoreline, but Matilda continued skiing until she reached the center of the small lake. "COME ON! The ice must be a foot think by now." CRACK! "Or maybe not." Matilda raced back towards shore as the snow and ice parted behind her. She climbed to solid ground a second before the ice split apart against the sand.

We ate our lunches in silence as we struggled to calm down. The temperature had become much warmer than the previous week, so we were able to eat all the food. Adrenaline was the best appetizer. What would I have done if Matilda had fallen into the lake? If I had gone out there I would have also fallen in. But I would have had to try. If Matilda died…. The concept felt so foreign. In some ways, the end of the season will feel like people dying---because some of them you will never see again. Most of them. All of them? Matilda and I talked about traveling together. There was so many places I wanted to see, and Matilda seemed just as excited to want to show them to me. But that was still half a winter away. Our feeling for one another---whatever feelings they were---might change by then. If I saw no one I met this winter again, would it feel like a mass murder? Or genocide?

The sun shined brightly, almost too brightly at times. I still hadn't bought a pair of sunglasses. If it was summer, it may have been a good time to take a nap. Winter wasn't as soothing. We talked instead. Matilda began. "When I was a kid I always wanted to live in a log cabin beside a lake like this."

"I just wanted some peace and quiet. Being around my mother wasn't very peaceful, and neither was being around my friends."

"We can have both here."

"If only that was possible."

"I would like to live in a log cabin one day."

"Can I come to visit?"

"You can even live in it with me if you like. It's cheaper for two to live together than one. It's sure peaceful out here. I don't even hear the snowmobiles. Sometimes I wonder if it wouldn't have been better living a hundred years ago."

"I'd rather think of the future. My people---people of color---were definitely not better off then, than they are today."

"If you could transport yourself into the future, would you?"

"I would strongly consider it. The world still has a lot of problems."

"But if people continue to escape from problems instead of

trying to fix them, then the troubles will never disappear."

"Well, I think the point is moot anyway. Time travel couldn't really happen. There would be too many paradoxes. Reality would be in constant flux."

"You're probably right. Time is better thought of as a river, constantly flowing downstream. Some memories get washed upon the shore and evaporate, others continue to flow through the channel."

I gust of wind coming off the lake nearly froze me to the ground. I put my cap back on.

Matilda put her food waste into her plastic lunch sack, then placed it in her backpack. "Unless we build a fire, or move into that cabin we talked about, we better start heading back. A little exertion will warm us back up."

We detoured around the fallen log that had blocked the trail. We began to climb back up, stopping at the fork. "That's the Mallard Creek trailhead. It's the most difficult trail in the area. We can attempt it after you get a bit more experienced."

"Can't we at least begin it today? We can head back when it becomes dangerous."

"Do you see those orange markers up there?" They were on top of the nearly sheer hillside. "Even if you can make it to the top of that, you still have to make it down. Going up is the easy part. And this is just the beginning of the trail."

With regret, I followed Matilda up to the pass atop the boulder bowl. We paused before descending. "I don't think I need to remind you to be careful when you fall." I noticed she said *when* not *if*. "You are as familiar with the trail now as I am. There are few flat areas. Don't be afraid to bail out if you begin to go too fast."

I didn't have to worry about bailing out. I fell enough before I picked up enough speed for it to become dangerous. Between my tumbles I had the best ski runs of my life. The slope was steep enough in most places to keep me moving without any effort on my part. That trip back from Mallard Lake felt like I was in the winter

Olympics.

17.   THE RESOLUTION RACE

The influenza epidemic hit the following week. In a small enclosed community, disease strikes swiftly and forcefully. It was easy to reduce fever in Yellowstone in winter, but chills became chillier. Eighty percent of the Snow Lodge staff was affected. It was closer to one-hundred percent, but only eighty percent were sick at the same time. Those who were not sick, or at least not very sick, had to fill in for those who were too ill to work. I didn't get the bug until my fourth day of work. I wanted to die during my fifth, but I didn't call in sick. I wasn't the kind of person who gave up, and going home because I was sick was giving in. Looking back on it, it wasn't that great of an idea being around food and guests when I was sick, but I was too young at the time to think through the consequences. If everyone who was sick stayed home, we wouldn't have been able to stay open. Which might have been for the best. Those guests who were infected probably infected others when they got home. The virus that began in Yellowstone may have spread all over the world. It took two weeks for Snow Lodge to fully recover, but most of the damage was done in the first week. The Resolution Race was almost cancelled.

I still felt like crap by race day, but I was determined to not back out. I had strongly encouraged Matilda to sign up. It was her decision, but she wouldn't have done so without my nudging. If she was going to race, I had to too. I had to work later in the day, but I had all afternoon to recover before I had to clock in at five. That was assuming I would reach the finish line by then. In the condition

I was in, that wasn't guaranteed.

The attendance was dismal, due to the flu epidemic. It was remarkable the race wasn't cancelled, or at least rescheduled. Snow Lodge had traditions though, and those that lived in its community weren't going to allow aches and pains and vomiting to get in the way. There were just a dozen of us. I was by far the least experienced skier. There was just one other woman in the race besides Matilda and me. She was a bubbly blond who worked in the snack shop. She wasn't the best athlete, but she was willing to try anything. She had just graduated from college and wanted an adventure before stepping into the real world. Some of the guys I had never seen before. One of them, I think, worked at the gas station. The other two were rangers. I knew that, for certain, because they wore their uniforms as they skied. Most of the others in the race looked as fit as those two who worked for the Park Service. When I thought of the Old Faithful area I only considered those working at Snow Lodge. The community I was part of was considerably larger, and more eclectic.

The race began at the base of the Water Tower---the hill, not the structure. Actually about 50 yards away from it, so every participate could be lined up together. I was at the fringe of the starting line, not wanting to get trampled once the race began. Matilda was beside me, but I knew that wouldn't last. Not only was she more experienced than I, and in better shape, she was also much healthier. She was infected early in the week, and had completely covered.

I expected someone to shoot a gun or something. I was disappointed when someone just shouted, "GO!" Some of the most fit racers had already distanced themselves by the time we reached the Water Tower. They appeared to almost run up the steep hill. Matilda was about in the middle of the pack. I was dead last. I expected to be, so it didn't bother me. My goal today was to finish. Only twelve of us raced today, but if I finished I could say I was the twelfth best skier in Yellowstone.

I had never skied up the Water Tower before. A few weeks ago, I fell down it, but I never went up. It snowed last night, which made it easier than if the hill was a sheet of ice. I didn't slip at all, but it did take me awhile to make it to the top. Every hundred feet or so I had to take a break. I looked around before I made my descent to the Howard Eaton. Only one other skier was in sight. It was the bubbly blond. She was at the bottom already.

I sighed, then pushed off. The side descent of the Water Tower wasn't as steep as the slope I came up, but it was still significant. I was determined I wasn't going to fall. I was weak enough from my climb and the flu that if I did fall, I wasn't confident I would be able to pick myself up. I ACTUALLY MADE IT TO THE BOTTOM WITHOUT FALLING! It was the first time I was able to do so on such a long, steep descent. The adrenaline rush created by my success, and the cooling, generated by my hasty descent, alleviated my aches and pains, momentarily, giving me a burst of energy.

Climbing Howard Eaton tapped it, almost immediately. But I was determined to at least make it to the top of the hill. And after that there was just one more major hill to climb. Then just a combination of level skiing with brief descents. Yes, if I could make it to the top of this hill I would be able to finish the race. The distance between myself and the bubbly blond stayed about the same. Wouldn't it be great if I could beat at least one person? I MADE IT! I had reached the top of that first hill, where the *Announce Your Descent* sign was.

I pushed on. I think I was beginning to gain on the bubbly blond. When I came to a significant straightaway it was confirmed. My enthusiasm abruptly waned when I hit the second hill. This was it, though. The last hill. My aches were returning. I pushed on never-the-less. They were going to ache even if I stopped. Might as well get something accomplished.

The bubbly blond continued to lose ground to me. I caught her near the top of the hill. "Track please." That was a polite way of saying, "GET OUT OF THE WAY!" She wasn't as happy as she was at the start of the race, but she did move off the trail and even gave me a weak smile as I passed her.

My victory was short-lived. Climbing that last hill sapped the last of my strength. I slowed down considerably. It felt like I was skiing through quick sand. The bubbly blond passed me. I liked to think this game of leap frog would continue throughout the race, but I was a realist. My energy was depleted, for the duration.

The only good thing to happen to me the rest of the way was when I came up to Amy and Lori. They manned---womanned?---a hot chocolate station. "You're halfway." Amy was trying to encourage me, but to me four more miles felt like forty.

"How long ago did Matilda come by here?"

"About 45 minutes." Lori handed me a steaming paper cup. "She was in 5th place."

"Good for her."

"You might do that well if you work another winter or two." If I worked ten more winters I don't think I would ever be as good a skier as Matilda. I don't think I had the right build. Why weren't there more Black skiers? Was their dark skin too much of a contrast to the light snow? Were they afraid they would stand out too much? Not to just other people, but to wild animals.

I continued to muddle through. I remembered to take my skis off when I passed Lone Star's runoff. When one is sick scrunching down like that isn't too comfortable.

The trail beside the Firehole River was groomed for the race, making it easy to skate on. The experienced skiers must have made good time over this leg of the race, but I was only able to move a bit faster. I tried to skate, but that required more energy than skiing, so I gave it up after a couple of brief attempts.

The last leg was beside the highway, up that hill I saw Barry practicing on, then a sprint to the open area in front of Snow Lodge. A crowd of employees and tourists cheered me on as I finally crossed the finish line. I was completely wiped out. But I did finish.

I was pleased with myself. I would have fallen on the snow, but that would have taken too much energy.

"Good job." Matilda skied up to me and gave me a hug. She knew how sick I was and how important it was that I finished the race. I could now say I was the twelfth best skier in Yellowstone.

"How did you do?"

"Fourth."

"That's great. Especially considering the competition. I heard you were fifth halfway through. You must have been able to pass someone."

"And he didn't like it---being beat by a girl."

"How did Barry do?"

"Eighth."

"That's not bad either, considering he was the heaviest person in the race."

"It took him about five minutes to pick himself up from where he had fallen after he threw himself past the finish line."

"How long have you been waiting for me?"

"Not too long."

"How long?"

"An hour and a half."

That's when I knew that Matilda thought as much of me as I thought of her. Our relationship may never advance to the next stage, but I now knew she liked me---more than a friend. And that was nearly enough.

The realization of Matilda's devotion to me caused me to lose my balance, resulting in me falling in the snow. The cold felt so good. I moved around in the snow, trying to take in as much of the tactile refreshment as I could.

Matilda looked down at me and smiled. "You make a pretty snow angel, but even more beautiful is a tray full of EDR food. I'm starving." Matilda helped me up, then we skied off together.

I fully medicated myself after I returned to my room. I slept as long as I could, allowing myself just enough time to shower and dress. I was too nauseous to eat dinner, but knew I should, so I ate a piece of bread and washed it down with milk. I preferred Coke, but it's acidity would have likely done a number on my stomach. I made it through my shift. Fortunately, I had the next day off. Two days would have been better, but with so many people out, the schedule had to be radically modified. I was much better by the time I had to return to work. What did they say? Starve a cold, compete a nine-mile race to reduce a fever?

18. FULL MOON SKI

Matilda had a visitor the following week. She was an old friend, from one of the summers she worked in the Park. Her name was *Susan*. They were inseparable the four days she was here. I felt more sick than when I had the flu. Matilda even took off an extra day of work. For me she hadn't even tried to switch her days off so we could have both of them together. There were times when I saw them together that Matilda giggled. MATILDA! Acting like an adolescent school girl. I pictured the two of them skiing to the same places Matilda and I skied to, doing the same things Matilda and I did. Susan was older than me, about Matilda's age. Maybe I wasn't mature enough for Matilda. How could I compete with someone who had more experiences? Who would prefer an 18-year old girl over someone in their 20's? Men maybe, but women were more profound. Personalities mattered more to us.

Matilda was polite during those four preoccupied days, but distant. She even asked me to sit with her and Susan once in the EDR, but I made an excuse to sit somewhere else. Having Susan and

I sit side-by-side would only make the comparison between the two of us easier. The thing that bothered me most about Susan was she looked like a normal person. She wasn't some exotic beauty. She didn't have overpowering social skills. And she was nice. Under different circumstances we might even become friends. I could be that ordinary person, but it might be too late.

I was in too much of a funk to do anything on my days off. I couldn't ski anywhere because I might see them. I read a lot, and cleaned, and straightened, and organized. With spending so much time with Matilda, I had let some things go. It felt good to put my life back together. And books? Most of the time there were happy endings in books.

After Susan left, Matilda returned her attention to me, like nothing had happened. It felt like I was given hand-me-downs. But it was enough. I had Matilda back. Maybe she would leave my life again, like she did during those four days, so I had to enjoy whatever time I had with her. Being upset with Matilda's ability to share her friendship would deter from that enjoyment.

Snow Lodge employees had a knack for keeping themselves entertained. In addition to the Resolution Race, they also created the No Talent Show. It was a hodge-podge of vaudeville-like performances. Embarrassment rarely occurred. When it did it was because a performer didn't understand the concept of the competition and attempted to display their authentic, but dubious, skills. The winner of this year's show were the employees of the Four Seasons Snack Shop. They did a skit to the tune of Grease, using that oily waste product as a prop. They made a mess in the pub, but they were the ones who had to deal with the consequences the following day.

Other activities included a cribbage tournament---self-explanatory. Ice ball---basketball played in a sub-freezing gym. The Super Bowl Coach---the only opportunity for many of us to leave the Park during the winter. But the greatest diversion, from being snowbound, was the Yellowstone Olympics. It was still a month away, but by the way some of the Snow Lodge employees were talking about it, it felt like we were already in the middle of it. Employee Olympic stories were almost as bad as old war stories, or about the fish that got away. I was happy they had experienced something so memorable, but it was difficult for me to get enthused about something I had never experienced. For all I know, those overzealous employees may have made all of it up, like us going to the moon, or getting old one day and dying.

The Full Moon Ski was going to happen much sooner. At least once a year a snow coach or two would take a group of employees up to a place called Divide Lookout. There was a ski drop there that I hadn't yet gotten around to taking. The trailhead was seven miles east of Old Faithful on the West Thumb highway. A two-mile ski that rose 700 feet brought you to a 70 feet tall lookout tower. I wasn't going to allow a once-in-a-lifetime opportunity like that pass me by, and neither was Matilda. We both got our shifts adjusted so we would be off by the time the coaches left. Having already changed her schedule once during the week, it must have been difficult for her to ask for another. I think it was her way of making up for not spending time with me during the week.

The two coaches were bursting with employees. Every time we thought no one else could fit, we slid over another few inches and somehow, they squeezed in. We all sacrificed for the general good. I had elbow indentations to prove it. Charlie was particularly generous. "Someone can sit on my lap." Lori actually took him up on the offer.

We left promptly at eight. The drive up to the continental divide may have been magical if so many hot bodies hadn't steamed up the windows so badly. The moon had just risen when we entered, but whatever light it had given off was overpowered by the bright lights outside of Snow Lodge. The trip was rocky. I think Lori might have regretted her choice of seats. She was bounced around like she was on a trampoline. "You're going to have to be my seat belt, Charlie." He wrapped his arms around her, being careful were he put them. Would he have been so gallant if Lori wasn't in a relation---with a woman?

We didn't have be told to unload when the snow coach stopped. It may not have even completely stopped when the first person leapt out. It was partly cloudy, so visibility was adequate at best, but even through the clouds the moon glowed, making it a magical night. We took head lamps with us as a precaution. It was light enough now to see without them, but if the clouds became any denser we would be glad we had them.

I didn't see a trail marker anywhere, but that didn't prevent most of the employees from skiing up and over a snow bank. There must have been a significant drop because they immediately disappeared. For the same reason I was on the fringe at the beginning of the Resolution Ski, I waited until most of the skiers were gone before I headed in the direction they went. Matilda didn't mind. She didn't like crowds either.

"Shall we?" Matilda strolled to the rim of the snow bank, then slid down its backside. She disappeared. At the top of the rise I saw the trailhead marker. It had been obscured by a snow drift. Matilda could be seen fifty yards away. There was enough of a downhill slope that she was able to coast that far, and she was still moving. It took me a hundred yards to catch up to her. The trail leveled off, briefly. In the distance, I could see it rising. A seven-hundred-foot climb was ahead of us. How high was that relative to the Water Tower or Howard Eaton? Maybe the two of them combined. Twice that? At least I wasn't sick today.

"Do you think it would help to have done this ski in the daylight first?" I asked.

Charlie skied by. "And it would have helped to have some training before being born too. Being pushed out into the unknown is more exciting."

We passed a trail on our right that dropped abruptly. "I hope there's not too many forks like that to look out for on the way down."

Matilda continued to stay in front of me, but I didn't allow the separation between us to be more than a few yards. "That's the only one. It's the Spring Creek trailhead. It leads to Lone Star Geyser."

"So, we could return to Old Faithful that way?"

"Only Charlie has been reckless enough to try it in the dark. There are many elevation changes and bridges."

"It's not as difficult as Mallard Creek?"

"No, but any intermediate trail can be dangerous at night."

"If I attempt it will you come along?'

"I'm your protector, aren't I? I will come if you insist to go, but I don't recommend it."

Up and up we went. At an overlook, many of the old-timers, including Charlie and Andy were cutting some turns down the ridge. We stopped to view Shoshone Lake below. It looked florescent under the moonlight.

The trail became steeper. I think we were now in the lead, because I didn't see anyone in front of us. At the top of the ridge, I expected there to be a great view, but there were too many trees in the way. The metal fire watch tower gave us hope. We took off our skis and climbed the metal, slippery steps. We clung to the railing as we prudently progressed. The door to the tower was locked, but the view near the top was still spectacular. All of Shoshone Lake was in view, as was Lake Yellowstone. To the south, a range of mountains stood out. "What are they called?"

"That's the Teton Range in Grand Teton National Park. South of it is Jackson Hole." I heard about that place. It was one of the touristy places celebrities hung out, like Vale and Aspen. There was steam billowing to the west. It must have been the Upper Geyser Basin.

Every minute or two someone arrived at the tower. The solitude didn't last. When Charlie walked up the steps, he didn't stop at the tower's door. He stepped onto the railing and climbed up and around like a gorilla on the Empire State Building. "CHARLIE!" Andy yelled from safety. "It's a thousand dollars to airlift you out. You can't afford to lose that much money. You still want to go to Florida, don't you?"

"I've done this before."

"But not in the dark."

"ICE CREAM AND ONIONS! The view is much better from up here." Charlie spent just a few minutes on top, but to those of us who were concerned for his safety, it felt like hours.

"Should we tell someone that we're not riding back?" I asked Matilda.

Charlie's ears perked-up. "Where are we going?"

"You already made plans," said Andy. "We'll tell the coach drivers when they do their head count."

"Do we have to go to Barry's party?"

"We'll be the only ones coherent. Who's going to prevent someone from jumping out the window?"

"Flint will be there."

"You think one chaperone is enough with that crowd?"

"I thought Barry was no longer taking drugs," I said.

"The illegal variety," said Andy. "He is still extremely proficient in drinking everyone under the table. Or in this case, out the window."

"The snow isn't deep enough yet, and some of Barry's friends don't have enough brain cells remaining to figure that out before they hit the ground," Charlie elaborated.

"Most of the people in my neighborhood, including myself, were pretty heavy into drugs," I shared. "I gave that up, but many of my friends didn't. Some of them aren't alive anymore."

"Most of the people at Snow Lodge live, work, and play hard," said Andy. "For some of them that means artificial stimulation."

"If drugs become a substitute for real adventure, natural methods will atrophy," said Charlie. "I don't want to trade temporary pleasure for a lifetime of disability. Drugs fill the void for something that's lacking."

"So, does reckless physical abandon," added Andy.

"I've become more cautious in my old age. Two years ago I would have done somersaults on top."

At the top of the drop-off Matilda told me, "The most difficult turn is at the overlook. It's about 120 degrees. If you aren't careful you'll see Shoshone Lake up close and personal. And don't forget to turn at the Spring Creek trailhead. The conditions are slick enough tonight to take us all the way there without stopping."

Matilda pushed away first. The steep downgrade took her out of sight in a few seconds. It was now my turn. Slow down and bank left. Slow down and bank left. I saw the opening of the overlook. I hit the turn perfectly, but then eased-up too much. My concentration was shot. I was still going fast, so I didn't have much time to react. I was maneuvering on instinct. My instinct stank. I swerved around one tree, but hit another. Fortunately, it was only two-feet high---the part of it that was above the snow. I tumbled head first, but landed to my left, away from the steep drop off.

I composed myself, picked myself up, then continued. As I started to slow down, I pushed off with my poles to add some momentum. My crash stole the velocity I needed to make it to the bottom without stopping. Near the Spring Creek trailhead, the grade increased again. I was so ecstatic that I forgot to turn. I was reminded when I saw Matilda off trail pointing to it. After I crashed at the bottom of the hill, Matilda skied down to meet me.

I made a snow angel where I lay. Matilda pulled me up. "We'll have no trouble finding our way back if you keep taking those breaks. It'll be light."

The moon was completely exposed now, but the going wasn't any easier. This part of Yellowstone was still foliated, causing many shadows. The most dangerous time to drive is at dusk and dawn. Nordic skiing was like driving, but with a narrower chassis and brakes that could sometimes slow, but rarely stop.

We varied our velocity, depending on the conditions. In the open, when we could see, we went as fast as we could. Through dense foliage we slithered, huddled together, as we scrutinized potential hazards. Our wild animals were hidden branches and sudden drops. There were times we permitted ourselves to be careless, so we could enjoy the full length of a good run. There was one major consequence.

Being the most experienced skier, by a substantial margin, Matilda led most of the way. Knowing she would lead us on the correct route at the correct velocity gave me permission to enjoy the adventure, without the burden of trepidation. We were traveling at a good clip, through a moderately lit cluster of trees, when Matilda dropped suddenly and veered to the right. I didn't, landing in a creek, instead of crossing a bridge. Even if there was daylight, it would have been difficult to see the hidden bridge and adjust in the seconds between the two.

I think Matilda was more scared than I. She immediately detached her skis and bent down to the creek bed. Most of the water was frozen, but enough remained to soak my lower torso. I've heard of people dying of hypothermia even in temperatures above freezing, so I became concerned. We still had more than halfway to go. Significantly more. Fortunately, the low was supposed to be about twenty this evening---a heat wave. Matilda helped me detach my skis and stand up. Nothing was broken or sprained. My soaked pants and long-johns actually didn't feel cold to me. Maybe hot springs ran into that creek. Or perhaps it was just my adrenaline. Matilda helped me wring out my clothing the best she could without actually taking them off me. She helped me get back onto my skis. "We need to get moving as soon as possible, before you start cooling down and freeze to death." She didn't have to add that last part.

We started moving again, Matilda still in front, but constantly looking back. After a couple of strides, I was stuck. I lifted my skis, one leg at a time, to examine the damage. Six inches of snow and ice was caked on both. I tried to kick off the freeloaders, but wasn't very successful. I didn't want any more delays. This adventure had suddenly transformed from fun to a burden. I took off my skis, scraped them, put them back on, and started moving. I repeated the sequence three times before all the gunk was removed.

The combination of anger and adrenaline kept me toasty. I was even able to dry out a bit.

We entered a narrow canyon, granite cliffs on both sides. A series of bridges zigzagged the creek that shared space with the trail. The route was relatively flat, so the crossings were accomplished without difficulty.

Our first and only major obstacle along the creek was climbing out of the canyon. It may have only been a fifty percent grade, but it felt steeper. More vertical than horizontal. It was too difficult to herring-bone, and nearly too difficult to side-step. Luckily, we only had to climb ten feet. If we had to, I guess we could have taken off our skis and climbed with our hands and feet.

Over the top was a gentle ride back down to the creek, and from there it was level all the way to the Lone Star Geyser trail. Maybe we were in time to see the geyser erupt. I only saw the last whimper the last time.

The intersection was near the halfway point of the Lone Star loop. Going counter-clockwise was the easiest rout, but it wouldn't take us past the geyser.

Matilda looked at her watch. "It's only 12:45. The pub isn't even closed yet. Let's see that geyser. It'll be a much prettier sight than the fountain I created the last time I was in the pub. I wonder how long we'll have to wait."

"I hope forever."

"I meant...."

"I know." Matilda patted my face with her gloves like I was a small child. I may have been insulted if it wasn't so endearing.

As soon as we arrived at the geyser, I read the last page of the log. The last entry was at 4 p.m. It mentioned an eruption. If I keep adding threes to it, the next one should go off about....

"Maybe we shouldn't wait for it," Matilda suggested. "It might be another three hours before it erupts."

"Or just five minutes. How about we wait for fifteen? If it doesn't start erupting by then, we'll head back." Matilda agreed.

The anticipation was building. Would I be right? I had to be. Wouldn't Matilda be impressed. I nearly peed in my pants when it began bubbling right at 1 a.m.

Matilda squeezed my shoulders from behind. She continued to make contact with me, her chest against my back, as we watched the entire eruption. I thought the contact might go further---I wished it might go further---but Matilda pulled away after the last sputter. "Time to go." But why? I knew after that perfectly romantic setting if we weren't able to hook up there it was likely we would never become more than friends. There was still hope, but not hope centered in reality.

Even with the added idiosyncrasies the partially illuminated night created, I was more successful skiing down Howard Eaton than I had been at the beginning of the month. The trail was less slick, but I also felt I was becoming a better skier. I wiped out just a couple of times, and my turns were much sharper.

Through charred trunks we saw the lights of Old Faithful. For once, returning to civilization didn't mean noise. The village was peaceful and welcoming. I convinced Matilda to take a run with me down Water Tower. For the first time, I made it all the way to the cabins without falling. I needed to get some sleep before going to work in a few hours, but I knew I would be too wound up to. There were too many things to think about, fantastic memories, and dreams unfilled.

19. MALLARD CREEK

Confidence in my skiing ability was at an all-time high. I felt I was ready for Mallard Creek. I did the Spring Creek Ski Drop on my next day off---by myself. Other people were dropped off, but I was the only employee. I needed to redeem myself. It was embarrassing falling into that creek. A veteran skier wouldn't have done that. And I also wanted more practice on that steep hill in the canyon. I was successful with each. I took Howard Eaton on the way back, but after stopping at Lone Star geyser. It wasn't erupting, but I felt compelled to reminisce---Matilda pressed up against me, her heart pumping inches from mine. I sighed, then resumed my athletic enlightenment. I fell a few times down that hill at the end of Howard Eaton, but who doesn't. It didn't diminish my confidence. I climbed back up and did the run three more times. I did the best on my third run, only falling once. I was either getting tired or over confident on my final run, because I did significantly worse, falling three times. Why couldn't I have just stopped after three runs? But what if I hadn't fallen at all during that last run? Sometimes it was difficult to know when to stop. There would always be second guessing.

It didn't surprise Matilda when I told her I wanted to do Mallard Creek. She recognized the increase in my confidence, and my desire to push myself. Why couldn't she have recognized my desire for her? Did she not want our relationship to turn into anything more? Or was she incapable of liking me more than a friend? Should I make the first move? She was older, more experienced, more established. It felt more appropriate for her to be the instigator. If I made a move on her and she didn't feel the same way about me, as I felt about her, I could lose her as a friend. It was hinted that something like that happened to Barry. A friend of his had made advances, strongly unwelcome ones. No, my friendship with Matilda meant too much for me to risk losing it.

Mallard Creek required not only technical prowess, but substantial endurance. The round trip from Snow Lodge was twelve miles. The only flat section was the return, below those power lines I followed on the way home from Fairy Falls. I was fully recovered from the flu now. If I was able to do Spring Creek twice in one week, I should be able to do Mallard Creek once. I was about as prepared as I could be. It would be highly unlikely I would be in better shape by the end of the season.

Matilda began to think of me more as a peer than as an apprentice. Now that I was becoming an experienced skier, and I had learned most of the trails, I led as often as she did.

Even with the training I did this week, that steep hill right after the Mallard Creek/Mallard Lake split nearly wiped me out. Half of it may have been the stress of anticipating skiing backwards down the hill, crashing into a tree or rock. There were two switchbacks that nearly turned back on themselves. Sometimes a human body just can't move a certain way with skis attached.

Down the back of the ridge there was some relief, but it didn't take long for the trail to become curvy. The only good thing to say about the trail was that it must have been more difficult before the fires burnt away most of the blind spots. An added burden the fires created, was a diminished wind break. It was windy on top of most of the winding hills. The persistent wind caused the powdery Yellowstone snow to become dynamic. Major sections of the trail were covered by the powder. Someone may have skied the trail earlier in the day, but there was no longer any evidence of it. We had to break trail, which meant not only wading through soft snow when we got off course, but also having to look out for orange trail markers that were occasionally covered by the blowing snow. Even Matilda began to tire.

Our first major hurdle was skiing through an oasis of green. One of the loopiest, twisting-ist sections of trail I had ever skied on was within that zone of near zero visibility. Matilda and I both crashed, which Matilda took as a personal affront. She tried again and again until she skied down the run without falling. We were both so low in energy after our devastating success, we ate lunch early, at least an hour before we normally ate our midday meal. We left our cookies, to be taken like medicine when we were drained again, preferably near the end of the ski.

The second hurdle came at something ominously called *the wall*. At the end of a long descending run, precariously close to a creek---fortunately frozen---was a ninety degree turn across a bridge, then up a sixty-degree rise. Not only would it be difficult to make the turn accelerating, if one does successfully accomplish it, their skis were in the wrong direction to climb. As my skis jarred to a sudden stop at the base of the hill, I bounced back, sliding against the bridge, then falling. If the bridge had a railing I would have broken something. This obstacle was easier to conquer in two, if not three parts, like a particularly difficult miniature golf hole. I should have slowed myself down enough to stop at the base of the hill, then cross the bridge, then somehow climb the wall.

I had the misfortune of being in the lead when we hit the wall. Matilda used the correct approach, either from experience, or from watching me mess up.

She determined she should climb the wall first. I graciously relinquished the honor. She looked like I did my first week of skiing. She kept on slipping as she tried to side-step up. We were in another phase of progressively slickening trails. Every time it snowed, skiing was great---for a few days. In contrast, a few days without snow, especially with full sun, made conditions atrocious. The blowing snow on top of the ridges and hills substantially improved conditions, but the gully the creek was in was well protected.

Sweat began to bead on Matilda's forehead. She took her jacket off and wrapped it around her waist. She began to climb again, with renewed determination. Sweat broke out again, but she was gaining ground. She made it to the top without additional disrobing. I did as well as Matilda, maybe even better, and I didn't even have to lose any clothes.

The remainder of the Mallard Creek Trail followed the creek's canyon to our left. The trail didn't have any more surprises. It consistently dropped. As long as we didn't slip too far left, or fall, we would be okay.

The last leg of our journey was boring, worse than the first time we skied under those power lines. Familiarity truly breeds contempt. If we had any enthusiasm left, we would have skied faster. The lack of variety, and challenge, in the trail completely wore us out. We ate our cookies early in our discomfort, so we were famished by the time we returned to Snow Lodge. We didn't have enough energy to ski to Lupine to wash-up before we ate, so we went into the EDR early and waited for the food to arrive. Someone woke us up when dinner was served.

20.   THE YELLOWSTONE OLYMPICS

The Super Bowl snow coaches left shortly after I rushed home after work and showered. Lunch wasn't particularly busy that day, so Milo benevolently permitted those going to West Yellowstone to get off work early. It also helped with his payroll, but it still made him look good.

The novelty of riding in a snow coach had worn off, so I just wanted to get to West Yellowstone as quickly as possible. We were dropped off where the coaches normally dropped off guests. We weren't given instructions were to go. We were just set loose. We didn't even have to see the Super Bowl if we didn't want to, but West Yellowstone was a small enough town there wasn't much else to do. "The snow coaches are leaving half-an-hour after the game," one of the drivers announced, "so unless you want to spend the night here, be back by then."

I almost wished I hadn't gone. Matilda was working, as were the rest of the Snow Lodgers I considered my friends. I followed a group of acquaintances to a bar that was already crowded. I eventually found a seat. The trick would be leaving---if I got bored with the game, or needed a pee break. The chairs were that tightly packed. My acquaintances ordered beer with their nachos, corn dogs, chicken strips, and pizza. Being just eighteen, I had to settle for a coke---but in a dirty glass. That wasn't my choice, that's just how all the drinks came. It didn't matter that much if alcohol was in it. Alcohol was an antiseptic. It killed bacteria. Maybe coke did the same. It was rumored that a glass of coke could completely dissolve a nail in a week. A group of large, tall men played with an oblong ball for about an hour-and-a-half, then there was some entertainment, then they played with the ball again. I don't remember who won. Most of the people in the bar were happy about the outcome, or maybe they were just happy to be drinking?

Someone got sick on the snow coach on the way home. We had to pull off the road. After she clawed her way out of the vehicle, she fell on the snow and puked. I always thought of snow as being pristine. If Seattle got more snow, like New York or Chicago, I probably would have thought differently. It looked so beautiful in movies. The multi-colored, partly dissolved sustenance was prominent against the white backdrop. Her barrage must have been imprecise. The coach didn't smell very good the rest of the trip. Peer pressure from our stomachs was overwhelming. It was amazing none of us added to the stench.

When I returned to my room, Samantha was already in bed,

but not alone. Fortunately, the lights were off, and she and Charlie were both asleep. I thought about turning around and sleeping somewhere else, but I was too stubborn, and too tired, to be any more inconvenienced by Samantha's indiscretion. The last thing I wanted to do was wake them. Who knows what they were wearing under the covers, if anything. I went into the bathroom, brushed my teeth and washed up a bit, then quietly pulled back my covers and crawled beneath them. I left my clothes on. It felt indecent wearing sleeping attire when a man was in the room. It didn't take long for me to fall asleep. When I woke up, both of them were gone.

The next two weeks were a blur. Every day there was at least one Olympic event. To maximize participation, most of them were held in late afternoon, when people began getting off work, but before others started. Schedules were modified to accommodate those who wished to participate.

The Olympic season traditionally began the day after the Super Bowl. Sign-up sheets for events were put up in the EDR a week in advance. Matilda hadn't participated in the Yellowstone Olympics much in the past, but after I strongly encouraged her, she signed up for most of the events. The two events we could do together were the three-legged race, and the chair pull.

Opening ceremonies were on February 1st. At 4pm there was a parade of sorts that began near the cabins and terminated in front of the EDR. It was quite a spectacle. Samantha skied in a bikini. Charlie carried a torch. He set it on a pile of wood that immediately erupted into flames. The fire almost got out of hand. The stack of wood was too high, and someone had put too much lighter fluid on it.

The first event of the 1989 games began after a brief tale about the crown prince of Norway being kidnapped. He was reclaimed and taken back to the royal family, after a harrowing escape on skis over treacherous terrain. To represent the approximate size and weight of the infant prince, backpacks were filled with a 12-pack of beer. It had to be relayed among members of three-person teams. Teammates were randomly selected, to discourage the creation of super teams. Being a novice to the event, I chose to be a spectator. Matilda's team consisted of two people I didn't know very well. Neither of them looked like they did much skiing. It was the luck of the draw.

Matilda chose to ski the first leg. She and a dozen other people lined up in front of their beer-laden backpacks fifty feet away. "GO!" There was a mad dash. A couple of people got tangled and went down, just a stride from the starting line. The first person to snag his backpack and put it on in front of him was already over the first obstacle, a five-foot high mogul. He disappeared down the other side. Matilda was third up and over. Some of the people had trouble getting over the small hill. As more skis pounded into the mound it became slicker. A third of the competitors failed the initial scaling.

I didn't stick around to see if everyone would make it. I rushed to the beginning of Howard Eaton, the end of the first leg. Most of the Snow Lodge staff must have either been participating in the race or watching it. As the first skier was seen dropping down the back side of the Water Tower, we cheered. IT WAS MATILDA! She had passed those two in front of her. She said she had a secret weapon. Most of the better skiers used high quality metal-edged skis. Precise waxing was required to maximize their efficiency. Some waxes helped with traction, but more traction meant a lessening of glide. Metal-edged skis were also heavy. Matilda chose to use a waxless pair. They didn't glide well, but they were lightweight, and great for climbing.

Matilda didn't slow herself down until she hit the road. She twisted her body. She skidded another few yards, then fell over. I thought she may have hurt something. Then she smiled. With her skis still eschew she got up onto her knees and half-threw, half-handed her pack to her teammate. He rushed off, skating down the road.

Another person was coming down the hill. Matilda got up, and out of the way. I gave her a hug. "You did wonderful."

"I hope it's enough. Some of the best skiers are on the anchor leg, and the skating specialists are on the 2nd leg."

"You should be proud. I don't think you could have done much better."

"I might have been able to get to my backpack quicker. I also had trouble putting it on."

"A second here or there won't matter."

"It might. Let's head back to the starting line. That's also where they'll finish."

As we started back to Snow Lodge, a skier fell about halfway down the hill. That would have been me, but much farther up. I probably would have fallen going up the Water Tower too. The racers had been close together at the beginning of the race, but they had begun to space themselves. Would the last skier to cross the finish line feel happy just to finish like I did during the Resolution Race, or would they feel bad for disappointing their teammates?

Shouting and clapping proceeded the first racer to cross the finish line. He wasn't on Matilda's team. The crowd continued to cheer, including a few tourists, as the second racer appeared, then crossed the finish line. Matilda's look of disappointment changed to one of resignation. Then her eyes lit up. The third member of her team could be seen. Someone was coming up behind him. My heart was pounding madly, and I wasn't even in this race. Matilda's teammate was able to hold on, but just barely. The crowd erupted more than it did when the first racer crossed the finish line.

"So, a few seconds doesn't matter?" Matilda and her other teammate congratulated the 3rd place finisher. "Finally. That's my first medal ever won in the Yellowstone Olympics."

"Third place is bronze, isn't it?" It may have sounded like I was being demeaning, but I really didn't know, not confidently. I was never that much into sports. Until five minutes ago there was never any drama in it for me. A team was either going to win or lose.

"Yep. But it's still a medal."

"How many events have you been in since you started working winters here?"

"This is just my forth. I didn't participate in any events my first winter, and just three last year. I was third down that hill in '88."

"So, your improvement was the reason your team won a medal this year?"

Matilda smiled. "Now, let's see if we can get you a medal, and me more. Tomorrow is the three-legged race."

To reduce the chaos, and the collisions, only two teams raced in each heat. A bracket system was used to keep track of everything. Most of the teams raced without practicing. Matilda was the type of person that if she was going to do something, she was going to give it her all. We must have spent two hours practicing over two days. Two problems developed. One, Matilda was taller than me. I couldn't help that. I suggested she find another partner, but Matilda insisted I was the only partner for her. The second problem was inferior skiing skill. I was decent now, better than some Snow Lodgers, but far inferior to Matilda. Being tied together, our racing results depended upon the weakest member of our team. And that was me. Speed-wise I was nearly Matilda's equal, but I couldn't turn as quickly as she could. When she tried to crisply cut a corner, I couldn't keep up. I became unstable, which caused me to fall, inadvertently dragging Matilda down with me. When it was time for the races to begin, I was much improved, but still not close to being as good as Matilda.

Odd-ball events, like the three-legged race, were fun to watch, but many of the more serious skiers didn't participate. Fewer participants meant a greater likelihood of success. We got a bad draw and got put against one of the better teams the first round. They started well, but stumbled down the stretch. Their awkwardness revealed they were one of the teams that hadn't practiced. We rushed past them at the end as they picked themselves up for the third time. "This is not a real race anyway," I heard them both say as they stomped away.

The second round we won handedly. There had been just fifteen teams competing, so after two wins we were already in the semi-finals. We lost the next one, to a superior team, but by just a couple of yards. It gave us confidence heading into the bronze medal match. We ran an almost perfect race. Our movements were in sync. I even nailed the turn at the turn around. The team that beat us ended up winning the final by a larger margin than they beat us by. Officially, we came in 3rd, but I liked to think we were the 2nd best team.

"So, when are we awarded our medal?"

"During the awards ceremony, on the last day of the Olympics. It's still twelve days away."

The chair that had to be pulled was on top of a pair of skis. Being much bigger and stronger that I, Matilda was the logical choice to do the pulling. I had no trouble sitting down. The one problem I had was having to drink a beer while Matilda was pulling me. Being a minor, I wasn't allowed to consume the alcoholic beverage. I was given a soft drink as a substitute. Some of our opponents complained, but I always thought beer went down easier than soft drinks. I think it had to do with the carbonation in soft drinks.

The race was bracketed like the three-legged race. There were fewer teams than there were for the last event---just thirteen. That meant three byes instead of just one. The Yellowstone Olympic Committee (Y.O.C.) must have thought a strong person like Matilda pulling a light person like me made us one of the favorites, because we got one of the byes. That meant we were already in the quarter finals.

I had some problems with the soft drink. I think I got more on myself than down my throat. Even with so much waste, we had to wait at the finish line for me to finish the tumbler. To show it was empty I had to tip it over my head. The few drops that dripped were insignificant compared to what was already on me. We won that first heat, but my drinking problem made it close.

In the end things tended to balance out. As unlucky as we were in who we were paired with in the first heat of the three-legged race, we were just as lucky in our pairing in the semi-finals of the chair pull. A weaker team had the fortune of playing only weak teams---their luck of the draw. I was determined I wasn't going to hold us back this time. As Matilda pulled me past the finish line I tipped the tumbler over my head. The other team had just made the turn. We had nearly lapped them.

"For the final we're going to try something different." Charlie handed Matilda and the other puller a bandana. "Tie this around your eyes."

"But I won't be able to see," whined our opponent.

"That's the idea."

Neither of the teams did very well. Matilda took a cautious approach. She walked slowly with her head bent over, with a hand in front of her. I had to guide her. We worked well together. The other team's approach was the faster we do this thing, the faster we'll get it over. They did sprint ahead of us, but near the turn they crashed into the side of the outdoor freezer.

On a particularly cold day, I went out there to retrieve a three-gallon tub of ice cream for Lori. It actually felt warm in there relative the temperature outside.

We passed them. With renewed determination, not only in an attempt to retake the lead, but to bandage their pride, they sped up again. This time they crashed into the EDR. In two events, I had won two medals, and one of them was gold. In three events Matilda had won three.

The remainder of the Olympics didn't go as well, not for me anyway. Matilda continued to finish in the top three in many of the events she competed.

We tried to pair up again, to do the tandem ski, where two people shared the same pair of skis, but weren't able to make our schedules work.

I did win one more medal. It was even a gold, in the snow sculpture contest. Matilda helped me build a three-dimensional representation of Yellowstone. If we could pull it off I knew we would win. Who could vote against Yellowstone? We even used food coloring for the lakes and rivers.

Matilda became known as the Silver Queen. In all four of the individual events she won medals in, she placed second. The individual events were broken down into male and female sections, which had something to do with her success. The one race she would have liked to do better in was the biathlon. It consisted of racing from one shooting station to another. Every point she scored with a dart was a second deducted from her time. She completed the course faster than any other girl, but her dart throws weren't that good. The event was too heavily weighted with the luck of the throw.

The first event she got a silver medal in was the Waitri 500. Waitri was a term Yellowstone uses for its servers. You have to give the powers to be credit for creating a gender-neutral version of waiter and waitress. But why did the term have to sound so stupid? To win the race a person had to ski up then down the Water Tower with a bowl of water carried on a beverage tray. A ski pole could be used in the off hand, but it was safer to carry the tray with both hands. Some water had to remain in the bowl by the time the skier reached the bottom of the hill. It was quite common for a skier to empty the bowl---as proof the bowl still contained some water--- seconds before crashing into the snow or a tree. Focus was more important than safety. Even if you didn't win a medal, you wanted to do better than your friends, to have bragging rights the remainder of the winter.

Matilda also placed second in the pub to dorm race, which included a person buying a beer out of the soft drink machine in Lupine's lobby, before returning to the pub. It sounded easier than it actually was. Try drinking something when you're huffing and puffing.

The 100-meter dash was a straight forward race for Matilda. She used her metal edged skis and skated the entire time.

The last medal she won was in the obstacle course. It included racing up and down hills, throwing Frisbees, and eating a peanut butter sandwich. Just peanut butter, no jelly. I also competed in the race, taking two minutes just to swallow the damn thing.

The only race I did better in than Matilda was the reverse ski. She never got the hang of it. I used to roller skate backwards, so that gave me a significant advantage. I finished 4th, and Matilda 11th, out of 12 female competitors.

Many of the events neither Matilda or I competed in. There were team events like volleyball, and Beer Ball, where after hitting a softball wrapped in silver duct tape---so it can be seen in the snow---a person had to drink a cup of beer before going to the next base. Some of the more dangerous events---which we weren't stupid enough to participate in---were similar to true Olympic events, like the ski jump and the luge. One of the employees broke his leg after landing poorly after jumping the five-foot high mogul built near the base of the Water Tower. The winning leap was over fifty feet. The luge consisted of riding an innertube down the Water Tower. Those two events had minimal participation, but were heavily watched. Who didn't want to see a good crash?

The awards ceremony was held in the pub. There was even an awards platform. The awards were given out sequentially, beginning with the Rainier Cup---named after the beer in the backpacks. Rainier Beer, pronounced RON-YAY, was the unofficial beer of Yellowstone, celebrated more frequently---and fervently--- in the winter. There really wasn't room for three people on each step, so the award winners had to use some creative maneuvering. A string was attached to each gold, silver, and bronze cylinder.

"They are spray painted Rainier Beer cans," Matilda informed me when she returned to my side after accepting her medal.

By the end of the ceremony I had three cans dangling from my neck, and Matilda eight. "I'm I allowed to drink these?"

Matilda had finished two beers during the ceremony and was working on her third. "I think you were overlooked, as being underage. I wouldn't drink them in public."

"Back in the dorm?"

"If you are discrete. Too many people are having too much fun to pay too much attention."

"Are you trying to finish all of yours before you leave?"

"That's the tradition."

"Won't that make you sick?"

"Probably."

"I think for someone who won so many, drinking half now and half later would be acceptable."

"You're probably right." I couldn't help associating Matilda's drinking with what happened during the New Year's Eve Dance. It didn't help that the Valentine's Dance was going to start in about an hour.

Minutes after the last medals were given out, the table tops were detached. Matilda began to head for the door. "I am working early tomorrow. I don't want to be sick on the job---again---not when I have to look at raw eggs all morning. You ready to head back?" I would have liked to stay for at least part of the dance, but I didn't want Matilda to have to ski home alone.

I didn't get very far when I heard a pop, then a fizz. The

tussling of the beer cans around my neck created enough force on one of the strings attached to a pull tab that the can opened, shooting beer all over my face, and into my hair. Great. I was covered in beer, and underage. I poured out what was left in the can and continued my ski home. Another can opened as I crossed the wintry meadow parking lot. Matilda wasn't fairing much better. She had her first can pop open prior to my second. There was always a reason behind a tradition. Consuming all the beers at the awards ceremony would have prevented this.

I made it to Lupine with that final beer still intact. I would save it for later. All I wanted to do now was…. "I'll see you later, Matilda. I need to take a shower, possibly with my clothes on."

21. MY OWN TRAILS

Matilda was at work, but with just three weeks remaining I couldn't waste my time waiting for her. Instead of trying to find someone to go skiing with I decided to wander off on my own. It was easier for me to think when I was doing something active. And I had many things to think about. Speaking with yourself was easier than trying to make polite conservation with someone you didn't know very well.

I didn't like skiing too far away when I skied alone, so I usually went to Fern Cascades or to the geyser basin. I was feeling a bit more anti-social than usual, so I opted for Fern Cascades. There were always people in the geyser basin, even in the more remote areas, like Daisy or Moring Glory.

I felt like exploring. The only part of the Fern Cascades canyon I had seen was at the rapids. At the top of the hill, I angled away from the trail, to the right. I expected to drop three or four feet into the snow, but actually stopped falling after about a foot. The snow had finally set up. It had become dense enough to support my weight. I had heard tales of people breaking trail in un-set snow for miles, being so worn out after an hour or two that they could barely drag themselves home. Large parties take turns breaking trail. Every five minutes or so the lead skier would fall to the end of the line. As he recovered, the skier previously behind him would plow ahead.

The gentle descent abruptly terminated at the precipice of the creek. I was now skilled enough to stop before I tumbled into the water that was more of a drool than a stream. I continued along the canyon's contour. It took me about ten minutes to reach the Fern Cascades overlook. The official trail, the one with orange flagging, would have taken less than five. The new trail couldn't have been that much longer. It was a new, exciting experience for me, so time must have slowed.

I continued to follow the canyon after the cascades, considering, briefly, that today was the day to cross that log. I had survived a fall into a creek during the full-moon ski, and it was warmer today...but Matilda wasn't here to help me up if I did fall. I would have more fun exploring with her anyway.

I spent the remainder of the morning creating my own trails. I was quite proud what I had accomplished. I would no longer be limited to skiing the same old trails every day.

I barely missed Matilda at lunch. The food and beverage employees ate early, sometimes before all the food made it to the EDR line. I liked to see Matilda as often as possible, but on Thursdays it meant just fifteen minutes in the morning, and whenever she got off in the afternoon.

The letdown of not seeing Matilda tapped my enthusiasm. I sat through the entire lunch period, occasionally listening to the diners, but more often staring into space.

The last group to eat, barely did so. They came in as the

food was being taken away. The EDR server didn't hesitate to allow them to eat. Everyone at Yellowstone was a friend, or at least someone that would be seen the next day. Making an enemy on an island wasn't wise. "The trail is ruined," spoke one of the newcomers.

"How could someone make that mess?" questioned another.

"I ski to relax, not stress out about which trail to follow."

"If I wanted to see so many roads, I would have spent the winter in the city."

I was becoming angry. HOW DARE THESE IDIOTS DETERMINE WHAT I SHOULD OR SHOULD NOT DO! They left after a few minutes, but I continued to sit there. I was even in a fouler mood than before. It was still two hours before Matilda was supposed to be off work. I hated to feel that way, and I definitely didn't want to when I was reunited with Matilda.

I skied to the geyser basin, and immediately became less depressed. Was it the natural wonders or the physical exertion? It didn't really matter. No more worrying---at least for the remainder of the day.

They were right. I shouldn't have made those trails of mine without thinking about the consequence. Everything I do may affect others, like a snowball rolling down a hill. I wasn't really angry at them. I was angrier with myself. Feeling bad, but not wanting to, or being capable of, directing it at myself, I took it out on others. Most negative reactions are caused be insecurities and shame.

One place I hadn't skied to yet was Solitary Geyser. It seemed to be the perfect place to be today. Off the Geyser Hill loop, a trail climbed into the forest. The hill may have been intimidating at the beginning of the winter, but all I could think about now was the great ski run coming down. Elk clustered near the trailhead. I was careful not to disturb them. They had as much right to be there as I did. And they were a bit intimidating,

especially when I was on skis. My maneuverability was better---
than the beginning of the season---but still significantly worse than
walking. Or running.

At the end of the trail the forest opened up. The ground
was clear of snow in the vicinity of a steaming pool. My timing was
perfect. The water rippled, then a column of water rose from the
pool, first three feet high, then growing to six. A cloud floated away
from me, towards a copse of un-burnt lodgepoles. They looked like
the frocked trees I saw at Norris Geyser Basin. Within seconds the
spectacle was over.

A sign mentioned eruptions occurring every eight minutes. I
could wait that long.

I was startled when I realized I wasn't the only person there.
Barry sat on his coat, with his legs crossed. His eyes were shut. I
worried that he might be dead. Then he twitched. It may have
been an involuntary muscle spasm, but more likely, it meant he was
still alive. Like the elk, I was resolute in not disrupting his
tranquility.

After he competed in the Resolution race, he reverted to his
sedentary ways. He didn't ski anymore, except to work. He even
gave up studying thermal features. That had been a hobby of his.
He was drawn to its primal nature. But he was here. Why now?
Why today? Was it another turning point for him or a final gasp
before he went under, forever?

Yellowstone's Buddha's expanding beard and gut was
making him look more like Jerry Garcia every day. I felt both sorry
for Barry, and envied him. What devotion he had for his beliefs.
Although the consequences of his lifestyle were slowly killing him,
he rarely deviated from his beliefs. The key was to achieve spiritual
enlightenment *without* destroying yourself.

Quietly I dropped down the hill. As I began to accelerate I
pushed off a couple of times to supplement gravity's pull. The trail
was narrower than Mallard Lake or Howard Eaton. I was constantly
on the verge of falling, but never quite did. If I fell in these dense

woods, the ground wasn't the only thing I would be hitting. The elk believed it would be a good time to graze in the middle of the trail. I dodged at the last minute, my skis turning sharply to the right, becoming parallel to the slope. Off trail, the forest was cluttered with naturally fallen debris. I intentionally fell upslope to prevent myself from crashing into a log.

I picked myself up, then headed back towards the trail, making a wide detour around the elk. Why did there always have to be a balance between beauty and danger? There were the frocked trees, the geyser, and the great ski run, but also elk and logs blocking my route.

I couldn't leave the geyser basin without stopping at Grotto. As usual it wasn't active without Matilda beside me. For once, the thought of her didn't remind me of her absence, but of the time we would be spending together. Tomorrow Matilda and I were going to discover Yellowstone's Northwest Passage. We were heading to Summit Lake.

22.   SUMMIT LAKE

Matilda and I stopped at the snow-incrusted log that spanned the creek. I eyed it critically. "It looks wide enough to ski across."

"Yes, but if it isn't, the least of our worries will be returning to Lupine to change into dry clothes. The delay will probably prevent us from making it to Summit Lake today. Skiing at night on a known, marked route, is relatively safe, but...."

"We'll be practically blind on one we create ourselves haphazardly. We can't risk returning in the dark. That means we'll also have to keep track of the time. Turn around by one?"

"Maybe a little later. We'll be mainly going downhill on the way back, and we'll have a trail to follow."

We removed our skis and held them perpendicular to our bodies to give us added balance. The crossing reminded me of the duel Robin Hood and Little John had on that log bridge---if they wore winter attire.

We put our skis back on---always difficult on unstable terrain. There was a narrow, level shelf beside the creek, but beyond that the land rose steeply away from the water.

We studied the detailed topographical map of the Old Faithful Area that was on the back of the Yellowstone topographical map. No matter the route we took to Summit Lake from Fern Cascades, we had to cross that ridge. It was just 250 feet above us, but on a pair of skis it looked much higher.

Once we climbed above the lip, and skied to the end of a small meadow, we scanned for a pass. There appeared to be one on the right. Weaving through burnt timber, we snaked our way up through the shallow chute. It was steep enough that we had to climb at a diagonal, then flip around in the other direction after one-hundred feet or so. Side-stepping the entire way would have taken twice as long, and would have been just as tiring.

The climb did end, and we took a break to celebrate, but not too long. We couldn't screw around if we wanted to reach the lake today. No one had reached the lake yet this year. Charlie and Andy attempted it from its trailhead at Biscuit Basin. Conditions prevented them from making it more than halfway. No one had been there since the fires. Would it still be a secluded paradise, or a scorched relic?

We took out the map again, and this time also a compass. The lake was west-southwest of us. The land continued to rise, transitioning to falling about halfway to the lake. Heading west, we could stay on the same contour line for half-a-mile, until we had to cross another creek.

Sporadically, we made good time. This was one of those occasions. I looked behind me intermittently, confirming our escape route. Snow wasn't falling, and it wasn't breezy. Our tracks should remain visible. But it was overcast. It could start snowing any minute. It would be problematic to ski home without a trail. Impractical during the day. Impossible at night. We had some protective gear, and matches to start a fire, but most of the wood in the area was already burnt.

It must have been a wet weather creek. Or, more accurately, a summer creek. Whatever water in it was frozen. Matilda slowly dropped to the bottom of the creek bed, then more quickly, skied up the other side. Trying to impress her with my skiing skills, I flew down the hill. My intent, to coast up the other side. My skis slammed tip first into the far bank instead, bending the skis and jarring my body. I fell into the creek bed, backwards. Matilda skied back down to help me up. "I'M OKAY!" I squawked at her, sounding harsher than I intended. Instead of impressing Matilda, I looked like a fool. Once again, she was helping me.

She said, after we were both up the bank, "I knew someone who broke a ski, and had a heck of a time making it back home."

"It didn't take me that long."

"You only broke your binding. I'm talking about someone whose ski actually broke in two. Fortunately, he was on Howard Eaton, so he had less than a mile to wade through the snow. If we broke a ski here I don't think we would be able to make it back until spring."

"I'm always going to be your little sister. The naïve, careless girl that needs to be looked after."

"In this setting, perhaps. We've talked about this before. I might be more knowledgeable about skiing and Yellowstone...."

"And life."

"When we leave Yellowstone, I look forward to you teaching me about...."

"What?"

"Seattle. Cities. I haven't spent much time in cities."

"Because you don't like them."

"Maybe that's because no one has been my guide, shown me the type of things that make cities great."

"You'll always be older, wiser, more worldly."

"Knowing more doesn't always make a person worldly. From what you told me of your life, you've probably experienced more in eighteen years than I'll have in twenty-five."

"Not the experiences that matter."

"All experiences matter."

I gave Matilda a hug, which was never easy on skis. At times like these I almost wanted to risk ruining our friendship for an opportunity to make it more. But we still had many more hours of skiing to do today, and limited daylight. But maybe before the season ended. Maybe.

We climbed another two-hundred yards, predominantly through moguls. Exhilarating, perhaps, coming down, but a pain in the butt having to weave around coming up. Then another level section, following another contour. By the time we reached a second creek crossing, we had traveled just one-and-a-half miles since leaving Fern Cascades.

Matilda looked at her watch.

"Do we have enough time to make it to the lake?" I asked.

"Plenty of time," she replied enthusiastically, but without conviction.

The third creek had flowing water. Matilda skied slowly down its bank, crossing it over a natural causeway. Snow shook from the branches of a fallen tree below her, in response to her abrupt divorce from them. Covered in snow, the span looked more stable. It no longer looked strong enough to support my weight. Psychological or structural, the absence of icy bonding material, created a less safe crossing. I took off my skis and tested the intertwined twigs. They gave a bit, but they didn't disintegrate. I held out my skis like I did during the initial creek's crossing. As

184

expected, the bridge gave the most near its middle. It became more stable as I climbed up to the far shore. Why couldn't all the creeks be frozen in winter? There had to be a thermal run-off somewhere upstream.

We entered a canyon, the uneven slope creating an awkward climb. Left leg compressed. Right, elongated.

After more than a mile the canyon terminated, a combination of herringbone and side-stepping bringing us to the top of the ridge.

The terrain on the other side was laden with green lodgepole saplings. Yes, we had found another pocket of Yellowstone untouched by the fires. Until a person skis through a burnt area, she doesn't realize how much easier it is than skiing through a healthy forest. Burnt trunks take up less space than low-lying branches.

The elevation was about 8400 feet at the top of the ridge, 900 feet higher than Fern Cascades. It seemed like more, but building your own trails changes one's perspective.

We looked at the map. Then at Matilda's compass. Then back to the map.

"We have to be here," she said, pointing to the map.

"Two miles so far?"

"More than that. We weren't going in a straight line."

"A mile...and-a-half to the trail."

"And another mile-and-a-half to the lake."

"We're not going to have time, are we? To reach the lake and get back before it gets dark."

"We'll see. It looks pretty flat down to the trail. It will be more difficult heading up to the lake, but we'll at least have a trail to follow."

"If we find the trail."

"When we find the trail."

This leg of our journey was the most enjoyable. The terrain *was* relatively flat, with occasional gradual downhill stretches. The green trees were a welcomed sight, and spaced evenly enough to permit maneuvering without contemplation.

About where the Summit Lake Trail should be, the terrain began to climb again. "Unless we are completely off course, the trail should be beneath us," Matilda stated.

"Let's stay in this valley and continue in the direction of the lake until we see a marker," I suggested.

Matilda screamed, then hugged me from behind, nearly knocking me over. She pointed to the orange marker that was nearly on the ground. And I had been looking up. "Let's eat lunch to celebrate," I suggested.

"NO WAY! I haven't skied all this way to dine next to an orange marker. If we push, we can make it to the lake in half-an-hour."

Except for the first hundred yards or so, ascending a narrow canyon, the final leg to Summit Lake was flat, straight, and without interest. I had hoped the lake would be surrounded by green, but regrettably the charred trunks returned.

A large, white meadow lay ahead. It had to be Summit Lake. The trail wound its way clockwise around the lake, but we went in the opposite direction, towards an isolated, green, copse a hundred yards away. A large, flat stone jutted away from the trees into the frozen lake.

We took off our skis and backpacks. As we sat down with our lunches, a sunbeam illuminated our stone. The hole in the sky enlarged, filling our hidden haven with light and heat. By the time we finished eating, the rock had become warm.

Matilda looked at her watch. She opened her jacket and pulled up her shirt, revealing a sports bra. "If you close your eyes you can almost imagine it's spring." Which she did as she leaned back.

With her no longer being able to see me, I gave myself permission to look at her belly. Like a person who was compelled to jump when standing on top of a tall building, I was tempted to kiss that soft, exposed skin. Instead, I imitated her. First, unzipping my jacket, then with much hesitation, lifting my shirt. Matilda sports bra looked more conservative than most bikini tops. My bra looked more indecent. It was more lingerie than swimwear. From how Matilda reacted to the exposure, I thought it would have been warmer---much warmer. Maybe a breeze had come up. I shrieked. Sometimes when a part of a woman's body gets cold it wants to tell you about it. Now I really felt indecent. I covered myself up, but not before Matilda saw me. My shocked utterance had woken her. She smiled. I didn't know if it was from what she saw or from me becoming so surprised from the cold. I zipped my coat back up. Matilda looked at her watch again, then closed her eyes and laid her head back down.

I laid back myself. I glanced at Matilda's belly again, then shut my eyes. I thought about us coming back here in the summer when it was warmer. I would kiss her belly---and perhaps more. What would it be like if we had that type of relationship? Would enough of society allow us to be who we were, or would we have to hide behind friendship? I contemplated some of the things we would do together, some of the places we would go. I didn't see us flaunting ourselves at a sandy beach in California or Florida. Homosexual women were much more reserved in how they presented themselves than heterosexual ones. I think it had to do with breeding. If they wanted to propagate they had to meet members of the opposite sex who wished to assist them. Going around half naked was definitely one way to get noticed. Will there ever be a society that will truly accept? Someone like me: a woman, whose ancestors came from Africa, that loves another woman. Will there ever be a religion that is truly accepting? How can a religion be universal if it doesn't include all?

"It's time to go." For a moment, I had forgotten where I was. I could have been in my bed in Lupine, or even at Grain's. I opened my eyes and looked over at Matilda. She had already dropped her shirt, and even zipped up her jacket. I yearned for a final peak of her belly. Who knows when, or if, I would ever see it again. "You look pensive."

"I was just thinking about what this place would look like in the summer."

"Let's return after the snow melts."

We quickly packed up, put our skis back on, and were off. We should have plenty of time left, but there could always be delays. As we followed our tracks back to Fern Cascades, I expressed some of the thoughts I had before Matilda interrupted my revelry. "Do you ever wish you could go off to some place like Summit Lake and start your own society, doing things your own way, the way you think they should be done? A complete overhaul of the society you were raised in, including creating a religion that fits what you believe in."

"That seems quite ambitious. And tiring."

"Maybe we could start slowly, beginning with the foundation. Aren't most societies founded in spirituality? Can you think of a religion that isn't saturated with doctrines of hate?" I was referring to the Bible condemning homosexuals. It actually condemned many things, but Christians tend to fixate on that one thing.

"Humans are imperfect, and they are the ones who create religions. God is not petty enough to want to control people's lives. Times change, but many see religious truths as absolute, and unvarying. To be fruitful and multiply is sensible when populations are low, but not when the Earth has too many people. If the Bible was written today it would discourage a couple from having more than two or three children. More people means more money going to the church. Maybe we can create a less complex religion, one that involves just a few people, maybe as small as just you and me."

"But doesn't a religion have to involve millions of people?"

"Why?"

"So, it can be respected, I guess, and become well known."

"Is it important that everyone believes the way we do?"

"It would make life easier."

"But life would become boring if we were all the same."

"But if we thought our religion was important, isn't it our duty to tell others so they might become saved?"

"I don't think our religion would work for everyone. No religion works that way, not even capitalism."

"Should we allow anyone who wishes to join our religion, to do so?"

"Religions are spiritual clubs, but clubs shouldn't be restrictive, so religions can't either. And we should allow people to be critical of us. And we shouldn't belittle other religions, because we would be affecting people's decision to choose. How about society in general? What is immoral? What is moral?"

"I think we should all work together for the common good. We should be humble. If we are, there shouldn't be anything to feel guilty about. Why must we sin in order to be saved? Why don't we not sin in the first place? Live the life we will not be embarrassed of, that we wish to take into the internal sleep. We aren't perfect, but we can try to do our best."

"We should cherish children, and only have them when they are wanted."

"How do we do that? Abstinence? That's not going to happen. Birth control only works if people use it properly. And even if they do, accidents happen."

"Maybe add something to the water. Like fluorine that is put in to prevent tooth decay."

"How would that effect people who can't become pregnant---children, the elderly---and men?"

"How about birth control implants, provided free, from the government?"

"Better."

"And we must provide for the elderly, and the disabled."

"Half our income for ourselves, and half for the community."

"We must provide safety and health."

"Reduce the disparity in wealth."

"How?"

"By forbidding monopolies. Allow a company to become as large as it wishes, but it must be under one roof."

"But democracy must flourish."

"With truth and not with trendiness."

"We should not harm one another."

"We must be careful to not over strive. Doing a bit is better than too much. Too many leaders sacrificed their relationship with their families for a perceived common good."

"Feed you family before you feed your community."

"And you must take care of yourself before you can do that."

"And if your community is in distress, how can you help your nation, or the world?"

Something seemed to change once we reached the top of the green pass and began our decent to Fern Cascades. It must have been how Dorothy felt as she stepped from her house into Oz, but in reverse. The excitement of reaching Summit Lake and spending time together faded, as abruptly as the pigmentation. The remnants, the continuation of my mundane existence.

Spring was arriving. The decay of winter had already begun. As the days got warmer, more snow melted, and less fell. It was now more common for highs to be above freezing than below. Snow was mushy in the afternoons and icy in the mornings.

The inevitability of my future was approaching. What was I to do now? I could return to Yellowstone in the summer---and I wished to experience the Park in that state at least once---but what was I to do between winter and summer. Most of the winter employees traveled or visited relatives. I didn't want to spend the little money I earned in Yellowstone. And it felt wrong returning to Grain for more than a couple of days. I was an adult now. I could visit her, but no longer burden her. Yellowstone had changed me. I had grown up. Grain would always be my grandmother, but she could no longer by my guardian, my surrogate parent.

Cresting the green pass seemed to effect Matilda as much as it did me, but differently. She became quieter, more pensive. We returned to Old Faithful, without saying more than a few words to each other.

I didn't see Matilda the next day. Could it have been something I did, or said? But it wasn't just me who hadn't seen her.

Christine appeared upset when I saw her in the EDR the following morning. "What's wrong?"

"Matilda moved out. I thought we got along pretty well as roommates. She never complained about anything."

"Where did she go?"

"Most of her stuff is still in my---her---our---room, but she's no longer living there. You know that room we fold sheets and towels in? She has begun sleeping in there. Did she mention anything to you about me?"

"Nothing. I don't think this has anything to do with you. Did she say anything about me?"

Christine shook her head.

Neither of us said anything for a minute, as we contemplated. I finally said, "She began acting funny when we returned home from that ski a couple of days ago. I think it had something to do with Spring arriving and us still having three weeks left."

"Matilda did mention she was getting tired of being around people. I thought she meant tourists, but maybe she meant me too."

"And probably me---everyone. Has she ever done this before? You've known her longer than I have."

"Do be honest with you, I didn't know her very well until this winter. People tend to hang out with the same people. Before she became my roommate, we hadn't spent much time together. I've seen other people get a bit moody at the end of the winter."

"Cabin Fever?"

I began to feel differently about Matilda. I felt sorry that she was feeling this way, but I also began to worry about her losing interest in me. If she can't cope being around people after three months---three weeks short of three months---how will she be able to spend the rest of her life with someone? Did I even want to be in a relationship that is doomed to whither?

23. CAMPING

With Matilda escaping from the world, except when it was absolutely necessary---such as going to work---I spent my last days off in February alone. I slept in my first day off. Then after lunch, I skied to Biscuit Basin. But no further. I would have liked to see Mystic Falls again, but that meant passing that sign for Summit Lake. Instead of returning through the Upper Geyser Basin, I skated along the highway. I wanted to do at least one more new thing before I left Yellowstone. I stopped at Black Sand Basin. Due to its remoteness, few people went there during the winter, especially skiers. Two snowmobiles were in the parking lot. Somewhere in the mist two bi-pedal beetles shuffled on the wooden planks and packed snow. The thermal features reminded me of Biscuit Basin, but without that area that was like a steam bath. When I returned to the parking lot the snowmobiles were gone. They must have been travelling in the same direction around the loop.

The following day I did the Lone Star loop, in the morning. After lunch, I skied up to Solitary Geyser. The peacefulness of the setting overwhelmed me. Before I could pull myself away, I had experienced half-a-dozen of the mini eruptions. Grotto Geyser was next. I contemplated making a clean break, but it may the last time in the geyser basin. For once it was erupting without Matilda beside me. As I made the turn to return to Lupine, to do laundry before dinner, I spotted Matilda. It looked like she was also returning, but from the northern end of the geyser basin.

I waited for Matilda to catch up with me. She stared at me for a moment, then snapped out of it, "You just missed Riverside going off."

"Crap. Do you know that I haven't yet seen it or the Grand erupt? Maybe tomorrow, before work. How are you doing?"

"I'll be better in a few weeks. I feel the isolation more every winter. I don't think I'll be able to return to Snow Lodge next year."

"That's too bad. It's been a significant part of your life, hasn't it?"

"It's exhausting seeing the same people every day in the same tight spaces."

"I'm sorry you weren't able to enjoy the winter."

"But I did."

"Even with you being my tour guide?"

"Especially with me being your tour guide."

"Is there something you wished you would have done this winter?"

"Camping. I've never camped in the snow."

That wasn't the answer I was hoping for, but if it could get her out of her funk.... "What do we need to do to make that happen?"

"Camping equipment for one thing. Most of my summer gear is stored away in my car in Mammoth. And even if I had access to it I would still need a better sleeping bag. It's colder camping in the winter than the summer."

"Then let's find someone willing to...loan...their winter gear to us."

"CHARLIE!"

"He's probably working, but we might be able to catch him

in the EDR. Or in the dorm tonight."

With reserved excitement Matilda returned with me to the EDR. It was still just mid-afternoon, but we were both starving. I made a peanut butter and jelly sandwich. Matilda poured herself a bowl of cereal, which she drowned in milk. I returned to Lupine to do that laundry I had put off---so unlike me. And Matilda? Back to the linen room.

"Sure, you can borrow my camping equipment, but Andy and I are coming along with you." That was unexpected. I thought with Matilda and I alone we had one final opportunity for romance to spontaneously combust. Considering our track record so far, it was extremely unlikely, so the more the merrier. If Charlie can't improve Matilda's mood, no one can.

"You sure you have enough equipment if we all go?"

Andy sat across from me with an empty cafeteria tray. It had been bulging a couple of minutes ago, when I first invited him, and Charlie, to sit at my table. "You don't know Charlie very well, then, do you? Yellowstone is like being in the Scouts. With Charlie as it's den mother. He'll make sure everyone who wants to go on one of his excursions has the means to do so. Which means having enough equipment to supply a small army."

"For people who have never been to the Park before they don't know what to bring," Charlie explained. "Everyone needs to have fun on their weekend."

Matilda arrived. She scanned the room. Upon seeing us, she went directly to our table without getting her food first.

"Charlie not only gave us permission to use his camping gear, he and Andy graciously agreed to join us," I told her.

Matilda sat down beside me. "This should be fun."

"How is this all going to work with everyone having different days off? You two have Tuesdays and Wednesdays off. I have Wednesdays and Thursdays. And Matilda, Thursdays and Fridays."

"I think I'll be able to switch my Friday to Wednesday next

week. It's easier when you only change one day."

I've been trying to get Matilda to switch to the same days off as me the entire winter, and now that Charlie and Andy are doing something with her, she can't wait to change them. "That still won't give us the same days off. Close, but...."

"You and I can meet up with the boys after work on Tuesday. We might even be able to get off early, if we're not too busy."

"By the time you arrive we should have camp set up," Andy said as he rushed off to the serving line for seconds. Matilda followed him.

Charlie stared off into space. "I wonder who else we can get to go with us."

I found out later that evening. Samantha was already packing. Supposedly for camping, but it looked like for the season. "This time of year the weather is very unpredictable," she explained. "It could be sunny and above freezing one day, and snowing and below zero the next night."

"How will you ever be able to carry all of that?"

"That's why God made guys."

Matilda continued to sleep in the linen room, but she did socialize more than she did the week before. We spent most of our meals together. Discussing the camping trip had created a frenzy. One thing we were afraid to discuss was the weather. The long-range forecast was for a cold snap to occur sometime late Monday or early Tuesday. Neither one of us wanted to call off the camping trip, but how cold would it have to get before it was unsafe to spend the night outdoors?

It was extremely cold Tuesday morning on the way to work. The moisture in my nose froze, making crackling sounds when I tried to breathe out of it. My face felt like someone was rubbing sand paper on it. After a while I couldn't feel my toes. Could someone get frostbite by just skiing to work? I tend to move slowly when I'm cold. Also slowing me down was the overnight pack. To save time Matilda and I agreed the night before to have everything with us so we could leave right after work. It was decided we were to camp at Shoshone Lake. In addition to there being a large body of water---frozen---there was a thermal basin. Matilda was quite excited about hotpotting---bathing in a natural hot tub. She had experienced the glorious activity many times in summer, but never in winter.

At 1:15, Matilda waved me over from the cooks line. The last lunch rush had finished a few minutes ago, but I was still busy clearing tables. After relocating a couple of table's worth of dirty dishes from a large metal oval tray to the dish drop, I walked up to her. "I've been given the red light to leave in half-an-hour," she informed me.

"About the same for me."

"It helps being the end of the month. Milo gets nervous about costs. If the EDR food wasn't already purchased, we would probably be eating peanut butter and jelly."

"On stale bread."

To conserve our warmth, we put our packs on in the EDR. Before we stepped outside, Matilda felt obliged to share something with me. "I heard it was supposed to get down to 40 below again tonight."

"You're not saying we should back out at the last minute? Everyone else already left."

"I was just trying to make polite conversation."

"It would have been more polite to say it was going to be 40 degrees *above* zero."

It was five degrees when we skied away from the EDR. I know this because there was a thermometer attached to the outside of the building. It felt almost balmy relative to this morning.

We worked most of the day, but we didn't feel tired. Adrenaline had something to do with it, but there was more to it. Skiing consumed energy, but a different kind of energy, than when working. It was less mental, and you used different muscles.

It felt like it took us just minutes to ski to Kepler Cascades. An hour later we were at Lone Star Geyser. It was steaming, as it always was. We didn't wait for it to erupt, or even look at the log to see how close it was to happening. We were exceedingly careful not to get our skis wet as we worked our way to the Shoshone trailhead. It was awful enough scraping snow and ice off them unburdened. It would be nearly impossible with an overnight pack. Having to take it off and put it back on was a cumbersome task at best. A near impossibility if buried in chest deep snow.

Skiing the Shoshone Lake Trail was a new experience for me. Why had I never done it? Because if I started a trail, I was compelled to finish it, to its completion. Self-preservation demanded I limit the type of trails I attempted. A less determined person could have just skied a couple of miles and turned around.

After crossing the Firehole River, we followed it for a mile or so. Someone was camped beside the trail. Camping was only permitted in designated sites, after being given permission by a ranger. Who had the nerve to camp there? Some might say *balls*, but being female that didn't apply to me. And that same someone had built a fire, nearly on top of the trail.

Matilda stopped beside the makeshift camp. "What's up, Barry?"

"I thought I might return to nature. My feet apparently like the city better." Barry raised his bare feet towards the fire. They were black. That wasn't a good sign.

"You camp here last night? Or plan to camp tonight?"

"Both. Or I was before my feet nearly froze off this morning. I don't work until four tomorrow. I still haven't decided what I'm going to do."

"Good luck with your feet. We're heading to Shoshone."

"The lake or the meadows?"

"The lake."

"Charlie, Andy, Christine, and Samantha are also camping there tonight."

"We're on the way to meet up with them," I said

"They passed by here about noon."

"That means about a four-hour head start. Thanks."

Matilda resumed her skiing.

I followed a couple of strides behind her. "Bye, Barry."

The terrain varied from minor thermal activity to meadows to forest. A mile past Barry, the trail began to climb. "We're heading to Grant's Pass." After two-and-a-half months Matilda was still my tour guide. "We'll be crossing the Continental Divide."

The trees began to look different. Not only were most of them green, they were of a different species than those found at lower elevations. The evergreens were taller, and their skirts appeared to be better tailored.

After we reached a sign that mentioned Grants Pass, the trail leveled off for fifty yards or so, then began to descend. The drop was as steep as the slope up---moderate---but it didn't last as long.

At the base of the hill, the forest opened up. It was beginning to get dark, so the meadow was welcomed. We looked up into the twilight sky. We could see both stars directly above us and to the east, and light at the edge of the horizon to the west, sharply accented by oranges and reds. We weren't going to make it to camp before dark anyway, so we stopped to eat a snack. Cheese and crackers, and a sip of water.

In the few minutes we had stopped, twilight had transitioned to a few lumens shy of complete darkness. With what light remained, we put away our food and found our headlamps. Our surroundings went dark as the area in front of us lit up. We put our packs back on and resumed our trek.

With the light went what little warmth remained in the air.

The heat loss couldn't have been that extreme, so the chill must have been more psychological than physical. After a few minutes of moving again, our discomfort abated, not completely abolished, but we longer felt miserable.

A creek meandered through the meadow. After passing a spur trail that mentioned Bechler Ranger Station, we crossed a narrow bridge over the waterway. I was tempted to take my skis off as I crossed, especially with it being dark. Tonight, would not be the time to take another plunge. With baby steps, I made it. Less safe, but more satisfying.

Shortly after crossing the creek, we reentered the forest. We followed the creek the remainder of the way to Shoshone Lake. The closer we got to it, the higher we climbed. I know, it didn't seem logical. The lake was upstream, not down. The trail didn't drop again until we were within sight of the lake, not too long after the creek diverged from the trail.

We saw a light ahead of us. Relief. Matilda's lamp had gone dark about a mile earlier. We had to slow to a crawl, especially on any of the downhill sections of the trail. To make it as safe as possible, I would ski down first. As Matilda caught up with me, I shined my light on the trail in front of her.

Two tents were erected about fifty feet from where the trail split into clockwise and counterclockwise spurs around the lake. Of the four people supposedly in camp, Charlie was the only one within sight. The others must be in their tents already. Charlie greeted us. "Welcome to Club Shoshone."

We unfastened our packs and leaned them against a tree. On a small backpacking stove, Charlie was heating what looked to be Ramen noodles. It smelled like chicken. He poured it into two cups. He handed one of them to Matilda, then the other to me. It was the best dinner I have ever had, or so I thought at that moment. And I don't mean just the flavor from the packet of powder. The soup comforted me as it went down, like it was giving me an internal message.

Now to other business. "Where are the...ah...facilities?"

"There is one of those open-air toilets down that way about a quarter-of-a-mile." Charlie pointed to the right.

Couldn't someone have told me that before I agreed to go on this excursion to hell? Wasn't Dante's ninth circle of hell a lake of ice? What did I expect? A heated toilet with a bathroom attendant handing me a warm towel afterwards?

"I'll be back," I muttered without confidence.

"I have to go too," spoke up Matilda. "I'll join you."

Normally I wasn't one of those girls that liked to make going to the bathroom a group activity, but in these conditions I wouldn't mind companionship. Misery loves company.

We skied away in the direction Charlie had indicated. After a couple of minutes of following the tracks that led to the north, we decided, simultaneously, that we had gone far enough. We looked at one another. I was first to speak. "Do you think there's some manual somewhere that describes the procedure?"

"I think it's just like when you pee outside in the summer." I gave her a blank look. "You haven't peed without using a toilet, have you? You just have to squat down, being careful not to fall over. It's more difficult on skis. Let's find a flat area off the trail."

I searched with my headlamp. "How about over there?"

"That will do."

I skied to where I had pointed. Matilda followed closely behind me. She pulled down her pants, long johns, and underwear in one pull. "YOW!"

I turned away from her, then I tried to pull my three layers down, in a single tug. Something very unladylike burst from my mouth. It felt like I was sitting on an iceberg. The most depressing part was that only the outer two layers fell. What would it feel like when that last thin layer of cotton disappeared. It wasn't significantly worse. Maybe I had become acclimated to the cold. Or too numb to feel anything. I heard what sounded like water dripping, but it was muffled. I envied Matilda. In a few more seconds she could pull her three layers back up. I squatted, being careful my skis didn't slip from beneath me. I attempted to release the flow. Nothing. Maybe it had frozen. I tried again. This time the urine burst from me, as if the ice-clogged damn had ruptured. After I was done I reached for the…. "Matilda, how did you clean yourself?"

"Just shake it dry like boys do."

We'll, boys don't make as much of a mess. They do, but not usually on themselves. I did the best I could to emancipate myself from the last few drops, then I tried to pull my underwear up with my other two layers, as I stood up. The only problem was I couldn't move, not immediately anyway. I was frozen in place. It was the combination of being cold and my muscles doing something they normally didn't do. With renewed determination, I jerked myself up, not caring if my clothes came up with me. Success. "Well, that was interesting." I was no longer exposed, but my backside hadn't fully recovered. It still felt numb. I looked down at the ground. It looked like someone had dropped a lemon snow cone. The frozen precipitation wasn't the only casualty. One of my skis also got sprinkled on. Matilda covered up her evidence by kicking snow on it. I did likewise, beginning with the ground, then my ski.

Charlie was still up when we returned. "The other three are sharing that tent, so that means we're sleeping in this one." He pointed to each of the tents as he described the situation. "I thought it best if they fell asleep early for us not to disturb them."

"You sure it's best for Samantha and Christine to be in the same tent?" I asked.

"Andy is between them. I think it's always been one of his fantasies to be the filling of a chick sandwich. Anyway, I think they're on the way to patching things up. With Spring Break arriving they better be. They each want to come along with Andy and me when we travel to Florida."

Charlie cleaned the cooking pot with snow, then made preparations for bed. "When you turn in tonight take your water bottle with you. Stick it in your sleeping bag. Your body heat will keep it from freezing."

For the second time since I was a young child I went to bed without brushing my teeth. Germs and tartar probably couldn't survive in temperatures this cold.

Matilda ended up sleeping between Charlie and me. I don't think I ever warmed up---or fell asleep. Charlie and friends had piled up snow against the tents to give them some insulation. How cold would it had felt if they didn't do it? Sometime during the night Matilda and I snuggled up to one another. It was the first time since meeting her that such proximity only made me think of stealing her heat.

We didn't leave the tent until a couple of hours after sunrise. With the sun shining against the tent, the temperature rose considerably. It had become a tug-of-war. Spending a few more minutes in relative comfort or emptying my bladder. After about an hour contemplating, the pendulum had swung, and peeing became a necessity. I leaned up in my bag. Inadvertently, I brushed against the ceiling of the tent. A thin layer of ice coated it. My movement was enough to rouse the others, who were apparently as wide awake as I.

"Our respiration in a more solidified form," Charlie elucidated. "In the summer it's water vapor. Damn." Charlie pulled out his half empty water bottle.

"From your reaction, I assume that was full when you put it in there," Matilda commented.

"That's the second odd thing to happen to me so far on this camping trip."

"What else happened?" I asked.

"I broke a ski yesterday. It was after we had set up camp. I wanted to see how far across the lake I could get. On the way down to it I fell into a depression. My ski bent too far and snapped."

"How are you going to get back?"

202

"SNOWSHOES!" was heard from outside the tent, likely from inside the other tent. It was Andy's voice. "CHARLIE THOUGHT THEY MIGHT COME IN HANDY! HE HAD NEVER BROUGHT THEM BEFORE ON A CAMPING TRIP! HOW LUCKY CAN A GUY BE?!"

"I still have to walk all that way out. After breakfast I'm going to begin. It's not only slower than skiing, but more tiring. I'll probably need to take a break every ten or fifteen minutes."

Did that mean we were also going to head back this morning? I had mixed emotions about that. I wanted to explore the Shoshone Geyser Basin and do that hotpotting thing, but it was very cold.

Noticing my concern, Charlie added, "But that doesn't mean y'all have to leave today. Andy and Christine have to work tomorrow morning, so they'll also have to leave today, but not until early afternoon. Samantha would like to stay another night if the two of you are staying."

"SAMANTHA LIKES TO SPEAK FOR HERSELF SOMETIMES! PLEASE STAY ANOTHER NIGHT! I KNOW IT'S COLD, BUT WE CAN ROAST MARSHMALLOWS AND SING CAMP SONGS! PLEASE."

I looked at Matilda. She nodded. "OKAY! WE'LL STAY ANOTHER NIGHT! BUT WHO WILL CARRY THE TENT OUT?!"

"We can share the load," Matilda insisted. "You carry the tent and I'll take some of your gear. Or I could carry the tent and you carry some of my gear."

"WHAT ABOUT ME?!" asked Samantha.

"I DON'T THINK WE'LL BE ABLE TO CARRY ANY OF YOUR GEAR!" said Matilda.

"THAT WASN'T WHAT I MEANT!"

Breakfast consisted of oatmeal, fortified with frozen chunks of sack lunch cheese and pieces of jerky. There was also cocoa. It was all good. The best thing, it was hot.

Charlie left after cleaning the breakfast pan and packing his gear. It had originally included one of the tents, but Andy insisted he carry it instead. "It's going to be hard enough on snowshoes without an extra five pounds to weigh you down." We waved to him as he slowly walked towards Old Faithful.

"Time to explore the geyser basin," stated Samantha.

"Or we could wait another hour, until it warms up a bit more," Christine countered.

"I think we should go to the geyser basin now," Samantha insisted.

"And I think we should wait," Christine repeated.

I looked at Matilda and Andy.

"I'm staying out of it," he immediately responded.

"Maybe we can flip a coin," Matilda suggested.

Christine sighed. "Okay, let's go to the geyser basin now. It's probably as good a time as any. Warmer is a relative term today. As long as we all agree." She looked at Matilda, Andy and me, intentionally turning away from Samantha.

The ski was bearable as long as we kept moving---keeping the blood from congealing---but not too fast to create wind chill. It didn't hurt that it was sunny. And it was just half-a-mile away.

Unlike geyser basins accessible to casual tourists, this one didn't have paved trails or boardwalks around the geysers, fumaroles, and hot springs. "Watch where you step," cautioned Andy. "Some of these pools are cool enough to get into, but most aren't. The only thing I wish to boil alive is lobster."

"Only lobster, huh?" commented Christine. "Not crab, or oysters, or...."

"You know what I meant."

"What I know is you aren't shy about eating what's in front of you."

"Sometimes even beside or behind you," added Samantha. "Andy doesn't feel it's rude to eat off another person's plate," she informed Matilda and me.

"It would be more rude to throw away good food," Andy declared.

Being so isolated, it felt like we had discovered the thermal area. Each new pool and geyser wasn't just new to us, but to the world. Many of them were labeled, which ruined my fantasy, but others weren't. One of my favorites was Minute Geyser. I wasn't sure if it was pronounced like the unit of time, or for the word that meant small. I was too embarrassed to ask. I felt I should have been able to figure it out. Just when I thought it had to be one way, a got an epiphany and switched to the other pronunciation.

I discovered a pool near the creek. "Is that a hotpot?"

Samantha squealed. "You found it. I soaked in it a couple of times last summer, the last time with Charlie alone after it go dark."

Christine made a gagging sound. "So that's why you two were gone so long. I'm definitely not going to go in there now."

Andy leaned down to the water and dipped a finger in gingerly, like he was afraid it might fall off from the contact. He wiped it off on his pant leg. "It's too cold."

"It's winter," I said matter-of-factly.

"If hot water drains into it, it shouldn't be that much colder than during the summer. I think it's tapped out. Thermal flows are constantly changing. Look at Minerva Terrace at Mammoth. All that chalky white was once as colorful as those areas with water still flowing over them."

Samantha pouted. "I was really looking forward to soaking in some hot water."

"There is always your bathtub back at the dorm," Christine suggested. The look Samantha returned would have melted the snow if the thermal basin hadn't done so already.

After an hour of exploring, we returned to camp. We ate an early lunch. What else was there to do when it was that cold? More oatmeal was cooked. We added just cheese this time. The apples were too frozen to eat. The Oreos were delicious.

Christine and Andy whispered to one another.   A moment later Andy said, "Christine and I are going to leave early. The only things to do here are sleep, return to the geyser basin, and ski. We still have those ten miles to ski back to Old Faithful, with full packs, so it doesn't make a lot of sense to wear ourselves out before we leave."

"We could play a game," Samantha suggested.

"Like see who can turn the deepest shade of blue?" countered Christine.

"I brought a deck of cards."

"It's too difficult to hold them with gloves. And it's too cold not to wear them."

"Bye, then."

"I'll help you pack that tent," said Matilda.

We waved as Andy and Christine skied off. Now we were down to three.

"Well, I can't just sit here." Samantha began to pace. "There has to be another pool the right temperature for us to soak in. You guys want to help me find it?"

"Sure," Matilda and I said in unison.

Once we reached the geyser basin, we split up. "Don't get too close to any of the pools," Matilda warned me. "The brighter the color usually means the hotter the water. Only get close enough to test the temperature if the pool looks dingy." Why couldn't it be the other way around. Hotel pools were always so bright and cheery.

I climbed to the top of a hill to get a better view of the basin. The pool I was looking for had to be warm enough to steam, but not too warm to promote the colorful microorganisms that created those bright colors. Nothing so far, but I did have a good view of the lake. Like West Thumb, the water beside the geyser basin was still liquid. It reminded me of that bear who got trapped on that island in Lake Yellowstone last summer. Sometime between reviving from hibernation and the lake thawing, it crossed the frozen lake to reach the island. Why wasn't it able to return to the mainland before the thaw? Was it not quite done with hibernating and took a nap during the breaking up of the ice? Was it so fascinated with the ice breaking and receding that it sat watching it, mesmerized? I guess there are some things one does there is no going back from.

Away from the geyser basin, near the lake, was a dark brown pool, almost black, that was steaming. If I hadn't climbed up there I would never have seen it. It was on a shelf adjacent to the hill I was on.

I skied down the hill in the direction I saw Matilda and Samantha. "I THINK I FOUND THAT HOTPOT!" I shouted when I got closer.

They skied towards me enthusiastically. As they got near, I turned away from them and began heading towards the pool. I almost didn't find it. It was so easy to spot from above. I was beginning to get frustrated when Samantha shouted down at me from the ridge she had side-stepped up. It was higher up than I thought. Matilda and I met up with her. We could feel the warm air rise up towards us. Most of the bowl was bare of snow, so we had to take our skis off and walk down the ten foot or so drop.

Samantha walked down to the water and stuck her hand in. "Perfect." She began to strip. "We should set our clothes as far away from the water as possible, to prevent the steam from getting them wet. And it would be a good idea to wrap them in our coats." There she was in her full glory, her modest breasts firm enough to barely move as she stepped towards the water. Then I saw just her backside, toned, but still enough flesh on it that there was no doubt she was a girl. The pool must have been shallow, because it just came up to the top of her thighs. She turned around, then sat, the murky water swallowing her to her neck. "Come on in."

Matilda and I looked at one another. "This could be a once in a lifetime opportunity," Matilda told me, or was she trying to convince herself? She took off her jacket. She laid it on a rock with its inner shell facing up. She shed her pullover sweater next, and the long-sleeve tee-shirt beneath it, revealing the sports bra I had seen at Summit Lake. Then came her gaiters, ski boots, two layers of socks, thermal underwear, and Gortex pants. She set them

207

carefully on top of her coat. She looked over at me. "Hey, you haven't even started." I was so fixated on watching Matilda undress that I had forgotten to do so myself.

I set my coat out like she did. By the time I was down to my underwear Matilda was already walking in the water. I briefly saw her bottom before it dropped into the water. It was larger than Samantha's, but with toned definition. Here I go. I unclasped my bra and set it on top of my clothes, then my underwear. I nearly tripped trying to get out of them, with standing on the uneven bedrock, and disrobing as expeditiously as possible. I almost made it before Matilda turned around. At least I was more fit than I was at the beginning of the winter. Matilda smiled at me. It was more sympathetic than mocking or leering.

I sat down next to the other girls. The bottom of the pool was muddy. Getting past my initial revulsion, it began to feel quite nice, like sitting on warm foam. It felt odd being naked next to two other people, but with most of our bodies being covered I adjusted to it. It felt no worse than being beside someone in the next stall. But, as you know, I have never been comfortable with that either.

Samantha scooped up a handful of mud and began rubbing it on her body. And I mean all over. "You're not comfortable with nudity, are you?" She was looking at me. "Others, or your own."

"I wasn't raised seeing other people's bodies, not even my grandmother's. The last time someone had seen me naked was when I was five, before I could bath myself."

"Not even a doctor?" questioned Matilda.

"No."

"You've never been to a OB/GYN?"

"No."

"You really need to, especially if...."

"I've been sexually active?"

"I was under the impression you weren't a virgin," said Samantha.

"I had sex when I was initiated into the Marauders, and then

208

after, with some of the gang members I liked best, but never out in the open. It was always in the dark or under the covers."

"You never showered after PE?"

"I either didn't dress down, or if I did, I tried to not get sweaty enough to need a shower. By the time I reached high school I rarely went to school anyway, so…."

"Nudity bothers you that much? That you're embarrassed for someone to see you naked? Or you to see them?"

"It was just how I was raised. The longer I went without exposing myself to others, or seeing them, the harder it got to not being completely covered."

"But we are born naked. How can nudity be that scandalous if we enter the world like that?"

"Maybe we develop morals as we get older."

"I think it might be just the opposite," Matilda interjected. "Isn't a child innocent until he or she is contaminated by society? I think if we remained naked after we were born nudity wouldn't seem taboo. You ever see those photos of nude aboriginals in National Geographic? Being naked isn't a precursor to an orgy. It's just their normal attire. If men can go topless, why can't women?"

I was less ashamed when the three of us walked out of the water together than when we entered it. In some societies, a woman couldn't expose her face, or even her ankles, because they were deemed too erotic. It seemed so silly. But how is that any different than how I choose to be attired? We tried the best we could to scrub off the mud, but I was confident I would find some somewhere when I showered the next day. I was becoming more comfortable with nudity, but I felt even more comfortable when the three of us were completely covered. Becoming accustomed to people wearing coats and gloves, how close was I to believing someone wearing just pants and a tee-shirt was indecent?

We felt refreshed as we skied back to camp. Was it the hot water, or the mud, or just that we were doing something other than sitting around? We cooked ramen, then toasted marshmallows.

Samantha even thought to bring graham crackers and chocolate. I felt good. And we had just one more night of sleeping in the cold.

When I woke up in the middle of the night, Matilda must have noticed, because she said, "I'm too cold to sleep."

"Me too," I immediately responded. Not completely accurate, considering I had just woken up, but I felt uncomfortable enough, now, that it was unlikely I was going to fall back asleep.

There had to be some way to warm up. We could start a fire, but that meant getting out of the tent, and our sleeping bags. Something like this happened in a movie I saw recently. They got warm by sharing the same bag---before someone murdered them. At least they died content.

"I could join you in your sleeping bag," I suggested. "Sharing each other's body heat ought to warm us up." To take it a step further we put my bag around hers, adding a layer of insulation.

The squeeze into Matilda's bag was tight. We had to lay on our sides. At first, I just lay next to her. She did feel cold, especially her feet. She was shaking. I put my arms around her and tried to squeeze my warmth into her. She clutched her hands to mine. They pressed into her breasts, like a mother trying to comfort a child. I don't know if she guided my hands or they made their way to between her legs by themselves. It was the only part of her body that felt warm. She rubbed herself against my hands, then she made a sound. I think she was crying.

She abruptly pulled my hands away. "I need to get some air." She squirmed her way out of the double insulated sleeping bag. She put on her coat, then her boots. After she unzipped the tent, the temperature must have dropped 20 degrees. After she stepped outside she quickly zipped the tent back up. I heard two snaps, then the sounds of someone skiing off.

What was that all about? She had wanted me to caress her, then suddenly not. Why was she holding back? Or was I just imagining it all again. I had to be more intuitive than that. We needed to have a long discussion after we got back to Old Faithful to sort this all out. I believed the problem was on my end, but now I wasn't so sure.

An excruciating howl shredded the serenity of the evening. Was it a bird? A coyote? A bear? The tone of its torment was so universal it could have been anything. If Samantha had been asleep, she wasn't now. "Where's Matilda?" It hadn't occurred to me until she said it. Could that have been Matilda? Then I knew it was. I went from *couldn't be* to *no doubt* within a fraction of a second.

We yanked our bags away from us, then put on our jackets, without buttoning them. It was suddenly too hot to wear them. After spastically pulling on our boots, we unzipped the tent and darted to our skis. There was enough light from the stars and the sliver of a moon reflecting off the snow to do what we had done so far, but not enough to ski by. We grabbed our headlamps from the tent, placed them on our heads, then turned them on. It was now very bright in front us, but dark everywhere else.

We began skiing in the direction of that sound, toward the geyser basin. We found Matilda about halfway there. She was crawling through the snow. It was slightly more than waste high on her. One side of her face looked like it had boils. "What happened?" Matilda wasn't able to answer. Her eyes were glazed.

Too cumbersome to carry, we had to drag her back to camp on top of the snow. Because the snow had set up, she skimmed on the surface, barely creating a trough in the snow. I held one wrist and Samantha the other. The skin moved more than it should have. We put her in the bag within a bag. I felt her forehead. She was a furnace, yet still shivering.

Samantha unzipped the top of Matilda's jacket and peaked under her shirt. Her chest was as bubbly as the side of her face. Puss began to ooze out. Samantha felt the skin. It ruptured at her touch. "We need to get help immediately."

"How? We're ten miles from the nearest ranger station.

You need to ski for help. I'll stay with Matilda."

"You're the better skier. An hour may make all the difference."

I nodded. I kissed Matilda on her forehead, then rushed out of the tent, zipping it up behind me.

The ski back was a blur. Under any other circumstance my skiing may have been called careless. I only fell once, and within seconds I had pulled myself up and was off again. I practically ran on the straight-a-ways. I would have skated, but the trail wasn't groomed for that, not until I hit Lone Star. At Kepler Cascades, I skied on the highway instead of the trail.

The rangers were surprisingly calm when I told them what happened, much calmer than my telling of it. It was a miracle they understood what I was saying. I wanted to go back with them, but they justifiably declined my demand, due to my fatigue and my frantic nature. Snowmobiles were used for the rescue with one of them having a stretcher pulled behind it.

24.   META INFINITI

Matilda died before the rangers got there. Even if they got there in time she wouldn't have survived. She had third-degree burns on 90% of her body. Dehydration was the major complication. No one could survive losing so much of their body's fluids.

We didn't close for another week, but for most of us the season had ended. Samantha and I were basket cases. What would it be like if someone died beside you, you being the only person for miles? Charlie also took Matilda's death hard. He believed if he had been there she wouldn't have died. Those of us most effected continued to work. Not working meant no break from our sorrow.

When I returned to Seattle I wrote Meta Infiniti, an attempt to sort out my life, while retaining my connection to Matilda and others I lived with for three months at Snow Lodge. Not only would Matilda survive in my eternal dreams, but perhaps, in some part, in the dreams of people who didn't know her personally. I miss her every day of my life, but at least I had that anticipation of doing things with her, and that was nearly as good.

For people who were interested, I told them my story, and shared Meta Infiniti. Like Barry, I drew followers without really trying. The first warders were born, and even some paladins. A commune was built near Carnation, Washington, where we pooled our resources. Each of us had more than we could have had on our own, including a vast wilderness within the circle of our individual homes. The language of peace and beauty was developed, and the words created randomly. The new millennium brought new communes into all parts of the world. Many of us, including myself, sought purity. Not only was I not going to eat meat, I refused to eat vegetables. I medically transformed myself into a solavore, receiving my energy directly from the sun. I never had a close relationship after Matilda. I became asexually pure, living platonically. As I entered tenth stage, I returned to Yellowstone, and to Summit Lake. I felt it was the place Matilda and I connected the most....

"Thank you, Bardula."

"*Thank you* is also not our word, because it is also always implied."

"So, you never really had a relationship with Matilda?"

"I do now, and that is all that matters. Our past is our foundation, but our present is what we experience."

"May I live with you at Summit Lake?"

"You are Jolairshay. I am Bardula. Because I choose to live

my life as a hermit, doesn't mean everyone must become a hermit. Because I'm an African homosexual female solavore, doesn't mean everyone must be so. Because I seek Homo Maturus doesn't mean everyone must seek Homo Maturus. You are Jolairshay."

That's how I remember my discussion with Bardula this time. I've been dead many years now, and the dreams change. Maybe she'll be an Asian heterosexual male carnivore next time.

The end...

...is the beginning.

META INFINITI

Creation

In the beginning there was nothing, but that was boring, so something happened. Something began as infinite mass and infinitesimal dimension. For a brief instant density was perfect, but perfection is only possible with nothing. Something's perfection decreased with its density. Deviations from perfection create personality. Matter changes, but doesn't disappear. Matter has always existed. Great spouts discharge matter. Great drains extract matter. Connectors condense absolutely, then contract. Matter in motion continues unless dampened by resistance.

God

God-energy-nature pushed. God is subtle omnipotence. God is the creative force. God is growing a branch on the left side, but not on the right. God is a seed blown into this meadow, but not into that meadow. God is chaos. We wish to become part of God. Creativity brings us closer to life's push. Spiritual shoves may come during consciousness, or not. Matter's perfection becomes more complex. Hydrogen begets helium begets gold begets uranium. Plants transform into animals, which transform into people, which transform into societies. Over complexity facilitates suicide.

Homo Maturus
Transformation alters predetermined consequences. Conformity is the norm. Deviating from expectations is heresy. Creativity is insanity. To grow, chaos must lead us. Multitude of growths are non-physical. Growth will eventually destroy unless equilibrium is achieved. Humans have always been violent and selfish. Humans cannot change, so they must evolve. Homo erectus begets homo sapiens begets homo maturus.

Warders
Homo maturus is a goal that can never be achieved. Each generation can become halfway closer to homo maturus. Warders will precede homo maturus. Warders will heal the earth and protect it. Earth is its people, animals, plants, water, sky, and land. Warders do what's beneath others to do. Warders are sought in every profession. Paladins are warders who are their own profession.

Religion
Religions are spiritual clubs. All organizations and clubs have agendas. Religion for one can be as beneficial as religion for billions. Worthy religions allow themselves to be criticized. Religions that belittle fear their own faults. Clubs with restricted membership force ideas to become stale. Religious freedoms must be within the laws of the land. Religions often prey on the weak. Worthy religions aren't a cure, and don't need marketing. Don't blame God for your own prejudices.

Science

For a species to survive, it must grow morally. The more intelligent the species, the more likely it will destroy itself. For technically advanced extra-terrestrials to survive, they must have advanced morals. Human morals aren't strong enough for us to be shown dangerous toys. Clones will be no more similar to us than twins, less so because they will develop in a different time. Artificial intelligences will seek citizenship. Citizenship should be granted, we reaping what we sow. Sports will replace wars, with spoils to the victors. Entertainment will be computer reproduced, with voices, physiques, and personalities becoming immortal in cyberspace.

Death

Death is eternal sleep. Death is remembrance of one's self. Souls are unique clusters of memories. Death is dreaming of mutated memories. How we view our life becomes our heaven or our hell. Celebrate one's life. Don't mourn their loss. Do not make a person's memory a burden. Remember a person's positive influence. Do not make someone's life unworthy. Add life to your death chain.

Dynamics

Most ill deeds are caused by insecurities. Love yourself so you can love others. Cherish the moments when existence is jubilant. Diminish loneliness by helping others in need. Illness will occur when physical, mental, or emotional/spiritual activity wanes. Hate harms the one who hates more than the hated. Forgive, so you may live life. Prejudice is being afraid of what lies beyond preconceived norms. Prejudice is unfairly associating unpleasurable events. Everyone has prejudices. Recognize prejudices to minimize their effect. Seek truth. Individualized truth is perception. History is truth mutated by perception. If drugs become a substitute for adventure, natural methods will entropy. Don't trade temporary pleasure for a lifetime of disability. Allow change, amending spirituality in light of new insight.

Society

Provide recreation for youth. You choose or they will choose. Prevent monopolies in commerce. Limit each proprietor to one location. Strive for democracy, but without trendiness. Democracy shall provide for all. Half for government, half for self. Become partners with nature. Half wild, half civilized. Provide education to prepare for life. Combine resources. Create neighborhoods with individual living spaces and group recreation.

Goals

Only take what you need to enjoy. Borrow from the land. The less moral we are, the more likely we will consume something like ourselves. Be humble. Do for self and the common good, not for fame. Chaos creates fortune and misfortune. The pleasant and the unpleasant. Appreciate and don't dwell. Don't be ashamed. Don't do things you're ashamed of. Faith until falsehood. Do, but without harm to others. Plan for children. Only have as many children as you can provide for. Creating children creates their priority. Feed yourself so you may feed your family. Feed your family before you feed your community. Feed your community before you feed your nation. Feed your nation before you feed the world. Do anonymous, unselfish acts of goodwill. Analyze all sides of issues. Don't desecrate or steal. Don't become a burden unless helpless.

Language

Language is part of self-identity. Beautiful language is simple and random, as are names. Twelve consonants. Twelve vowels. Twelve notes.

Development

First stage, we are created. Second stage, we are born. Third stage, we walk and talk. Fourth stage, we begin formal education. Fifth stage, we show independence. Sixth stage, we reach sexual maturity. Seventh stage, we leave the nest. Eighth stage, we become aware and prominent. Ninth stage, we begin to decay. Tenth stage, we retire from formal activity. Eleventh stage, we become decrepit and feeble. Twelfth stage, we dream.

The Language Of Peace And Beauty

1	d	a	c
2	f	air	c#
3	g	ar	d
4	h	aw	d#
5	j	ay	e
6	k	ee	f
7	l	er	f#
8	n	i	g
9	p	o	g#
10	sh	or	a
11	t	ow	a#
12	w	u	b

www.ingramcontent.com/pod-product-compliance
Lightning Source LLC
Chambersburg PA
CBHW071905220626

47052CB00002B/212